BEC McMASTER

HEART
of
FIRE

LEGENDS OF THE STORM SERIES ·

D1319739

Edited by: Hot Tree Editing
Print formatting by: Cover Me Darling and Athena Interior Book Design
Cover Art © Damonza.com

ALSO AVAILABLE BY BEC MCMASTER

LONDON STEAMPUNK SERIES
Kiss Of Steel
Heart Of Iron
My Lady Quicksilver
Forged By Desire
Of Silk And Steam
Novellas in same series:
Tarnished Knight
The Curious Case Of The Clockwork Menace

DARK ARTS SERIES
Shadowbound
Hexbound

BURNED LANDS SERIES
Nobody's Hero
The Last True Hero

OTHER
The Many Lives Of Hadley Monroe

Heart of Fire

The old eddas speak of *dreki*—fabled creatures who haunt the depths of Iceland's volcanoes, and steal away fair maidens.

Freyja wants none of such myths. *Dreki* seducing young ladies? Ha. They probably eat such foolish girls. But when the local *dreki* steals her last ram—costing her any chance of feeding her ill father through the winter—Freyja intends to confront the fearsome myth.

Sentenced to a life of exile from his clan, Rurik is fascinated by the furious woman who comes to claim her ram. She reeks of mysterious magic, and challenges him at every step. He intends to claim the passionate firebrand, but to do so he must take mortal form.

It's the only time the *dreki* are vulnerable, and with a dragon hunter arriving on the shores of Iceland, he can barely afford the risk—but lonely Freyja, with her elf-cursed eyes and pragmatic soul, tempts him in ways he's never felt before. Is she the key to reclaiming his heritage? Or will she be his downfall?

GLOSSARY FOR
LEGENDS OF THE STORM

Álfar - Elves. Comprised of the *svartálfar* (black elves some commonly think are more dwarfish in nature, who work metals), *Dökkálfar* (dark elves that live within a hidden world within the earth) and the *Ljósálfar* (light elves who are fairer than the sun to look at, and live in *Álfheimr*). Some Icelanders say that to speak the word '*Álfar*' is to draw their attention, and so it's safer to call them *Huldufólk*, which technically, they are not.

Álfheimr - Land of the Light Elves.

Cycle - Sixty years or so. *Dreki* consider time in cycles. A *dreki* is not considered an adult until they are two cycles old, and they often live for twenty-five cycles.

Chaos-Bubble - a small side-world made purely of Chaos magic. Held within each volcano, this is the heart of the *dreki* court and guarded by magic. No human can enter a *dreki* court, unless they have a certain amount of magic within them, or have been rewarded with a *dreki* talisman, which grants them passage.

Clan - A group of *dreki* who share familial ties, and live together. The term is commonly used throughout Europe and the North Americas. Each clan rules a certain territory, the edges of which are formed by treaty with other clans.

Court - The official term for a clan or tribe of *dreki*. Also a place each clan refers to as home. Generally within a volcano.

Dreki - *Dreki* were created when the Great Goddess tore her soul to pieces, and imbued each piece into flesh within the Fire of the volcano, Hekla. *Dreki* therefore, are creatures created of Fire, Earth and Air, who also have an affinity for Tiamat's Chaos magic. Commonly mistaken for their lesser brethren—dragons—they have the ability to change forms if they desire. *Dreki* prefer to live within volcanoes, where they can be close to the elements of Earth and Fire. There are many *dreki* clans in the world. Many clans rule the West Coast of Canada, and the Americas. Another hotspot is along the East coast of Russia, and the string of islands that leads down through Asia. There are also a few scattered courts along the Mediterranean and throughout the East Coast of Africa.

Dragons - lesser children created by Tiamat, but borne from her flesh, not her soul. Monsters that hunger for *dreki* power, and emulate them by finding volcanoes to settle within. Lack the magic of the elements. It is considered an insult by the *dreki* to be called a dragon.

Great Goddess - Tiamat, Goddess of Chaos and Creation.

Huldufólk - "Hidden Folk". Those creatures from Scandinavian folklore.

Mate - To choose the one who will bear your children, and whom you will live out the end of your days with.

Plague of dreki - human term for a collective group of *dreki*. Insulting term to the *dreki*.

Sarratum Zamani - "Queen of Lightning"

Serpents - Created at the same time as dragons, sea serpents were hunted to extinction by ancient sailors.

Tiamat - Ancient Sumerian goddess who was killed by the Storm-God, Marduk, when she was in serpent form. The North Wind took her soul North, where it hibernated within the volcano, Hekla, for many eons, drawing power from the Earth and the Fire within. When Hekla exploded, she used the eruption to tear her soul to pieces, giving birth to the first of the *dreki* race, in one last act of Creation.

Tribe - African *dreki* term for 'clan'.

Trolls - creatures of myth in Iceland. Rarely seen, they have an affinity for the element of Earth.

Twin Flame - a *dreki* concept for the other half of one's soul. A soul-mate. *Dreki* consider their souls lacking, as they were created from pieces of Tiamat's soul, therefore to find the other half of their soul completes them. A rare occurrence, which goes beyond mating.

Wyrms - another name for dragons.

Zini Clan - Spirit of the Wind Clan, rules Iceland.

Zilittu Clan - Spirit of the Mist Clan, rules the north of Norway.

CHAPTER
ONE

Iceland, 1880

"HERE, FATHER," FREYJA murmured, tilting the steaming cup of broth to his lips. "Perhaps this will take away the chill?"

Her father slurped at the watery soup, his eyes blue and vacant as his trembling hands tried to cup hers. "It's delicious, Freyja. One of your best."

Freyja pasted a smile on her face, even though he couldn't see it. Bitterness burned in her throat. "Yes, Papa. It is, isn't it?"

There were more vegetables than lamb in the broth, and more water than both, but the fact that he sought to spare her feelings made her shoulders hunch. It had been such a long winter, with little food or respite from the storms. The few coins they had left were drying up and her small herd of ewes was dwindling. She couldn't justify slaughtering another just to add more flavor to their soup.

Her father coughed, that same dry, hacking cough that had haunted him all winter. Freyja grabbed a rag and helped to dry his cheeks with it. Sometimes she wondered if he would survive to see another winter.

A fluttery feeling rose up to choke her, and she forced it down ruthlessly. No point in being maudlin. He was here and this was now. The future could wait.

"How was the village this afternoon?" her father asked. "You didn't see Ingmar's boy, did you?"

If she had, then Benedikt would have no interest in her. Not a respectful interest anyway. He had already hinted that he might have means to offer her coin to keep her larder stocked through the spring. Telling her father that, however, might send him to an early grave. He had such hopes. Freyja intended never to enlighten him; with his poor health, their dwindling resources, and her eyes, she was unlikely to make any sort of respectable match.

"He must have been busy, I'm sure," she replied, squeezing his hand, then levering to her feet. Gathering the ceramic bowls together, she crossed to the kitchen. "He has all that land to tend, after all."

Some of it theirs—or what she'd been forced to sell after her father's eyes faded and he could no longer work the land. She'd done what she could, but tending to him took a lot of her time.

The shutters banged on the windows as the winds lifted. Freyja glanced through the glass toward the enormous storm clouds boiling on the horizon. A storm from the north then, and bound to be bitter with the kiss of Arctic winds on its breath. She could feel it in her bones, tingling beneath her skin as if she herself were tied to the storm. It would blow a mighty gale, tearing its way through the mountains that shielded their little homestead, then blow out by morning. She knew it, with some inexplicable sixth sense.

Most of Iceland suffered from bitter chill at this time of year, but the area surrounding Akureyri was somewhat warmer thanks to a trick of the coastline, of cliffs and mountains. Of course, out here they were virtually alone. It was a day's sail to Reykjavik and longer overland, if one even dared.

"I have to fetch the sheep in," she called, watching the dull gray edge of the clouds roiling. Lightning flickered in the distance. "We're in for a storm."

"Be careful," her father called, sinking into his shawl and coughing again. "Don't be too long."

"I won't, Papa."

"And take Loki."

She rolled her eyes at the small bundle of white fur that nestled by her father's feet. "Come."

The little arctic fox yawned at her, seemingly content to stay where he was. Another mouth to feed when she truly couldn't, but then a part of her couldn't throw him out the door. He'd been with them since he was a pup.

Freyja frowned, reaching out with the inner part of herself that had some sense of connection to the creature. *Come.*

Loki rolled to his feet and shook himself, discarding strands of long white hair. Underneath, his summer coat grew darker. Another week or two and he'd lose the rest of his winter coat. He leaped with agile quickness to dart beneath her skirts, and threatened to trip her.

"You will make me a nice fur muff one day," she threatened, though he ignored her and scratched at the door, knowing full well the threat was harmless.

Skirts wrapping haphazardly around her legs, Freyja fought her way across the yard. It was almost five in the afternoon and evening was falling. In the village, most of the men would be retiring to the tavern to talk and laugh beneath the smoky eaves, whilst the goodwives tended their children and tucked them in for the night.

Not so out here. Freyja had been raised on these rugged slopes, beneath the looming volcanic mountain of Krafla. In the distance its constant plume of smoke seemed almost invisible against the gray clouds.

Still, its presence was more than felt. Freyja crossed herself. "Blessed Father, watch over us," she murmured, glaring at the mountain. "Let *dreki* sleep another night."

The small flock of ewes must have sensed the ominous press of the storm, for they were at the woven stick fence, bleating to be let into the small barn. Two snowy white lambs with black markings peered at her from beneath one old ewe. Despite her mood, Freyja couldn't help a smile.

Loki watched them with avid interest, licking at his cheeks with his long pink tongue.

Don't you dare. She snapped the thought at him and he sat down obediently, giving her a sly, long-suffering look.

It took little effort to draw the small herd into the barn, coaxing them into the separate stalls. Her boots shuffled over the thin straw, the air still and musty here. One pen remained empty and she hurried back outside to fetch the battered old ram from his own paddock.

Loki yipped as she stumbled. The skies were darkening swiftly now, large fat drops of rain spattering down. One struck her cheek like an icy bullet, wind whipping her skirts and shawl. Her long blonde plait slapped her in the face. The whisper of the storm drove through her, setting her alight with a feverish excitement, her heart quickening. This was the time she felt most alive.

"*Henrik!*" she called, her voice stolen from her lips by another gust. The pen was empty; or no, not quite. The ram cowered against the wall, head bowed as if to fight the force of the wind.

"You stupid beast," she muttered, grabbing her skirts and straddling the fence. Loki darted in and snatched a mouthful of skirt, almost hauling her back onto his side.

"Curse you," Freyja cried, trying to shake him free. A sudden sharp spatter of rain made her gasp. "Do you wish me to be soaked? Then I shall catch a chill and you must find your own dinner!"

The little fox worried at her skirts, his ears flat to his head. Freyja scraped the wet strands of hair off her face and tugged the material, her curses lost in another hammering echo of thunder.

Let go!

But the little fox would not.

Henrik bleated suddenly, turning in circles as if he didn't know where to go. Freyja shot him a frustrated look, then reached down and grabbed Loki's ruff. A blast of wind knocked her into the ram's pen. She landed flat on her back in the mud, breathless and cursing—

A sudden roar echoed through the air, cutting through the thunder as if it were nothing.

The scream of it beat against her skin, pulsing in her ears until she was forced to clap her hands over them. The primal shiver of it seemed to be inside her, in her head, in her pounding heartbeat— everywhere. It was the type of sound that echoed down through ages past, and sent both man and animal fleeing in mindless fear.

It cut off and Freyja choked in her first gasp, lifting her head in disbelief as a sinuous tail flew directly over her.

"Wyrm," she whispered, the heat draining out of her face.

Not just a wyrm, but the Great One. He who haunted Krafla's depths, slithering out to stalk the night and hunt his prey.

She'd never seen him this close before. Golden scales gleamed even in the stormy darkness, each wing sweeping out an impossible forty feet wide. She shouldn't be scared; the village paid its tithe and had for decades in exchange for being left alone. But there was something distinctly primeval about the sight of it directly above her. Some ancestral fear that made her feel like prey.

Then its forelegs curled up, claws plucking delicately at its victim. Henrik bleated one last time, and she could sense his fear as the wyrm thrust its wings downward again, launching itself into the air.

With her ram in its talons.

"No!" Freyja pushed herself upright in disbelief, mud squelching through her fingers. Without the ram she couldn't breed. It wouldn't matter *this* spring, but next year.... "*No!*"

Leaping to her feet, she chased after it. *Curse you! We pay the tithe!* Each week a lamb or goat was tethered out on the hilltop as sacrifice, though eddas told of a time when the sacrifice had been virgin flesh. Her father's face flashed into her mind, thin with lack of nourishment and color fleeing his cheeks as he coughed.

"Come back!" She snatched up a stone and hurled it skyward.

A pitiful effort, for the wyrm sailed high, soaring beneath gray clouds with mocking disdain, both for her and the weather.

Freyja sank to her knees in the mud, the fist in her chest tightening. What was she going to do? Hope and pray that one of the undropped lambs was a male? There were only two ewes still due to deliver, and even if the lambs were male it would be years before she could breed them.

She and her father didn't have that time.

Something broke inside her. Tears that she hadn't shed even when her mother passed away three years ago, finally tore free. Since then she'd been holding on, trying to keep it all from washing over her as she looked after her increasingly frail father. Slamming her fists into the dirt, Freyja heard the lash of lightning strike the hill nearby. Again. And again. Lightning crashing down in answer to her fury. She would not accept this. She would not fail.

Not even if she had to take her ram back.

The cold rain washed away her hot tears as she looked up. Loki slithered through the wickerwork of the pen and licked at her hand tentatively as if to appease her, but Freyja shook him off.

"I'm going after him," she told the fox. Dragging her shawl tight, she lurched to her feet, wet through, her skirts caked in mud.

The creature had terrorized her village long enough.

And Freyja was not without her defenses.

CHAPTER
TWO

FREYJA WAITED UNTIL her father was tucked in bed and snoring before she began ruthlessly stripping off her mud-encrusted clothes. Cold was a constant enemy out here.

Slipping into a pair of her father's old trousers, she belted them tight and dragged her boots on. An oiled sealskin coat went over her shirt to keep the rain off, and she dragged her father's bow out of the chest by his bed.

The storm was blowing itself out by the time she ventured forth. Loki scrabbled at the door behind her, yipping to be let out, but Freyja ignored him.

She strode with cold purpose across the plains behind her house, feet sure on the mud-slicked sides of the hill. Her anger boiled beneath her skin like a storm of her own, frequently sending belated strikes of lightning down nearby. A crater still smoked as she passed by it.

The terrain grew rocky, and soon she was striding past the enormous standing tors that no farmer dared remove. Goodwives whispered that trolls lived there, lurking beneath their rocky bases. Freyja had never seen one, but the hairs on the back of her neck tingled as if *something* was watching her. Glancing around, she loosened her grip on the bow.

Come on, she thought. *If you dare*. For anger was her ally tonight, and though the storm was abating, she could summon its fierceness to life again if she wished.

But nothing confronted her. She was almost disappointed as she set her body against the long climb ahead of her.

Stubby grass soon gave way to rock, and then ice. No matter how much she wanted to hold on to it, her anger waned as exhaustion began to tax her heavy limbs. Her father wasn't the only one dining on broth these days.

Lightning flickered in the distance, highlighting the smoking caldera of the volcano. Steam billowed from fumaroles as though hell itself rested beneath the mountain. Though she ached to rest, the sight urged her on. She had to hurry, or it would be too late; perhaps it already was, but somehow her mind was set on saving her ram. It couldn't be too late. It simply couldn't. She wouldn't believe it.

The Great Wyrm had haunted the depths of Krafla for over three decades, plundering what it wanted until the villagers agreed to pay it the tithe. Nobody knew where it had come from, though rumor whispered that there were more throughout the center of Iceland and the southern coast, following the volcano trail, for that was where they lived.

Cold-blooded creatures they were, difficult to kill, and incredibly dangerous. She could remember the tales her mother used to tell of them. The fabled *dreki*. Constantly hungering for heat and slumbering close to the volcano's depths.

Freyja's favorite tale had been that of Marya, the virgin shepherdess who had been staked out for the tithe of the mighty Beirammon, back when wyrms still thirsted for human flesh. Instead, a young soldier named Alvar hunted the wyrm and his prey back to the volcano, and killed it in a dangerous duel.

Her mother had rolled her eyes as Freyja tried to enact the sword blow that lopped the mighty wyrm's head off. Helga much preferred the story of Anika, who had enticed the local *dreki* into mortal flesh and become his lover until the village had turned against them, and she'd flown off on his back, never to be seen again.

"He probably ate her," Freyja had said, practically ruthless even at the age of twelve.

"No. No, I don't think he ate her, my little one." And then her mother had laughed, as if she knew something Freyja didn't.

Thunder rumbled around the peak of the mountain as she climbed, her thigh muscles aching. Slipping on moss, Freyja scrambled up over the last rocky hill and stared for a moment at the gaping caldera. Sulfurous fumes leaked from crevices, and bubbling mud pools threatened to drag in the unwary traveler. Freyja avoided them as easily as if she had been this way before, *listening* to the earth's trembling beneath her feet, the aching groan of its bowels and the blistering hiss of its exhale.

Any local knew where the opening to the *dreki's* lair was. As lightning flickered, Freyja stubbornly dragged herself up over the ice-crusted rocks. There was no trail, for the wyrm had no need of it. As she climbed, the smoldering coal of anger burned to life in her chest again. She almost fancied that she could hear something bleating, but then thunder rumbled, low and ominous.

Her very own battle cry.

Finally, she dragged herself onto the ledge that opened into a fissure into the volcano. It was warmer here, though not unbearably so. Krafla had not erupted for many years, and no doubt the wyrm would not have returned if it were going to do so in the near future. *Dreki* had ways of listening to the earth's rumblings; the same sense that Freyja herself had.

Right now the earth beneath her creaked, but it was not angry. No, that was all her.

Leaning under the overhang of the cave mouth, Freyja knelt and untied the small lantern from her belt. She dragged her gloves off and cupped her hands around the wick. *Come. Dance for me.* Her breath stirred the small wick and then a tiny flame sputtered to life, flaring up and almost singeing her hands.

Something shifted in the darkness; a sense of the mountain listening, as if it felt her small magic. Freyja placed a hand on the barren ground. *Easy.* She soothed it, stroking it with the awareness within her, feeling it tremble beneath her touch.

An alien presence brushed against her mind and Freyja froze, sucking in a sharp breath. The pressure was almost overwhelming, a mountain leaning down upon her. Then suddenly it was gone.

Freyja closed the small glass door on the lantern, and stared into the darkness of the lava tube. "That is right," she whispered in Norse. "You know I am here."

The lantern guided her into the heart of the mountain. The air reeked of sulfur and burned cinnamon, smoky spices. A scent that was incredibly appealing. She breathed it in, feeling it sweep through her, warming her from within. Somehow she knew it, though she had never breathed its like before.

The scent drugged her, luring her ever deeper. Ice gleamed in a thin sheen over the entrance floor, melting with each passing step as the air warmed. The walls were smooth, with rough bands at interval heights where lava had flowed, like the tidemark on the caves by the sea.

As she turned a corner, taking careful, stalking steps, something gleamed white and stark at the corner of her vision.

Freyja spun, holding the lantern high. A leering skull stared back at her, the owner slumped forever against the wall, his pitted armor tarnished and rusted. A sword hung clasped in bony fingers. Swallowing hard, Freyja crouched beside it, and tugged the skeletal fingers away from the hilt as she exchanged it for the bow.

She could feel that other awareness watching her, listening as if it could hear her.

You won't frighten me. You won't.

The tunnel opened into a larger cavern, enormous stalactites stabbing sharp fingers down from the roof, some touching the floors in dripping columns much like melted candlewax. Piles of gold coins glittered in the darkness, heaped at the sides of the cavern as if the press of the enormous wyrm's body forced them there. Winking gemstones. A dozen rubies at least. For a moment Freyja couldn't think. She could only stare at the veritable hoard in front of her. Wyrms were said to be voracious for treasure, guarding it with their fierce tempers, but here was coin enough to see her father fed forever. The entire village. Perhaps even all of Iceland.

Her fingers itched to take just enough to buy a dozen ewes and several rams to replace what had been stolen. The gold meant little to her, but the concept of what she could buy with it was incredibly tempting.

She could buy a future for her and her father.

As if sensing her thoughts, a warning rumble smoked its way through the tunnel. Freyja tore her gaze from the glittering piles. The *dreki* were possessive of their treasures, it was said. To even think of taking but one coin was to bring her own death down upon her.

It was warmer here; sweat trickled down the back of her neck and between her bound breasts. Freyja held the sword in front of her, sweeping the darkness with the lantern. He was here. Somewhere. She could feel the dark energy of his power, dwelling in the shadows like some enormous smoldering volcano.

"So now they send my tithe to me?"

The thought-whisper almost crushed her, and her fingers clenched around the sword hilt as she ground her teeth together. Pressure built behind Freyja's left eye; a stabbing ache that promised to make her head throb for days. She drew her focus in on herself, creating a shield against the immense presence. The pressure eased.

"I'm not your tithe," she called back. "The village pays you its tithe! And you have stolen my ram!"

A husky chuckle rumbled in the darkness, like a cat purring. Movement shifted, diamond-hard scales rasping over the polished stone floors. Freyja took a step back, her breath catching as she raked the darkness for signs of the wyrm.

Don't be afraid. He can't kill you. We pay the tithe, she told herself. Still the sensation of the *dreki* watching her made her nerves thrum with anticipation. She held the sword low, sweeping it in front of her.

"Tithe?" the dragon whispered. *"Your village has not paid its tithe in three moons. So, I will take what is owed. Your ram was… delicious."*

Freyja's lips pressed tightly together. *Too late to save Henrik.* Something hot and impotent burned at the back of her eyes.

Then she realized what he had said.

The tithe hadn't been paid.

The dragon was no longer bound by his word not to harm her.

Freyja placed the lantern on the ground and crept behind a stalactite, sword held at the ready, her heart thumping in her ears, drowning out all other sound. What had she done? Trapped herself in here with a creature that might just eat her? A creature that was near invincible with its plated scales and impenetrable skin.

The only place that showed any vulnerability was the smooth skin under its jaw or behind its forearm, where a sword just *might* pierce it, if she believed the eddas.

"You tremble?" His voice echoed with his delight.

Shadows of a long sinuous neck and the devilishly shaped head shifted on the wall. Freyja spun back around her stalactite, breathing hard. She darted a look to the left, and then ran, her boots silent on the stone floor. The shadowy head whipped around and Freyja threw herself onto her knees in a slide, spinning behind a larger stalactite, and pressing her back to it.

"Do you know how many have ever dared enter here?" A whisper slid hot along her nerves. He was hunting for her, his mind darting over hers.

Freyja pulled her senses in small, trying to hide, limning herself in shadows, and wrapping them around her. Pressure washed over her, as thunderous as the storm outside, but her small shadow-shield protected her from the worst of it and the storm rolled over her, searching elsewhere.

"Do you think you can hide?" Another rustle in the darkness. *"I can scent your skin, your hair… the soap in your clothes. Did you think to come here to steal from me?"*

"To steal—? The only thief here is you! I came to take back that which was mine!" The thought flew from her before she could stop it. Freyja's grip tightened on the sword hilt.

24

What a fool she was. Always her temper got the better of her.

She'd expected the wyrm to lunge for her, but only silence greeted her. Silence in which she sat with breath held, desperate to track him through the cave.

"To take back your tithe?"

She wouldn't be drawn. Not this time. Freyja glanced toward the opening, and froze as she saw the liquid shadow of a tail lash against the cave wall.

Curse him. He was waiting by the entrance for her. She looked to the right, deeper into his lair. But perhaps there would be more tunnels there? A way to escape that he would not expect? Levering to her feet, she glanced around the rock, and slowly stepped toward the next one.

"Come out, little mouse. I will not hurt you."

The same tone she cajoled her ewes with when she led them for slaughter. She had to get out of here.

"Even if you do escape, do you think I will not know where to find you?"

Freyja froze.

Scales rasped against the walls. That alluring scent of cinnamon-spice flushed through her as he came closer. Freyja's head swam, her body shifting toward it. That scent. Calling her. Filling her with a liquid heat that pooled low in her abdomen. She shook her head to clear it, forcing herself to breathe through her mouth until she could think again.

"You smell... delicious. Like something that I used to know of." A pregnant pause. *"What are you?"*

"The woman whose ram you stole—" She stopped the thought there, but he caught some of it because that purring rasp sounded again, as if he were laughing at her.

"Come out." Shadows danced on the wall. His head, darting suddenly around one of the enormous rocks near her.

Freyja looked up. Sharp, dagger-shaped rocks clung to the roof far above. Did she dare?

Shadows rippled over the wall. Stalking her. Coming closer. Swallowing hard, she pressed her hand to the rock and closed her eyes, *reaching* out.

The cavern trembled, just enough for a few tiny pebbles to rain down. Freyja stretched her senses out, reaching further, trying to meld the earth to her touch. One of the enormous jutting stalactites shuddered above the *dreki*, and then she felt the tiny crack snake through it, breaking off the end.

Gasping at the sudden exertion, she snatched a breath as rock rained down from the ceiling, directly where she thought the wyrm to be. A rumble of surprise greeted her, and Freyja took her chances. Sword in hand, she darted back toward the entrance she'd come through.

Something lashed toward her feet.

She saw the whip of his tail too late, and screamed as her feet went out from under her. The sword skittered across the floor as she fell, staggering into a pile of golden krone and silver rigsdaler coins that cut her hands. They scattered everywhere, one of them rolling with mocking slowness toward the feet of the great beast behind her.

Freyja scrambled onto her bottom and hands, shoving backward with her feet toward the sword. Her breath caught as the dragon loomed over her, faint light playing over the iridescence of his scales.

Freyja froze.

She didn't dare take her gaze off him. He'd tricked her with his shadow, making her believe he'd been far closer to her than he was, and now he loomed over her, golden wings stretching out as if to intimidate, the enormous head stretched forward with eyes narrowed and dagger-teeth bared.

Beautiful and horrific and terrifying. She couldn't take her eyes off him, could barely breathe at the sight of such lithe magnificence, dancing around the cave on surprisingly quick feet. Savage death dwelled in his amber eyes. What a beautiful fury he was, like the storm outside. If she had to die, then she could almost think of no better beast to fell her.

But dying had never been her plan.

Freyja's hand closed over the sword and she wrenched it forward, pointing it at him pathetically. One last defiant act as she lay tumbled on her sealskin on one of his piles of gold.

"You think me beautiful?" His head lowered, resting on his forelegs, those razor-sharp claws flexing. *"You are fierce."*

Freyja's arm grew heavy as a low rumbling purr filled the cavern. Her eyes narrowed and she slowly let the sword fall to her lap, suspicion creeping through her. She was right! He was laughing at her.

Without taking her eyes off him, she climbed to her feet, dragging the sword with her. The futility of it struck her. She could see from the polished gleam of those scales that she would never have been able to pierce it. Still, it gave her something to lean on as she stared at the mighty wyrm.

"What do you intend to do with me?" Freyja asked defiantly, her nerves itching. Why was he just waiting?

The pupils of his eyes were slit like a cat's. The eyelids lowered a fraction, an almost smug gesture that wasn't lost on her. *"What do you think the penalty should be for stealing into my lair?"*

He wasn't going to kill her? Freyja's shoulders slumped. Suddenly she wanted to cry. As if the thought spurred them on, hot tears flooded her eyes. "I don't care," she said. Her voice lost its edge. "Do what you will and be done with it. I'm too exhausted to waste words with you."

The wyrm rumbled deep in his chest. *Words are all you have.*

"I have cold steel too," she muttered.

"And it provided such wondrous protection for its previous owner."

Freyja stared at the wyrm mulishly. Not only did he laugh at her, but that was definitely sarcasm. She tossed the sword aside and crossed her arms, blinking away her tears.

"Better." He settled again, entire body relaxing into a lazy sprawl on the floor. *"I do not like it when humans try to stick sharp things in me."*

"I don't like it when wyrms steal my sheep."

The wyrm yawned, exhibiting an array of wicked-sharp white teeth. *"Make more of them."*

Freyja actually took a step of startled anger toward it. "I would, but that was my last ram. I don't have another, hence I cannot breed more. I hope your belly's full, for you shall be getting no more lambs from me!" Again the tears threatened. "And neither shall I. My father and I shall starve for your greed!"

Those eyes narrowed. *"It was you humans who broke the tithe first. I only took what was promised."*

"From one who had not promised it," she retorted. "Each family knows the roster, and who must make the sacrifice. I paid mine months back!"

The dragon suddenly launched itself to its feet, and Freyja stumbled back in fright, tripping on a pile of kroner.

"It would not do," he said at last, *"to see such a fierce little mouse starve."*

28

Freyja's fists clenched. "I am *not* a mouse."

"No?" Again the satisfied rumble. *"No, you are not. What are you? You smell so familiar."*

What are you? Words she had been taunted with all of her life, for the oddness of her eyes and the strange intuition she had always suffered. *"Don't let anyone ever know what you can do,"* her mother had whispered. *"Not even your father. You are special, Freyja. Like me...."*

"Am I a changeling?" she'd asked.

Her mother had smiled and leaned down to kiss her forehead. *"Ignorance is your best weapon, my love. You are special, that is all you need know."*

Freyja stared up at the mighty wyrm. "I am a woman," she said carefully, for he would taste on her breath any lie she spoke. "I am human."

"You are a mystery," the *dreki* murmured. *"And there is nothing I like more than mystery."*

"What do you mean?"

A claw lashed out and swiped through one of the glittering piles. Gold coins scattered toward her, tumbling over her boots and brushing against her trousers. *"Take as much as your cupped hands can hold as payment for the ram. It would not do to see you starve now I have found you."*

Now I have found you.... Freyja didn't move.

"Each new moon, you shall come and visit. I find myself curious about you. That is the punishment for daring to enter my lair, and price for your continued existence."

She was right; he did have some plan for her, some perverse desire to... to.... She didn't know. Couldn't even comprehend why he would ask this of her.

"Next time I would suggest that you do not bring the sword." The wyrm glanced at her, its lips curling in an odd way that one would almost think a smile.

Freyja knelt down and dug her hands into the gold. The price was more than she wished to pay, but she was pragmatic. Refusing his gifts would see both her father and herself starve, and some part of her doubted she would be allowed to refuse. She had been granted a reprieve. For whatever reason he granted it—wyrms were not human after all, and bound by their own whims—the truth was the same.

She had survived.

She had actually challenged the mighty wyrm, and won.

Still, Freyja did not feel as though she had won as she stood and pocketed the veritable fortune. Staring into those amber, cat-slit eyes felt as though she stared into the burning furnace of the sun. He was not finished with her, not yet.

"Now go." A whisper across her senses, one that sounded eminently satisfied with itself. *"You look weary and should sleep."*

Freyja took a step back toward the entrance, not daring to turn her back on him at all.

"I shall see you soon, little mouse."

After she left, Rurik exploded into the storm-lashed sky with heavy thrusts from his magnificent wings, barely feeling the faint sting of rain.

Exhilaration danced through him, sending lightning crashing down again and again, dancing in tune to his desire. He pinwheeled through the sky above a ridge, gliding in and out of the flickering stabs of lightning, whipping it to a greater frenzy.

Fierce joy rode him, and a hunger he had not felt in many years. He felt as if the cobwebs had swept from his drowsing mind, as if a dash of icy water had splashed over him whilst he lazed on the heat-baked stones of his tunnels. A shock of life, returning.

Who is she?

Rurik circled high, his eagle gaze lighting on the tiny, bedraggled figure far below, fighting her way across the bleak landscape. She would not see him, but he watched over her. The *dreki* loved puzzles, and she was a curiosity wrapped up in a mystery.

Fierce.

His female. Appearing in the heart of the storm to challenge him in his own lair. Of course he could not resist her.

And then there was the mystery of her power. He could remember the taste of it in the air between them, crackling like lightning. It reminded him of something, though he could not bring the thought to mind.

What is she?

For the first time in decades his interest, long dormant, stirred. The male in him had looked and seen a creature of flame and shadow, of mighty power, utterly bedazzling. A treasure beyond any he owned. He wanted her. Therefore he would have her, and together they would burn the world until he tired of her.

Rurik dipped his wings, feeling the lash of the winds. It turned him into a free fall, wind whipping past him with dizzying intensity until he banked at the last moment, sweeping over the moors and alighting on a crag. A shudder swept through him, an electric tingle lighting across his skin.

It had been a long time since he walked as a man. A long time since he had desired it, indeed desired anything.

Lightning flickered in the distance and in front of him his shadow quivered, then shrunk, wings disappearing, and his serpentine neck folding in on itself. Rurik fell to his hands and knees, feeling the power of the land roil beneath his touch. Rain stung his skin, a whiplash of sensuous pleasure as he bowed his head and waited for the shock of his transition to fade.

Nude. Glorious. Full of immense power that boiled beneath the heavy muscle of his skin. Rurik lifted his head as water sluiced down over his naked skin and smiled fiercely, his teeth bared.

Time to go hunting.

CHAPTER
THREE

THE PROBLEM WITH gold was that nobody in her village or the neighboring farms would be able to trade for it, nor was it wise to show too much of it, in case someone decided to see if she had more.

Freyja spent three days debating the problem, then finally harnessed their small Icelandic pony, Hanna, to the cart. Telling her father that she intended to buy a new ram in Akureyri—without revealing the precise details of the demise of their previous one—she set out toward the trading town. The cart was stocked full of wool and eiderdown, for trips to the trading town were rare and she was practical enough to take this opportunity to sell what she had stored.

One day to travel, one to trade, and one to get home. He'd be fine. He'd lived in their little house his entire life. He wouldn't need his eyes to get around, and their distant neighbor had promised to keep an eye on him.

Sunshine washed down over her as she guided Hanna along the marshy plain toward Akureyri. The thin track was barely marked by passing traffic, as the last thaw had obliterated it. Only several *kerlingar*—small pyramids of stone shaped much like old women—marked the way.

"Easy now," Freyja murmured, as Hanna crested the rise and Akureyri revealed itself below.

The trading town was nestled in the heart of a fjord, with a natural harbor and warmer waters that kept the bay ice-free. Red houses lined the bay and several Danish merchant ships lingered in the harbor. Sometimes the English came to trade for fish, but it was done under a cover of secrecy, for the Danish held the trade monopoly. One could often see them swaggering about the town, turning their noses up at the natives.

For a woman travelling alone, it wasn't wise to venture too close to the docks, but Freyja had been born with one mostly green eye, and one brown. Witch-born or elf-cursed, depending on which religion or superstition you believed in. People still crossed themselves when they saw her, and few would dare accost her.

She hoped.

Finding a room and board at a small inn, Freyja hastily brushed Hanna down, the gold in the pouch at her neck seeming to weigh her down. She felt as though eyes lingered on her as she left the stables, though that was ridiculous. Nobody knew what she had on her person.

"Hey now! Be careful with that!" someone bellowed as she hurried to the inn.

A large merchant ship had docked close to shore, and men were hastily trying to rig up some sort of contraption to swing what looked like an enormous crossbow on wheels from the ship deck to the dock.

Freyja tucked her bright red shawl around her shoulders as she sidestepped through the growing crowd. "What is it?" she asked no one in particular.

A young lad in a dark blue seafaring coat with brass buttons up the sides of it glanced at her, his hair covered in a knitted woolen cap. "It's the dragon hunter, miss. From Norway."

All about her people were lured out of their homes. Freyja stood on her toes to see. *Dragon hunter.* Chills of premonition edged down her spine. "The only *dreki* in these parts is the one beneath Krafla."

"Aye," the lad replied. "Some of the local villages have put together a fund for the dragon hunter's reward. They want no more of this tithe, or this wyrm's demands. Iceland should have no master anymore."

It would take more than a group of villagers to pay for the dragon hunter. It had to be Benedikt. He and his father made their fortune mining sulfur, and then buying up as much land as they could. He'd long been vocal about his hatred for the tithe and the demand it placed on the villagers. Not that she thought his desire to rid himself of the wyrm was truly guided by his concern for others. Benedikt's pride was enough to resent any overlord, no matter how little the wyrm stirred their affairs.

"Where is the dragon hunter?" she asked, stumbling over the words.

The lad pointed. "There!"

Freyja's breath caught as an enormous man strode into view, yelling harshly at the engineers as the ballista was levered off the ship. It dangled over the gulf between water and wharf, swinging precariously.

He was a tall man, wearing archaic chain mail and a long fur cloak. His hair shone moonlight-silver in the dying light, and even from this distance she could see he was handsome. Around her, several whispered murmurs assured her she was not the only one to believe so.

Freyja couldn't tear her gaze away as the ballista swung toward the wharf. Unease twisted in her gut as she tucked her hands into the narrow crevices of her elbows. The gold seemed to burn in the pouch around her neck.

"Has he hunted many *dreki*?" she asked. "I did not believe them so easy to fell."

"He has ways," the lad assured her. "They say he's hunted three of them in Norway."

Three. A man who knew how to kill them then. Freyja shivered. In hindsight, the wyrm seemed curious more than anything else. With time to think over the incident in the cave, she was swiftly realizing he never meant to kill her.

If he'd wished such a thing, he could have done so immediately.

An odd knot of guilt warmed in her chest. She shouldn't get involved. After all, what could she do? Warn the beast?

The dragon hunter stepped to the edge of the wharf, lifting his hands for silence. "My name," he called in a strong accent, "is Haakon Haraldsson. I am here to rid you of the foul beast that lurks beneath Krafla."

Clapping sprang up, women cheering for him and waving handkerchiefs. One would think him a feudal king for the way he carried himself.

A slight smile curled over Haakon's mouth, though his eyes remained as cold as the glaciers further south. The precise same color too, she noted, as his gaze locked on her. "My team have destroyed three of the foul beasts, and sent them back to the hell they came from." At this he crossed himself, and half the crowd echoed him. "They tell me that Iceland is burdened by such creatures. And I say, no more!" He roared the last words.

Excitement ran through the crowd, trailing over her skin. Freyja was the only one not clapping, and he saw it, his eyes meeting hers with a challenge.

"I hear many words," another voice called out in a low baritone. "But I do not hear how you will perform this"— the voice dropped to a mocking drawl—"miraculous feat."

All eyes swung toward the back of the crowd. Gasps rang out as people stepped aside to reveal another man, sunlight gleaming off the golden thread of his embroidered waistcoat.

He did not move, gaze locked on the dragon slayers, and his arms crossed over his firm chest. Both men were of a height, though the newcomer's shoulders were broader, and he held himself as though he were the tallest man in the crowd.

He was the sun to Haakon's moonlit coloring. Silky golden hair raked back from his brow, his watchful eyes the color of amber. Someone long ago had broken his nose, and the imperfection only heightened the severely handsome cut of his features. He was breathtaking. The kind of man she'd pictured as the prince of all the stories her mother told her, though the predatory nature of his gaze told her that he might not be quite as noble as she anticipated.

Definitely a stranger. Powerful and at ease with himself, as though he knew his worth. Freyja couldn't stop her gaze from dropping to those muscular thighs, encased in superfine buff breeches. His coat was dark bronze wool, and a spill of snowy white lace at his throat highlighted the golden hue of his skin. She'd never seen the like in her life.

"And who are you?" Haakon called.

"You may refer to me as Rurik," the stranger replied, with a slight accent. His voice was smooth, yet everybody strained to hear it. "And I study myths. Including this *dreki* that you speak of killing."

"A scholar." The way Haakon pronounced the word spoke volumes. He smiled. "Perhaps you should leave the talk of killing dragons to those better suited for it."

Laughter spilled around them.

"Knowledge is its own weapon," Rurik countered, an amused gleam warming his eyes. There was a challenge there.

Haakon turned and gestured toward the ballista. "This shoots solid steel bolts at a hundred yards a second. It's strong enough to pierce even a dragon's hide."

"He must stay very still for you then."

Haakon tilted his head slightly to the side. "There are ways," he said, with a chilling little smile.

"And the chainmail? Do you think yourself a knight of old?"

Haakon trailed his knuckles over the smooth rings. "This saved my life three months ago. A dragon has sharp teeth. This stops them."

A whip crack of sound drew everyone's attention, including Haakon's. Freyja's gaze jerked to the far rope holding the heavy machine in place. As she watched, one strand of the hemp unraveled with devastating swiftness. The other held for a second before the pressure snapped it in half too.

"Secure that bloody thing!" Haakon roared as the ballista tumbled onto its side, dangling by two precarious ropes.

Another broke, and the ballista jerked closer to the water below before the final rope lost its fight, and snapped with a mighty crack.

"No!" Haakon raced forward as the ballista tumbled into the water below with a chilly splash. It sank without further aplomb and he cursed at the engineers who had rigged the harness, barking orders in a brutally authoritative tone.

"A pity," a voice, darkly amused, murmured by her ear. "Now he shall find it most difficult to hunt *dreki*."

The words whispered over the smooth skin behind her ear. Freyja shivered, and spun on her heel to face the man. Rurik stood closer than he ought to, his body cutting the cool slipstream 'of the wind so that she instantly warmed. Or perhaps that was the heat that lingered in the air between them.

She hadn't even heard him moving. Tugging her shawl tight around her shoulders, Freyja glanced up at him as if daring him to stare at her eyes.

And he did.

But not the way most men usually did, recoiling in horror. Instead he leaned closer, seeming to stare right through her as if he could see something that no one else could. As if somehow he stripped her naked—not of her clothes, but of every pretense and inhibition she'd ever owned, every lie she'd ever told, every little smile she'd used to mask her hurt.

And it burned. The connection between them was irrevocable. Freyja was lost, unable to look away, drawn like a lodestone to iron filings, lured by the smoky amber of his gaze. Her breath trapped itself in her lungs, as though she wore a steel corset.

"You have beautiful eyes," he finally murmured, and the spell was broken.

"Beautif—" she blurted, then stopped herself. Nobody had ever called them beautiful before, and this conversation was incredibly daring for a man who had not even asked her name.

Small lines creased in the corners of his eyes, as though he smiled without moving his lips. "You doubt me? Do you not own a mirror?"

"This is most unseemly," she murmured, dropping her head so as to draw as little attention as possible.

"I did not take you for a seemly woman at all."

Freyja looked up with a steely glare. "Sir, you have spoken out of turn. I will thank you to move out of my way."

Those amber eyes sharpened, as though he had unearthed precisely what he wished to find. "My apologies. I did not mean to offend. I merely meant to point out that you are a rare blossom in a garden of"—his gaze raked the crowd—"ordinary blooms. You're not the type to conform. I find the effect stimulating."

And then he hit her with the full power of his smile.

Freyja stepped back, tucking her shawl tighter as though it could somehow protect her or help sort her whirlpool of sudden emotion. "You offer compliments with a practiced ease."

"I speak the truth and always have." He offered her his hand as if to bring her fingers to his lips. "My name is Rurik."

"So I believe you said." His fingers were long and elegant. She eyed them as one would eye a toad. She didn't want to touch him. Instinct had never let her down in the past and it was screaming at her now. Touch him and she would be lost. Touch him and all manner of dangerous, life-changing moments existed in her future. "And if honeyed words are the only weapons in your arsenal, then I fear you shall have a fruitless hunt."

"Are you challenging me to prove my intentions?"

"All I am saying," she stared at him defiantly, "is that I will not succumb to flattery."

His eyelashes lowered as he realized she had no intention of taking his hand. "I don't believe I caught your name."

"I never offered it," she replied, and gathering her skirts, moved to step around him. "Good day, sir."

Freyja could feel eyes on her as she hurried toward the inn. Watching her. Smoldering. And then she realized that Rurik wasn't the only person watching her.

The dragon slayer glared at her, his arms folded across his chest and his face expressionless. Behind him, his men dove into the waters of the bay, to attach cables to the ballista, but he paid them no mind. No, his attention was all for her.

Freyja faltered. Her ears began catching hints of the murmurs that surrounded her. The flickering glances of the crowd.

"...curious how it fell like that? All at once, as if the ropes were cut...."

"Cut by what?"

Silence greeted the question. Nobody quite looked at her, but she saw an older lady cross herself.

Somehow Freyja forced herself to take another step. Then another. Moving stiffly, though she tried not to. Her pulse started to race. They did not burn witches anymore, but she was suddenly aware of her vulnerability so far from home. There were none here to protect her or protest her innocence. No one who knew her.

It was not so bad out in the countryside where the goodwives told their tales, and everyone knew it was wise not to disturb the tors for fear of earning the wrath of trolls. Changeling, the local bonders whispered behind her back, but they did little more than whisper. Here in the town, religion had a stronger hold.

Freyja tried to ignore the dragon slayer's stare as she reached the inn door. The crowd was not where the danger lay.

"Here."

Rurik frowned down at her, offering his arm. He too understood the whispering vibe of the crowd. Somehow he looked different, as if the lazy, handsome wastrel had washed from his countenance, to be replaced by something infinitely feral. Meaner. His cheekbones seemed harshly cut, and his eyes glittered like a smoldering furnace. He placed his body between her and the crowd; cutting off the dagger-glance the dragon slayer gave her.

She shouldn't trust him.

"Take my arm," he said. "Dine with me."

Freyja slid her hand through the crook of his arm, swallowing hard. The press of his body against hers filled her with heat and an odd longing. Dare she trust it? Him?

"I won't let them hurt you. Come." He pushed through the inn door, holding it open for her. A slow smile curled over his mouth. "Be brave, my lady. I did not think you the type to retreat from anything."

Freyja sucked in a breath. He was right. If she could face down the mighty wyrm by herself, then she could certainly handle a crowd of superstitious, narrow-minded gossips.

The thought brought an ill-timed smile to her lips, and Rurik's gaze sharpened on them. "You are amused?"

"I have an odd sense of what to be frightened of. If you knew what I have faced… and yet I quail at this." She laughed softly. "Foolishness."

Rurik guided her through the door with his hand in the small of her back. The low-beamed ceiling was stained with peat smoke and several locals leaned on the bar, smoking their pipes. Mostly men, for women rarely frequented a place like this, only those like herself who were forced to trade for lack of menfolk in their lives.

"People are frightened of what they do not understand," Rurik murmured, the pressure of his hand warming the small of her back. For a moment she caught a hint of his cologne, and turned her face unconsciously toward his chest to breathe it in. Spicy. Smoky-hot. *Delicious*.

Their eyes met. Something about his gaze frightened her. Darkly knowledgeable. Patient. As if he knew precisely what sort of reaction she was having, and simply waited for her to succumb.

"Perhaps they have cause to be frightened," she murmured.

"And are we speaking of you or me here?"

His gaze raked over the plain black cloth of her *skautbúningur*. It was her best gown, with gold leaf embroidered around the neckline and skirts, and a spill of white lace at her throat. It covered her from throat to toe, but for a moment she felt dangerously unclothed.

Both of them. For he had a certain power too.

"Thank you," she murmured, drawing away from him and ignoring his implication. "But I do believe—"

"You are not walking away from me again, are you? And here I thought the North was known for its hospitality."

Freyja's words died in her mouth. With such a distance between farmsteads, and the harsh climes, to turn a man or woman from your door was unthinkable. To suggest she lacked in hospitality was an insult, and he knew it, from the amused twinkle that lit his amber gaze.

"This is not my home," she said, using precise, clipped words. "You may come or go as you please."

"Then I shall stay to dine." He stepped past in a swish of scent that left her breathless. Freyja's hands curled into fists, but Rurik seemed not to see. A smile curled over his sensual mouth as he glanced behind him. "And look. There is one table left. If you ask me nicely, I shall share it with you."

Arrogant devil. She did not wish to dine with him, but her stomach clenched as if reminding her of how long it had been since breakfast. And glutton that she was, she had been dreaming of baked kipper pie or roasted salmon for the entire journey to town. A rare treat, and now that she had coin she could indulge herself.

But he was dangerous.

For she'd never felt like this before: as if she had a secret that he somehow knew. A secret carnal craving that had never flared 'til now, as if her body knew things that she herself didn't. Perhaps having men shy away from her eyes had been a hidden boon in the past. Rurik's frank interest in her unnerved her in so many ways.

"I wish to know more about the *dreki* beneath Krafla," he said, starting toward the table as if she'd given her assent. "To further my studies. I would be most appreciative if you would join me."

Curse him.

What could it hurt? She did not have to speak overmuch. And his insinuation of her inhospitality irked her. Her mother would have been shamed, and Freyja herself…. Had she changed so much in recent years? For a moment she remembered the joy of being a child, when she had been sheltered and protected out there on the plains, not understanding quite why they had so few visitors, or why she was often sent to bed early when there were. She'd been hungry for human company once, before she'd learned what the world was truly like.

His manner had been uncondemning. Freyja's heart gave a small twist in her chest. More than anything, she longed for that.

Rurik glanced over his shoulder as he wove his way through the crowded seats. Eyes watched him as he went, conversation dropping to a murmur. An outsider. Like her.

Freyja didn't realize she'd taken a step toward him until the hardness leeched out of his eyes.

"My lady," he almost purred, holding a chair out for her.

She sat and let him push her chair in, his knuckles brushing against her shoulders. A spark of heat went all the way through her at the touch. Freyja half glanced over her shoulder, but he was moving, circling the table with fluid grace and sinking into the chair opposite her.

"Now come, my lady." He leaned back in his chair. "Tell me about yourself."

CHAPTER
FOUR

"WERE WE NOT speaking of you, and your fascination for *dreki*, my lord?" His little mouse countered.

She smelled like wildflowers and a spring morning, of dew wet on the grass, or the breeze that cut the mountain passes. Wild and free. Untamable.

The look on her face, however, was almost frigid; a cool, biting wind from the south, coming straight off the glaciers. Rurik leaned back in the seat, perusing her with lazy fascination.

Her manner ought to have left him cold, but he found himself only curious. She had not been so wary of him when she faced him in his lair. Only now, as a man before her, did he make her nervous, and he knew precisely why.

"I am not a very interesting man."

She arched a brow. "I beg to differ. After all, you didn't deny the courtesy title I just bestowed upon you."

Clever mouse. He gestured to the serving maid to bring them wine. "You demand all of my secrets, and here I have not even your name..."

That made her pretty mouth purse. "Freyja. Freyja Helgasdottir."

Freyja. Of course. "Goddess of love and war, beauty and death. It's a lovely name."

"I am no goddess."

"That depends upon whose eyes you look through."

Pink darkened her cheeks. "I have no wish to offend the gods."

"So, you still believe in the old gods?"

Freyja hesitated. "I have been baptized, but I believe there are some things in this world that defy explanation." Those mismatched eyes locked on him. "And you are doing an excellent job of not answering my original question, I notice."

"I am not a noble man, by the very definition of the word," he said carefully. "I own no lands,"—*technically true*—"I have no specific title, and I claim no king."

"Do you mean you do not recognize the Danish king? Iceland has a limited constitution now, and some autonomy. Were you a follower of Jón Sigurðsson? My father had older copies of his annual magazine, and I have read his thoughts on democracy."

This was where she came alive. Each flicker of her eyes toward him—those beautiful, unique eyes—made his body harden.

So she was curious about his thoughts, but immune to his flattery. How intriguing.

"No. I have not heard of this Sigurðsson—I've been absorbed in other matters of interest—but I do believe that no... no man rules the earth beneath him. Not here." He examined the bottle of wine the serving maid brought him, then nodded. "This will do."

Freyja's cheeks colored. "I do not drink wine."

"Have you ever tried it?" He remembered delicious vintages from his youth, when he'd drifted through Renaissance Italy and France, curious about these mortals around him.

"No."

"Do you wish to?" he asked, ordering his meal.

Freyja hesitated, but there was a ruthlessly mercenary look in her eye. "I shall make do with ale." She looked to the serving maid. "And I should like the ptarmigan stew with sliced rúgbrauð bread."

He kept catching hints of her thoughts, thrown into the world about her with careless abandon. And right now, she was thinking of gold coins. As much as he liked gold, he couldn't quite imagine what it had to do with wine and ale. "I never make do."

She eyed the cut of his magnificent coat. "Of that, I have no doubt."

Hmmm. "Bring two glasses just in case," he instructed the serving maid, "and my lady will have ale on the side."

Images of his hands hit him as he stroked over the table, and the way his collar tugged open when he shifted, baring the tanned, smooth skin of his throat. Freyja liked the look of him, and Rurik fought a predatory smile as she threw the thought around her.

A curious thing, to see himself through another's eyes. *Dreki* were strictly forbidden to enter another's thoughts and pillage them, though anything she projected was fair game. And her thoughts danced over his skin like rainbows, so vivid and colorful that he almost tried to reach out and catch them.

A bad idea. The stiff slant of her shoulders alone told him that. If she felt his psychic touch… if she knew precisely what was sitting at her table, then he would lose all chance at seducing her.

Not yet. She was too wary. More timid than he would have ever believed of his fierce mouse. His brows drew together momentarily. What had made her like that? The idea twisted inside him like something with claws.

"So," she murmured, "where *do* you hail from?" For a moment her eyes lingered on the fine cut of his coat.

Tailor-made, all the way from London. He'd paid a small fortune for the extravagance of having it and others so swiftly finished, before he returned to pursue her. But he was *dreki*. He would no more clothe himself in peasants' garb than wallow in a piggery.

"I come from the south," he murmured, eyeing her strictly cut black dress. Freyja ought to be in silk, or better yet, naked, lying on silken sheets. She deserved finer things, and he would see she had them before he was through with her.

"And you come here to seek tales of *dreki*? Of local superstition?"

Careful here. He could not utter a lie; the *dreki* were bound and honored by their word. "I am curious of what you think of such creatures," he replied, as the wine, ale, and their dinner arrived. "Many don't believe their existence. Mostly those in the cities, or on the Continent."

"I have seen... proof of their existence." Freyja frowned into her ale. "The cursed creature ate my ram."

"Your ram?" *Always that bloody sheep.* Would she never forgive him for it? It had been delicious and it had brought her into his lair, when he might never have seen her.

"My village pays a tithe," she explained. "For thirty years we have been bound to sacrifice one of our livestock each week to the wyrm, so that he might leave us alone. My father tells me that he and the rest of the local farmers gathered together many years ago, and struck a bargain with the beast."

Beast? "They were either very courageous, or foolish to brave such a fierce creature."

Freyja shrugged. "Perhaps they knew their offer would be accepted? Wyrms are lazy. Why hunt when a lamb shall be tethered out for you once a week? He used to hunt more frequently, my father claims, but now he spends most of his time lazing in his mountain, soaking up the heat of the volcano."

"I thought wyrms to be fierce, powerful predators."

"When they wish to be. Most of the time he leaves us alone. He is bound by his word not to harm us...." A frown tightened her brow. "Though now it seems some of the local bonders have broken *their* word, and hired a hunter."

"I would not think this would trouble you."

"It doesn't." Yet the worry etched on her expression didn't fade. She sighed. "If they've broken their oath, then the wyrm is no longer bound by his. They are vengeful creatures, according to legend. I don't particularly wish to incur his wrath. I can't afford to lose any more livestock."

And she wouldn't. Her fierce desperation in his cave scoured him. *My father and I shall starve....*

"Perhaps other tithes might appease him?"

At that her mismatched eyes locked on his, a flare of her temper lighting the beautiful green and brown of them. "A virgin sacrifice, you mean? We do not take part in such barbaric practices anymore."

"They are rare," he admitted. "A pity."

"Virgins? Or the act of sacrificing one?" she countered.

Rurik allowed himself a smile—and didn't answer. "You speak as though it is a crime."

"No woman should be forced to such depths."

She was definitely angry now. Her eyes blazed. And Rurik caught the edge of her thoughts. There were few virgins around her farmstead. Most of the young women were either married, or still children.

Except for her.

"In olden times, women offered to be made sacrifice," he said, sipping his wine, and watching her eyes spit sparks. *Beautiful.* "It was an honor."

"To be eaten?"

So innocent.... "Oh yes. To be devoured."

Freyja's lashes fluttered against her cheeks, which were filling with heat. Yet she did not respond to his playful innuendo, deliberately it seemed, for she certainly understood it. "You are speaking of those foolish eddas, where the *dreki* walk among us."

"Do you doubt such a thing could be possible?"

"Why would they wish to? My mother said it is the only time they are mortal and vulnerable to injury. So why would one of the *dreki* risk such a thing?"

"Perhaps he is lonely."

"You are ascribing human attributes to an inhuman creature."

"Inhuman, yes," he countered, his own temper flaring. "Don't ever mistake that, but perhaps all creatures yearn for companionship."

"There are other *dreki*," she replied. "Every volcano in Iceland is plagued by one. Sometimes more."

Rurik's fingers stilled on the edge of his glass. "Not all of the *dreki* welcome others. Nor are all of them welcomed. If one of their laws are broken, sometimes they cast a *dreki* from their ranks, exiling him to years of loneliness."

Freyja lifted her gaze at the coolness of his tone, as if she sensed something underlying the words. "How do you know so much?"

"I have eyes. And ears."

"You sound like my father," she growled under her breath. "You speak, but say nothing."

"I am curious as to how a man would allow his unmarried daughter to travel by herself?"

Rurik reached out, and captured the wine bottle, leaning forward to fill her glass. She sat so still, yet tension vibrated through her body. Captured lightning. Just daring him to reach out and touch it.

"My father is blind and ill, so he cannot travel with me." Those glorious eyes narrowed, and a chilling little smile tightened her soft lips. "However, I am not without protection."

As well he should know. His little mouse had claws and teeth, though neither would be truly effective against him. Still… he liked it. Liked that snap to her tone, and the way her pretty eyes narrowed as she examined him.

A challenge.

Rurik handed her the glass, their fingers brushing against each other's as she took it. The touch of her skin sent lightning dancing through him. Like to like. What in the Dark Goddess Hel was she?

Freyja's eyes widened slightly as if she felt it too, and then she jerked the glass close to her mouth. "Thank you."

He watched the wine wet her lips, and leave them reddened. Plush, glistening lips he ached to trace, to caress.

Then her eyes widened and she peered into her glass. "This is delicious."

"I know." He wasn't to be distracted. "You do realize you have nothing to protect yourself against when you are with me? I have no intention of hurting you."

"Who says I am frightened of you?"

"Your manner."

You couldn't hurt me if you tried.... Freyja arched a sleek, honey-blonde brow, as if she hadn't just thrown the thought at him. "Then what precisely are your intentions?"

"You intrigue me," he admitted, watching her lick a trace of wine from her lips. Gods, how he wanted her. "It has been a very long time since such a thing has happened. Perhaps not ever."

"Do they believe such honeyed words in the cities?"

Rurik smiled, and turned her words back upon her. "You do not like to be complimented. How curious. Is it because you believe yourself unworthy of such words?"

"I am unworthy of nothing," she snapped.

"Then you admit that you are intriguing? That I might see you as such?"

Her mouth opened... and nothing came out of it. Then she pressed those lips firmly together. "I know what you intend when you look at me."

"Do tell."

"I am not that kind of woman," she replied haughtily. "Your empty compliments and blatant desires shall earn you nothing more than this meal shared."

"That still tells me nothing of my supposed desires."

Freyja glared at him. "You wish for carnal relations."

Rurik leaned closer, careful not to let the predatory heat of his desire leech out. Best not to frighten her. Not yet. "I intend to have you in every way possible, Freyja. I intend to discover every last little secret you own, to know you... in every manner. This is a game of seduction, and I will not harm you nor make your choices for you. I speak of courtship only. But I think you would enjoy what I intend, very much so." At her swift intake of breath, he leaned back. "And I am not ashamed to admit I intend to chase you. Fair warning, fair maid. You will be mine."

Freyja tilted the wine glass to her mouth. "Fair warning, handsome stranger... you're wasting your breath."

How delightful she was. At least she'd relaxed at his stated intentions, as if she were so set on denial that the thought he'd win her over couldn't possibly prevail. "I like a good chase, Freyja."

"I hope you like a long and fruitless one then. Especially if the choice of consummation is in my hands."

"Are you not curious?" He reached out and stroked her hand suddenly.

There was that flash fire of connection between them, and her gaze jerked to his. "No," she said as she withdrew her hand, but she'd hesitated.

"Do you know what I find so fascinating about you?"

A faint hint of pride and scorn mingled on her face as she swiftly restored herself. "My lips? My hair? My *eyes*?" The dancing flames of the fireplace lit her cheeks and skin with gold, until it seemed as though he stared into the face of a creature made of fire itself.

"Your fierce temper," he whispered. "And that dare you throw at me every time you look at me. It tells me that I cannot have you, that you shall not succumb... even as your body reveals it for a lie."

Heat colored her cheeks. "You won't have me."

"You want me to have you," he murmured. "Don't lie to me."

"Your compliments are empty, and your declarations even more so." Standing, she glanced at the empty carafe of wine. "Do you care for more?"

Rurik glanced up from beneath his lashes. "Run, Freyja." He smiled dangerously. "And yes, I would enjoy more wine."

"I shall fetch it then."

Wending between the tables, she made her way to the bar. Eyes watched her back, lingering on her. Not all of them in suspicion or distrust. The very set of her shoulders defined her untouchability, and with it, part of her allure. He was clearly not the only one affected, and she could not see it, mired in distrust, and ingrained with suspicion. Rurik scowled, his lashes lowering as he leaned back in the chair and surveyed the room. With one lash of his temper he could destroy this room and all of the men in it. Men who hungered for her.

A dangerous hunger, marred as it was by their beliefs, for there were ways to force such a woman as she to heel, and such was anathema to his *dreki* nature. Women should never be coerced. But a whisper in the right ear and she could be accused of things she had no control over.... Thunder rumbled outside in the clear sky at the vile thought. He watched eyes glance toward windows and smiled, more a hint of his teeth than any sign of humor.

He would protect her. Whether she thought she needed it or not.

An odd tension filled him, and his gaze went to the entrance.

It opened, wind sending a man staggering through the light-filled doorway. The sharp scent of tar, fur, and the sea filled Rurik's nostrils as the dragon hunter stepped through the door, tugging his wolf fur close around his shoulders as he surveyed the room. His tangled blond hair whipped into chilling blue-gray eyes, and their gazes locked.

Rurik inclined his head slightly. A dangerous man, and one he would not underestimate, for the man spoke the truth on the docks as he spoke of killing three dragons. His lesser cousins were no match for *dreki*, but still monstrous creatures. It was a remarkable feat for a single man to have engineered.

"Would you care for company?" Haakon asked, as Freyja returned with the wine.

Rurik lifted his foot and slid the other chair back with a beckoning gesture and a hint of a wolfish smile. "Please." The last thing he would ever do was fear a puny human.

And perhaps it would be fun.

Dragging off his gloves, the heavily muscled man took the seat and offered thanks to Freyja as she returned to the counter to fetch another glass.

"How go your recovery efforts?" Rurik asked, faintly amused.

"Badly. The tide is coming in, and the dockhands seem to think it madness to attempt to retrieve my ballista now."

"A pity."

Haakon shrugged, icy blue eyes watchful. "A brief setback. I'm a patient man."

So was he. "The mark of a true hunter."

A dangerous smile curved the hunter's lips as Freyja settled again at the table. "What would a scholar know of such things?"

"I know many things," Rurik countered. "Wine?" At the other man's nod, Rurik took the carafe and poured before Freyja could. He had no intention of seeing her serve another man. Not when she was his.

"Mistress Helgasdottir." Haakon nodded politely.

"I see you've been enquiring about me," she replied.

Enough to learn her name, and no doubt more. The amount of information the locals owned about the unusual young woman was immense, and offered generously. A growl curdled in Rurik's throat. For what he could learn, so too could others.

"What man does not enquire about such a striking young woman?" Haakon asked.

This time the compliment brought no heat to her cheeks. She remained cool, and on her guard. "You are not the only one who can learn about another. You come to hunt the *dreki*," she replied, sipping her wine. "To kill him."

"I make no lie of my intentions," Haakon replied. "Word reached my ears of this particular beast, and so I have come to try my hand at him."

"Word of the beast? Or word of the reward?" she asked.

"A significant sum." Haakon leaned back in his chair. "But no, it's the beast I'm most interested in. I am told you come from the village at the base of its lair. That you know of the creature."

Freyja's lips thinned. "I know the creature. It stole my ram, and so I was forced to enter its lair to try and save him."

Haakon's eyes sharpened.

"Without luck, I assure you," she replied primly.

"All here know of the mighty creature," Rurik murmured. "You should be warned: this is no lesser dragon that you hunt. This is one of the mighty *dreki*."

"There is a difference between dragon and *dreki*?" Freyja interrupted. "I thought 'dragon' was simply another term used in different countries?"

"No. They are cousins, but far different creatures. Many, many years ago, the *dreki* were born to this land. Spirits of earth, air, and fire, created by a goddess into a single creature with the powers of all three of the elements."

"Which goddess?" He'd captured her curiosity now.

"None of yours," he murmured. "Only she that is sacred to the *dreki*, born many, many eons before your gods were but a thought. Some call her Creator, some Chaos, and her name was Tiamat, or Thalatte. This mighty spirit tamed the salt waters to her mastery, and of her children there were many, which some called gods. When these gods went to war with her husband, Apsu, and killed him, she created monsters with poison for blood, to fight them. The descendants of these creatures are what we refer to as dragons. The lesser of them bred serpents of the waters, vile beasts with limited thought that we call leviathan and serpents.

"But the *dreki*... they were different. They say that when the great goddess used her powers to turn herself into an enormous serpent in the sea to fight her husband's killers, she was slain by the storm-god Marduk. He scattered her body across the world, but her soul remained, formless yet still powerful. The sea and her waters had failed her, and when the north wind blew her soul around the globe, her soul sought solace in the warm, dark earth, where fire brewed."

Both of them were focused intently upon him. Rurik continued, "Long did her soul brew in the heart of the volcano, Hekla, and her spirit strengthened with the force of the element of fire. She sought life again, but to form a fleshly body was beyond her. Her only hope lay in creating more children, ones that spun to life from the earth, were gilded with the power of fire, and ruled the air. Using her waning powers in one last act of Creation, the volcano exploded and with each gout of fire, the goddess created her new children. The goddess tore her soul apart, pieces of her power imbuing each spirit with strength. These were the *dreki*, and they carry a part of the goddess within them. Powerful spirits who ruled the elements and could tame the sky itself; those with the goddess's own ability to shapeshift.

"The wyrms, leviathan, and serpents were slowly hunted by men, the last of them dying out centuries ago in the Persian Gulf. But dragons remain, and some say they haunt volcanoes, seeking to steal the gift of fire that eludes them." He tilted his head toward Haakon, "These are the creatures you have faced. Fierce beasts with poisonous blood, but no breath of fire, nor mastery of the elements. Jealous creatures who yearn for more."

"And *dreki* breathe fire?" Haakon asked.

"Some do," he replied. "You have to understand that there have been many generations of *dreki* born. They are not immortal, though they have long lives. Now, only the purest of bloodlines have the gift of fire."

"Hekla," Freyja murmured, "the gateway to hell."

"So say many who believe in such a place," Rurik agreed. Now it was the home of the *dreki* court, though he would not breathe word of it here.

"I have never heard such a story told," Haakon said. "Where did you come by such information?"

Rurik shrugged and drained his wine. "Years of listening, perhaps. There are many who will exchange an old tale by a hearth on a cold night. And perhaps you were not asking the right questions?" Setting the empty cup on the table, he leaned forward, "Such as why a man sets himself on such a dangerous pursuit as hunting dragons or even *dreki*? Especially when he does not know the difference between them?"

Haakon's expression tightened. "One of them stole my wife six years ago."

"Stole?" he asked thoughtfully. "You come from Norway, yes?"

"Yes."

"There are no *dreki* on the mainland in Norway," Rurik mused. "Which means that one travelled far to take her, and I assure you that *dreki* do not take that which is not given freely."

"Are you calling me a liar?" Haakon's face darkened.

"I am wondering how you were so certain your wife was taken by such?"

Haakon pushed his chair aside with a scrape, leaning his knuckles on the table as he growled, "Because I saw her enter the grove, and I saw the beast launch itself into the air directly after she screamed. By the time I got there, all that was left was her basket, and scattered bread loaves she'd been taking to my sister. I have not seen her since and I have spent *many* a long night searching." Haakon closed his eyes briefly, his voice becoming raw. "The last thing I remember is the sight of her face as she glanced one last time at me, and the look in her amber eyes...."

"Amber eyes?" A curious tale. Rurik frowned. "Describe the *dreki*, please."

"What?"

"Describe him," Rurik repeated. "What size? What shape? What color—"

"Gold," Haakon spat. "The beast shone like newly minted coins, which is why I'm here. I've heard that Krafla's beast is the same color."

Gold. Rurik sat back in surprise. Dragons could not change shape into mortal form. But *dreki* could. And there was only one golden *dreki* that he knew of, beside himself.

Oh, Hel.

"*Árdís, what were you thinking?*" He threw the thought out into the world, and felt someone far away turn toward him as she heard it.

After a rather tense supper, Freyja escaped to check on Hanna before she returned to the inn. The wine had gone to her head, and though dinner was delicious, it left her feeling a little unsettled.

Haakon had stormed out in a huff after the confrontation over his wife, and even Rurik gave up any pretense at trying to charm her, dwelling on his wine with a frown. The story of Haakon's missing wife bothered him more than he'd like to admit.

A storm rumbled overhead as she found herself in the courtyard behind the inn. Freyja looked up with a harsh intake of breath. Lightning lashed the mountains that surrounded the town. The houses were spread far enough apart that there was little protection from the wind.

"What is going on?" she whispered. This mood; this itch. It didn't feel entirely natural. Reaching out, she felt the rage of the storm slip through her fingers as though it were a herd of savage horses, whipped to fury by masters she couldn't see.

"Come." A warm hand slid into hers, and Freyja looked down in shock as Rurik took her hand. She hadn't realized that he'd followed her out of the inn. His gloves were warm and he was the kind of hot-blooded man a woman would want in her bed on a cold night.

He wasn't looking at her. Instead he stared toward the west, toward the origin of the storm, and that intense expression on his face deepened. His fingers slid between hers, locking their palms together.

"They say that *dreki* ride the wings of such storms," he finally murmured. "It would not do for either of us to be caught out this night."

"I have to check on Hanna."

Rurik stared at her for a long moment. "Follow me."

Then he hurried her into the shadows of the stables. And madness of madness, she let him.

CHAPTER
FIVE

THE HORSES WERE restless. Freyja moved among them with a quiet murmur, soothing where she could and darting glances over her shoulder at the man by the doors.

Rurik peered through the slightly ajar door, lightning flickering over his masculine features and carving shadows across his stark cheekbones. He didn't move, but his eyes darted, searching the skies above as if he truly expected to see something there.

"This is ridiculous," Freyja murmured. "The wyrm will not be out this night. He will be sleeping in his lair, purring like a kitten."

"*Dreki*. Not wyrm." A flash of irritation crossed his face, then his eyes turned cunning. "You have seen him, you claimed."

Her hand slid to a halt against Hanna's neck.

"For few would describe it quite like that," he continued, lightning turning his face stark for a moment, his eyes as intense as the storm as they locked on her. "You have seen the *dreki*."

Freyja turned her face away, stroking Hanna's velvety muzzle. "I just wanted my ram back. I paid little attention to the *dreki*."

"Liar."

Freyja's head jerked up. Rurik eased the door shut and turned to her with a smile in the near-darkness.

Moving toward her on graceful feet, he reached out and held his fingers for Hanna to sniff. The mare snorted and backed away, but Rurik never took his gaze off Freyja.

"Where did you see him, Freyja?" Soft words, barely a whisper, but oh, it set her body on fire.

And that was foolish, for she had never felt this way for a man.

She moved to step around him, but he reached out and shoved a palm flat against the partition between each stall. Freyja's breath caught as Rurik pressed close, heat swimming in the air between them. She couldn't stop a gasp from escaping; her hands came up between them as if to shove him away. Or perhaps not. She wasn't certain. What did she know of him truly? Dark stables, no one else in the vicinity. Freyja's eyes narrowed. If his intentions were less than noble, then he was about to get the shock of his life.

Reaching out, she tasted the storm, feeling the coiling power within it. *Come then*, she dared him as she stared into those gleaming eyes.

"I would not hurt you," he replied slowly. "You have nothing to fear, not that way. I told you this would be your choice."

That voice. She shivered, her clenched knuckles brushing against the edges of his coat. Soft wool. So warm from the heat of his body. The desire to reach out and touch him was staggering.

I have everything to fear.

Rurik's face darkened as he watched her. "You are so wary. Has a man ever tried to… to hurt you?"

Benedikt. She shoved the thought away. It didn't matter, and she'd proven she was hardly defenseless. Benedikt had stopped trying to force kisses on her years ago, and had begun to threaten instead. *"You should be kind to me, Freyja. Your father is frail—who shall you turn to when he is gone?"* Leaning close, hissing in her ear, *"Perhaps I should tell him what his daughter has been up to? What man would want to defend her if I name her witch?"*

Rurik saw the truth in her face. His eyelashes fluttered down, obscuring those magnificent eyes, but for a second she thought she saw rage there.

Outside, the storm suddenly broke over the town, wind screaming through the streets and tearing the shutters from their moorings. The horses spooked, even as a lash of sudden power swept through the air. A fierceness. A fury. For a second, she could almost believe his talk of *dreki* that rode the storm with their anger, whipping it along.

His face lowered, cheek pressed almost to hers, his lips not quite brushing her ear. "Tell me his name."

"He is nothing," she replied, feeling strangely protected. The cage of Rurik's arms, his body, sheltered her from the chill, and some part of her felt safe for the first time in years. It was insane. She barely knew this man.

Hot breath against her skin made her shiver. "Tell. Me. His. *Name.*"

"He is a local landowner near my village," she blurted. "What does it matter? You will never know him. You are a traveler and shall move on soon, and I—"

"Freyja."

"His name is Benedikt!" she snapped, her chest heaving. "For all the good it shall do you. You'll be gone in days, collecting your stories, your eddas. Seeking your dragons!"

"*Dreki*," he corrected again, thumb stroking her trembling lower lip. "They are *dreki*. Ancient spirits. Ancient power. And what makes you think I am going anywhere?"

She could barely see, but knew he turned to look at her, for she felt the stir of his breath move across her heated skin. Her heart hammered in her chest. "Don't pretend elsewise. I know men like you."

"Oh, Freyja... you know no one like me. That I promise you." Fingertips brushed against her other cheek. "Why do you always defy me?"

"You have not seen defiance yet. I barely know you."

"You know me," he replied. Fingertips brushed over her dress, between her breasts, the backs of his knuckles pressing against the racing thud of her heartbeat. "You know me here."

She had set him a challenge in the inn, to prove that his empty compliments were not the only arsenal he had. And he had accepted it, for the words, his touch, burned through her until she could scarcely breathe.

"I wish I'd never dared you," Freyja whispered. A single beam of light from a hole in the roof cut across his face as it lowered to hers. Her heart erupted in a flight of dragon wings. She could have said no. She knew his intentions.

But though the words hovered behind her lips, they didn't cross them.

What would it feel like, just once, to let a man kiss her?

For a second that lonely urge pushed aside the ruthlessly practical voice in her head that told her she was being a fool.

"Curious female." His soft laughter caressed her lips. "Did you think I only decided you were mine when you dared me? You were mine the moment I laid eyes on you."

The brush of his mouth against hers tore her apart. Somehow her hands caught his upper arms. To push him away or to draw him closer? She didn't know.

A hail of rain drummed on the roof above her as Rurik tasted her breath. The brush of his mouth whispered against hers, back and forth. Drawing her in. Luring her. Tongue darting out to wet her lips. His assault was so tender that Freyja's shoulders relaxed, her fingers no longer digging into his arms. She couldn't fight this slow seduction.

She didn't want to.

Heat speared lower, in her abdomen. Freyja moaned as Rurik stepped closer, his hard body pressing hers against the stable door and trapping her there. "Kiss me, Freyja. Kiss me, *sarratum zamani*."

She didn't understand the words, the way he rolled over them with his tongue, but she felt it shiver through her. His mouth opened over hers.

Rurik had power of his own. Power to shatter her defenses and leave her gasping. Freyja kissed him eagerly, hands sliding up his chest where she could feel the steady thud of his heart beneath her palms. Her first kiss, and it was divine. *He* tasted divine, the scorching heat of his skin warming her all the way through. Suddenly she couldn't get enough.

She wanted him all over her, inside her. Penetrating her. The sharp stab of the storm lashed over her skin, and Freyja opened herself to it, power crackling through her.

The tips of her hair flickered with static. As if he felt the change in her, Rurik thrust his hips against her, hands shackling her wrists as he pinned them above her head.

Hard lips captured hers, brutal and ravenous. No kiss to steal her breath, not this time. This was meant to own, to possess her.

And it did.

Freyja threw her head back, breathless with need. Thunder rumbled through the building, the storm lancing the air outside. She felt it within her, lightning flickering along her nerves as Rurik's roughened cheek rasped against her throat. Her heart pounded like a drum as his arms slid around her, bringing her into his powerful embrace. Hands slid up her back, locking her in place as his tongue darted down to the crevice between her breasts. The sharp nip of teeth stung against her tender skin, marking her. Freyja dug her fingers into his scalp, helpless to resist.

What was she doing? With a stranger, no less?

But then his hand slid over the black wool of her dress, cupping the unbound weight of her breast in his palm, and Freyja's protest died on her lips.

For she was curious, despite knowing the danger to her reputation, her heart, her body, despite everything.... Not once had she ever felt such desire for a man. *Just a little taste*, she told herself. To see what he would do, how it would feel.

Thunder cracked, rattling the iron sheeting on the roof. A drop of icy rain splashed across her face, shocking her. Then Rurik brushed aside the neckline of her dress, his hot mouth capturing her nipple.

There was no more thought of protest. Freyja gasped in shock, throwing her head back as his tongue traced torturous circles around the aching bud. Then his hands were beneath her bottom, hauling her up, moving her legs around his hips. His body nestled between her thighs, the hot surge of his erection brushing against her hip.

Yes. Yes. More.

"Curse you," Rurik breathed, drawing back just a little. One hand thrust against the stable wall behind her for stability, the muscles in his forearm tightening. "I'm trying to go slowly." He laughed, breathless as he nipped at her jaw. "You taste delicious."

Don't stop. Freyja dug her nails into the hard muscle of his shoulders.

"I won't." The rumble came deep from his throat, the sound trailing over her skin. Then his mouth captured hers again and though her mind fought to latch on to something, she couldn't chase the thought down.

Not with his hips thrusting against hers, the rasp of his buttons riding over the sensitive skin of her inner thighs. Not with his tongue pressing into her mouth, practically daring her to meet him back. Not with his hand sliding over the small of her back, and pressing her harder against him.

His erection brushed between her thighs, thick and heavy, and Freyja's eyes shot wide open at the sudden shock of sensation that streaked through her. Outside, lightning flashed, the light searing her eyes as it flickered between the gaps in the timber door. All she could see were bands of light as she shut her eyes, her moan fading against the thunderous wind as Rurik's body rode over hers, again and again, taking her closer to an edge she wanted to throw herself off—

A primal scream filled the air, echoing across her skin and rattling the roof of the stable.

Freyja felt Rurik freeze, his face lifting from hers and his hard body pinning her to the wall. Her heart thundered a ragged vibration in her ears.

"What is it?" she whispered, her hands still clasping his shirt.

He looked at her, eyes drugged and dazed in the low light, his body easing away from her. Wind battered the stables, another piercing war cry shattering the fury of the storm. It reverberated through the village like the call of an enormous horn.

A chill spiraled all the way through her.

She knew that cry.

She could feel the might of the great beast soaring past, its wings thrusting a downwash of wind over the tiny buildings and his power pulling at her.

Rurik shoved away from her, striding toward the door. He cracked it open, rain whipping over his hardened frame and wetting him instantly. Lightning flickered in the streets, too often for it to be natural. It stabbed the ground again and again, as if driven by something beyond the whim of earthly law.

"The *dreki*," she whispered, and hurried after him.

Rurik's body spilled heat through her as he glanced down, lashes wet with rain. "Stay here."

Her thighs were wet with need, her body still trembling. One kiss, one touch, had shattered her resolve. How lucky for her that the *dreki* had broken the moment, for she had little doubt that she would otherwise be lying on her back in one of the stalls right now, with her skirts around her hips and a "*Yes*" on her lips.

Freyja didn't know what was more dangerous. The wyrm outside? Or the man watching her with hot need still burning in his golden eyes?

"He won't hurt me," she whispered, pressing between him and the door to see. Rain stung her flushed lips, little razors of sensation against her cheeks.

The lightning lit the sky again, revealing the flash of wings over the rooftops. Light gleamed silver over scales.

Beautiful. Dangerous. And so compelling that she almost stepped out into the rain to see more of him.

Rurik hauled her back against his chest with a hiss, his arms locking over her breasts. "Do you have no sense, woman?"

He muscled her inside with appalling ease, slamming the door shut behind them and leaving her light blind in the darkness. Another primitive scream cut the air above them, and she looked up. Something whipped against the roof and Freyja screamed as Rurik drove her down into the straw, his heated body covering hers. Shards of timber lashed them both, an enormous sheet of iron tumbling where they'd just been standing. The noise ricocheted around the stables. Hanna squealed, and another horse snorted.

Then it finally fell silent.

Freyja trembled, feeling the press of Rurik's hips against her bottom. His weight shifted as rain drove inside the hole in the roof, and he let her lift her head.

"You're not hurt?" he asked.

"There... there are two of them," she whispered.

"Aye." A grim tone. "Foolish Freyja. Did you not see?"

"See what?"

"You spoke of the golden wyrm beneath Krafla," he said, looking up with a hard expression darkening his face. "And the one outside was silver."

Not her dreki. As if he read her face, Rurik's gaze softened. "Not yours, no." He levered himself to his feet. "Stay here. And do not come out until I come for you."

"Where are you going?"

"To see who dares to enter the golden wyrm's domain," he replied, in a hard-edged voice.

CHAPTER SIX

RURIK STRODE THROUGH the storm, the rain plastering his shirt to his chest.

Spreading his arms wide, he summoned the power to transform, a surge of fury igniting in his chest. How dare these interlopers intrude in his lands? When he'd been banished from the court at Hekla, he'd claimed the north of Iceland, and none dared trespass. The *dreki* queen insisted that Rurik was not to be roused; both out of a sense of wariness for his might, and simply because she knew how much the isolation would cut at him.

Amadea was more serpent than *dreki*, in some ways.

And this could not be tolerated. He felt his arms lengthen and—

"Where did it go?" a man bellowed.

Rurik froze, power whispering through his veins. He stood on the knife-edge of the shift, the *dreki* punching inside his ribs as it waited for him to free it.

A hand caught his arm and Rurik suppressed the change as he whirled, his head swaying for a second at the sudden loss of momentum.

"Which way?" Haakon demanded, searching the skies. Raindrops clung to his blond eyelashes, highlighting the arctic blue of his eyes. In them, Rurik could just make out the faint madness of obsession.

A good thing Haakon looked away, for Rurik's face tingled just enough to know that he'd not been quite human in that moment.

"There are two of them," Rurik said, gesturing to the south. "They went that way."

Toward his home.

Fury caused the vein in his temple to throb. His gold, his lands, his volcano. If they thought for one second that he'd tolerate—

"Two?" Haakon met his gaze. "Mother of God." He crossed himself, then turned for the stables. "I need to get the horses."

Rurik was seconds away from tearing the dragon hunter's throat out and simply erupting into flight when he caught sight of Freyja, peering through the stable door.

It swayed his intentions as nothing else would.

This was not done between them.

She'd surrendered to his touch, moaning beneath his kiss in a way that made his blood run hotter than lava.

But the second he revealed his hand, her wariness would return and he would lose all chance at claiming her.

Rurik let his power ebb until he could feel the rain stinging his skin once again.

"Have care, Haakon," he said quietly. "You know not what you face."

A twisted plot that threatened to sweep innocents into its midst, for the arrival of two *dreki* could mean nothing more than war, and he was certain he knew who sent them. Amadea wouldn't care if humans were killed. But he did. There were rules—*dreki* laws—that he abided by, and they were innate to his nature. The queen and her brother cared little for moral restraint, but there were enough *dreki* still at court who did.

Honor and honesty were vital to *dreki* nature.

"Perhaps it is the wyrms who don't know what is coming," Haakon growled, swinging up onto his black Friesian when his man brought it out for him. Haakon reined the beast into a tight circle, shooting a look at his men.

Rurik caught the reins. "I doubt that."

The two men stared at each other.

"This is not your fight, scholar," Haakon spat. Tension knotted in his clenched knuckles. "And I will not yield to pleas nor empathy."

"Nor sense, so it seems."

Haakon's lips thinned. "The last time I saw a storm like this was the day I first laid eyes upon my wife. She was lost in the forest, and the clouds brewed like this above me. I swore then that I would have her, and that I would protect her forever." He tugged the reins free of Rurik's hold. "And I failed her. If the *dreki* has her, then I will take her back. If he has killed her, then I will have vengeance, pure and bloody. And nothing you say can sway me."

There was one thing Rurik could say, but he did not know enough of the story to speak of what he knew. This was Árdís's secret. Wasn't it?

"Gunnar, get the men ready! We'll lose them if we wait too long!" Haakon yelled over his shoulder.

"What about the ballista?" called the man he'd addressed as Gunnar.

"Leave it." Haakon whirled his horse, but it balked as Rurik's grip tightened on the bridle. "Here, now!"

"You're a fool to leave your machine here," Rurik told him, with strangely glittering eyes. "You face two *dreki*, and you have not the ability to defend yourself without it. Don't let vengeance blind you. Or all you shall do is see your men dead, and your bones blistered with *dreki* fire."

Haakon bared his teeth. "Let go of my horse, scholar."

Rurik considered him for a long moment. He let go of the reins, stepping out of Haakon's way. "Let their deaths be on your head then."

"Bring the ballista, Gunnar! You can join me at Krafla," Haakon snapped, and drove his horse into the dying beats of the storm. But he glanced over his shoulder toward his men as he went. "Hyaah!"

"So be it," Rurik whispered, still full of doubt about whether he had done the right thing. He believed in fate, and no *dreki* should pit his will against that capricious entity. He had done his best to sway the man.

Let Haakon ride into his destiny. Rurik had other matters to resolve.

These newcomers, these challengers, would find no entry to his lair. He'd sealed it with his power when he left, and there were few still left on this earth who could cut through his magic.

They would know that, which made him wonder just why they were here.

What mad scheme did Amadea plot now?

"You think he won't return," Freyja said, as Rurik stared after Haakon. She'd heard their argument, and a part of her knew that Rurik's focus on her had shifted.

Lanterns filled the night, and Haakon's men tried to hitch his supply wagon to the horses. They'd thrown a tarpaulin over the ballista, but the rain was coming down in steady sheets now.

"*Fool.*" Or at least that was what she thought Rurik murmured. The wind snatched the word from his mouth as he turned back toward her.

"Why did you warn him?" Freyja asked, wiping the hair from her damp cheeks. She didn't wish to see that ballista make its way inland. "He'll kill one of them with that ballista, and I thought you were on the *dreki's* side?"

Rurik glanced toward the south darkly. "I have no wish to see that machine pierce any *dreki's* hide. But I think that without it Haakon will be little more than a delicious morsel to those *dreki,* and that I do not wish for. There is a debt to be repaid there, and his golden *dreki* will pay it when he finds her."

"Her?"

Rurik looked at her sharply. "Krafla's *dreki* did not take his wife. There is only one other who wears golden scales, and I think that Haakon's fate leads him toward her." He shrugged, and she couldn't help noticing the way his shirt clung wetly to him. "I believe they are... destined to meet again."

Freyja watched Haakon as he vanished at the edge of the town. "So, you save his death for another?"

"What makes you think that death is his fate?"

Freyja frowned. "You're playing word games with me."

"Perhaps. You seem awfully insistent upon the fact that *dreki* eat humans."

"Unlike others," she snorted, "I do not fall for those foolish romantic stories people like to tell."

"No?" A faint smile touched his lips. "Did your *dreki* eat you all up, Freyja? Or did it leave you alone? You still haven't told me the story of your meeting."

Freyja frowned, and wrapped her arms around her. "It ate my *ram*. Perhaps its belly was full when I saw it?"

She almost imagined that Rurik growled under his breath. "You eat lamb, do you not? Perhaps the *dreki* likes lamb too? That does not mean it eats people. There are treaties in place to help promote peace between both species. I think the last thing it would do is break the treaty. Besides," he looked thoughtful, "those foolish, romantic stories had to come from somewhere."

She threw her hands up in disgust. Virgin tributes, and happily-ever-afters.... They belonged in fairy tales, and nothing else. "You're as bad as my mother. She too dreamed of forbidden romances. Of *dreki* walking among us in human form, and seducing stupid girls."

That faint smiled deepened. "Who says they do not?"

"Have you seen one? Has anyone? Not in recent times, if ever. Even though they can change shape, there is always a touch of the *dreki* still in them. They say their eyes remain lizard-like in appearance, and that the sight of the holy cross reveals their true form."

"And when they say this, are they speaking of *dreki* or of your devil?" he mused. "It sounds like someone shaped *those* particular stories."

Of all the.... "You are a very frustrating man."

"I would like to believe. That is all. One day I think you will meet a *dreki* in mortal flesh, and then you will believe too. We all need a little bit of romance in our lives. A little bit of magic. You shouldn't trust all of the stories, but you should believe some, Freyja. After all, you've met Krafla's *dreki*. And he is clearly interested in you, if nothing else, from the sounds of your story."

Freyja snorted, and gathered a handful of her skirts as she headed for the inn. "You're as big a fool as Haakon is.

And I'm going in to bed. This is quite too much excitement for me for one night. Goodnight."

"Freyja—"

She turned, wind whipping her skirts past her and blowing his hair back off that clean, masculine face. For a second she thought he was about to plunge them straight back into that reckless, passionate moment they'd shared in the stables. A moment when something inside her— something she'd never even encountered before— overruled logic and sense, letting the storm erupt within. Freyja's heart skipped a beat.

"Would you like to break your fast with me?" he asked, instead.

Freyja hesitated. A part of her still felt that foolish, breathless moment in the stables, and the roughness of his hands on her skin. Heat flooded her cheeks. This man was dangerous. "I'm sorry, but I intend an early start. I need to get home and see to my father."

Thought raced through his amber eyes, but then he merely smiled and slid his hands into his pockets. "I will bid you adieu then. Until we meet again."

"I doubt that," she whispered.

Somehow he heard her. "You should not doubt fate, Freyja. That is like spitting in her eye."

Freyja shivered, one hand on the inn's doorknob. She could not escape this mysterious man fast enough. "I don't believe in fate. I don't believe in anything that I cannot touch with my own hands, or see with my eyes."

Rurik turned to eye the storm. "Why does that not surprise me?" His smile widened, or the half of it that she could see did. "Run, Freyja. You might not believe in fate, but I do. We will meet again. I am certain of it. And when we do...."

He looked back toward her, amber eyes ablaze in the darkness of the storm, and Freyja jerked the door open. That look in his eyes spoke of inevitability, and she had the breathtaking feeling that she wanted to run toward it, throw herself off that cliff.

She no longer knew whether she could trust herself. Not when Rurik was involved. For she wanted something that only he could give her, and while a part of her yearned, just once, to touch the sun, another part of her remained wary. Perhaps he could teach her what passion felt like, what love felt like, but there was always the risk that he might shatter her well-protected heart instead.

And she'd long known what it felt like to have your feet swept out from under her, time and time again.

Freyja ducked inside the inn, shutting the door and pressing her back against it. A rush of exhilaration swept through her veins, and she couldn't, for the life of her, understand why.

Fate, indeed.

CHAPTER SEVEN

THE SMALL VILLAGE near Freyja's house bustled with excitement as she drove Hanna past. Dozens of nearby farmers strode about the village green, and the enormous wagon that housed the dragon hunter's ballista loomed nearby. It had beaten her here, and so too had most of Haakon's men. Sweat foamed on their horses' flanks, and she saw one man leading his bay and patting its velvety nostrils as its head hung in exhaustion.

"Shame on you," she muttered. Pushing horses like that so hard on this treacherous terrain would only end in tragedy at some stage. It wasn't as though Haakon could mount an assault on Krafla immediately, so it made little sense to her.

The dragon hunters were clearly distinguishable from the locals; hard men, wearing furs draped across their shoulders and chain mail beneath. Clearly mercenaries that Haakon had scraped together, and she had to wonder where, precisely, he'd found them. Especially when one of them shot her a dark leer.

"Mistress Helgasdottir," someone called.

It was tempting to pretend she hadn't heard. She kept her gaze straight ahead, wishing Hanna would move a little faster as a blur of movement shifted in the corner of her vision.

"Freyja!" the voice bellowed.

Curse him. Freyja reluctantly eased Hanna to a halt, just as Benedikt caught hold of her bridle. The young ram in the cage on the back of the wagon bleated in shock.

He wore his finest coat, but after seeing Rurik in all of his glory, it looked a pale imitation. Benedikt was tall, his muscle soft and his face pale and pampered, with round cheeks and a boyish look that did not fade with age. He often reminded her of a petulant child deprived of some toy. The problem was that he and his father considered the village and its people to *be* that toy.

Particularly her.

"What do you think of the news?" Benedikt demanded, his eyes alight. He continued before she had a chance to reply, as usual. "We're going to take back our lands, Freyja. Father and I intend to drive the creature from Krafla. Or kill it."

"Let us be honest," she interrupted, before he could descend into one of his infernal monologues. "You've hired a man to *attempt* to kill the *dreki*. I'm not entirely certain whether the cursed *dreki* will think those dragon hunters a nice little gift to assuage his temper, considering you've been breaking the tithe and owe him several months' work of meat, or whether he will take serious affront at this notion, and burn our village to the ground. There's a reason we bargained with him in the first place."

Benedikt's fleshy lips pursed. He might have been handsome, in a sulky way, if the interior of the man weren't quite so repulsive. "You always see the worst outcome. At least my father and I are doing something about this

80

menace. And I have faith in Haakon and his men." His lip curled in a sneer. "You would too, if you knew what faith meant."

A vague threat. Hanna jerked in her traces, and Freyja took the moment to settle the flighty mare—and her own temper. One of these days....

"Your father thinks it's a good idea," Benedikt continued. "I spoke to him yesterday."

That ignited her temper. She didn't want Benedikt anywhere near her father, where he sought to please with a honeyed tongue and silver lies. Sometimes he laughed at her, knowing her father couldn't see her frustration when Benedikt was playing the charming local son.

"Leave my father out of this. He is not well."

"You coddle him. He's a man, Freyja. Not an invalid for you to siphon away his will."

"The only leech here is the one I'm looking at," Freyja seethed.

"Ah, Mistress Helgasdottir," Haakon called, distracting both of them. He strode across the green. "Have you reconsidered? Are you here to inform us of the layout of the wyrm's lair?"

Benedikt's hand curled around Hanna's bridle, and Hanna winced at the restriction. "You have met my Freyja?" he asked Haakon. "But I assure you she is of little assistance. Nobody enters Krafla and returns unscathed."

"I am not *'your Freyja,'*" she muttered.

"That's not precisely my understanding," Haakon countered, ignoring her words, and Freyja suddenly found herself the recipient of a pair of stares—one cool and considering, and one dark with thwarted rage. "I met Mistress Helgasdottir in Akureyri, where she was concluding some business. She claimed to have entered the dragon's lair."

Benedict shot her a shocked look. "You entered Krafla?"

Freyja rolled her eyes. "Let go of the harness. And yes, I entered the *dreki's* lair. He stole my ram and ate it, thanks to your cursed meddling."

"Why did you not tell me?"

Hanna jerked her harness out of his grip, startled by Benedikt's tone, and Freyja collected her calmly. "Because it had little to do with you."

"Everything around here has to do with me," he snapped. "Or my father."

"So some would think."

They glared at each other. Benedikt cursed under his breath, and backed away. "One day you're going to regret the way you speak to me."

As he turned and stalked across the grass, she pursed her lips. One day she was going to spear him with a stab of lightning and watch his boots smolder, and feel nothing but satisfaction.

As if the sky heard her, a distant rumble of thunder shook the horizon.

Haakon patted Hanna's flank, his lips quirking in an almost smile. "I see your winning touch extends to the gentlemen of your village, mistress."

"I see no gentlemen here."

"Touché." He didn't bother to plead his innocence. "There's been no sign of the two dragons."

"*Dreki*," she corrected, almost absently, and for a second she heard Rurik's voice in her mind. "Perhaps they flew south, over the glaciers? There's nothing for them here."

"Nothing but death and carnage."

She didn't like the way that sounded. "The *dreki* is dangerous and powerful, but he causes us little grief,

Haakon. If you do this, you might only stir his rage. There are people here who cannot fight against that."

"I don't intend to fail," he replied. "And you seem rather sympathetic toward a monster."

"Maybe I know what is like to be an outcast," she murmured. "All he wants is something to eat once a week. He's never caused us any other trouble. I see no monster there."

"Not everyone feels that way. Tell me, what was it like?"

"He was curious, more than anything. And he laughed at me, as though he considered me little threat. I don't think he ever intended to truly hurt me. But he could if he so chose." Freyja shivered, recalling the enormous teeth and the impenetrable scales. "He looked like he was covered in gilded armor, and the weight of his power nearly crushed my lungs...."

"I have iron and steel, Freyja. I will pierce his hide."

She shivered at the tone of inevitability in his voice. "Then we are done here. I will not help you, nor will I accept any blame for your deaths because I refuse to aid you. You've been warned, and you will not accept that." She gathered up Hanna's reins, easing the mare away from him. "I hope it is worth it, when the *dreki* is picking his teeth with your bones. Come, Hanna." She cracked the reins on the mare's shaggy hide.

Hanna leapt forward, and Haakon stepped out of the way.

"Be careful, Mistress Helgasdottir," Haakon called, patting Hanna's shaggy flank with a parting pat. "One might suspect your sympathies lie with the wrong party here."

A shiver ran down her spine. She didn't think Haakon would hurt her, but then she'd thought the same about

Benedikt when they were younger and he'd first set his sights on her. It was only once she'd said no that the ugly side of his nature emerged.

I am not without my defenses, she told herself again as she drove off.

Even if her powers set her apart and left her standing in a world alone, at least she could never be forced into something she didn't want.

The first sign that something was not right at her home started when she saw all of the ewes huddled in their stone pen together, big eyes wide with fright. The bleating set her nerves on edge, but she couldn't see anything to cause such distress.

Leading Hanna up the lane, Freyja frowned. "What has my ladies in such a dither?" She couldn't resist scanning the skies. Evening fell like a curtain of inky shadows from the east, with paler golden tones lingering in the west where the sun took its time to descend. A few stars sparkled in the night sky.

But no *dreki.*

A shiver ran through her as she put her new ram and Hanna away, tending the sweet mare and slipping her a slice of dried apple that she carried in her pocket. She had the same feeling in her stomach that she'd felt in Akureyri when she bid adieu to Rurik.

Fate, he whispered in her memories.

"Foolishness," Freyja muttered, and shut the stable door behind Hanna.

Wrapping her shawl around her shoulders, she scurried toward her father's house with her basket of goods. Night had finally vanquished day, but light glared from the kitchen window and the small sitting room next to it. What was her father thinking? They barely had enough kerosene to spare, and she hoarded it like the *dreki* in Krafla protected his gold.

"Father?" she called, pulling the door shut behind her and dragging her shawl off her shoulders. The heat inside the house enveloped her like a warm cloud. Good grief, he had the fire blazing as well. The dwindling woodpile in the corner of the kitchen looked alarmingly low. "Father, where are you?"

"Through here, Freyja," he called from the sitting room, and her heart skittered a beat at how well he sounded.

Thank goodness. Freyja squeezed her eyes shut, then let out the breath she'd been holding. Leaving him alone for a time was always a worry.

"Have you had dinner?" She could smell the lamb stew she'd left in the cool room simmering in a pot on the stove. "I've bought fresh bread all the way from Akureyri, and a wheel of cheese."

"Ah, leave all that!" her father called, "and come in here. I have a guest who is waiting to meet you."

Freyja set her basket of produce on the table, and crept toward the sitting room. Who would be visiting them out here? Benedikt and his father were in the village, as well as Haakon and his men. There were few others who would willingly step foot in her household, even with the iron horseshoe nailed upside down over the lintel.

"A guest?"

The chair creaked as her father levered out of it, and she caught sight of his shadow on the wall. Another shape shifted beside it, a tall man sitting in the armchair by the window, by the look of it.

Freyja stopped dead as she entered the room. "Rurik?"

85

What was he doing here?

Rurik sprawled in her father's second-favorite armchair, balancing an old chipped teacup in his hands with feigned nonchalance. Everything about his posture screamed that he intended to pose no threat, but his eyes flared amber the second he saw her, and everything in her body screamed at her to *run*.

"Mistress Freyja," he purred. "I was just telling your father here about our meeting in Akureyri. He has some interesting stories about *dreki*, which I am collecting for my book, if you remember?"

Book? He hadn't said a blasted thing about a book.

"*What are you really doing here?*" she mouthed.

"Freyja!" Her father looked up from the small platter of honey cakes he'd been destroying. Those filmy eyes turned vaguely in her direction, and he smiled.

He looked well.

Freyja scurried to his side, pressing a kiss to his brow in a surreptitious way to measure his temperature. "Where did you get the cake from?"

"Master Rurik bought it in the village as a gift." Her father hugged her. "He intends to do some research in this area, and someone directed him to my door." Pride swelled his chest. "He wants to learn about the local *dreki*, and I know all of your mother's stories. I offered her books to him, and offered him board for a few weeks."

Weeks?

"You shouldn't have," she murmured to Rurik, embarrassed that he'd noticed their poor plight enough to bring a gift of food with him. The little house no doubt looked like a hovel in his eyes, with its thatch of grassed roof, and the bare necessities that were all that remained of their furniture. The house was spotless, and the furniture gleamed with beeswax she'd lovingly rubbed into it, but she'd been forced to sell pieces of it over the years, and empty spaces gaped where stuffed chairs had once stood. Even her mother's precious books had thinned out over the years as one catastrophe after another—their crops failing, or the fence breaking and precious lambs going missing—had struck their little farmstead. She'd never even told her father she'd sold some of them, and he'd clearly not noticed.

It would have broken his heart.

"We don't have a spare room," she told him bluntly.

Her father sucked in a sharp breath. "Freyja—"

"That's quite all right," Rurik replied, lazy-lidded in front of the fireplace. He looked like he was soaking up the heat of the flames. "It wouldn't be right for me to share a roof with a young unmarried woman anyway. So I bargained with your father for room in your stables. I can pay good coin."

In the stables.... For a moment she almost felt guilty. But then he gave her that faint smile that rubbed all her hairs the wrong way, and guilt evaporated.

"Freyja will see you to the stables," her father agreed amiably, leaving her with little recourse. "Won't you, Freyja?"

She'd see him to the door, in any case. Freyja jerked her head at Rurik as he stood, and then tried to paste a smile on her face for her father. "I certainly shall."

After all, she couldn't say what she really wanted to say with her father in the room, could she?

"What are you doing here?" Freyja whispered harshly, the second they were inside in the barn. "And don't feed me that lie about a book."

"Who says it was a lie? I am considering writing a book. There are too many wrong stories about *dreki* in circulation."

She ground her teeth together. "I'm not an idiot. And I detest it when men think they are smarter than I am, and try to smugly protest otherwise. If you continue to pretend that you have not a *single* ulterior motive in being here, at my home, when last I saw you was many miles to the north, then I will be done with you."

Rurik paused, assessing her face.

"Why are you here?" she demanded. "Truly?"

"You're right. I didn't come here for a book. I came here for you. Fate, Freyja." He stepped forward, touching her cheek. "That's why I'm here." His breath warmed her lips as he loomed closer, and her heart gave a kick behind her ribs as he smiled at her. "Our destiny is incomplete."

Rurik's fingers tucked a strand of hair behind her ear. Freyja froze. She'd thought what happened between them at Akureyri was simply a result of the storm pounding through her veins, igniting the passionate fury in her blood. But the second his touch landed on her skin, her blood seemed to fire again, and a shiver ran through her. A distant storm, but one that could be stoked with but a few simple touches.

"Oh no, you don't," she muttered, ducking beneath his arm and whirling in a storm of skirts.

The damned man simply stood there with a smile, crossing his arms over his chest.

His rather impressive chest.

Freyja growled under her breath, pressing her fingers to her temples. She didn't want to examine her anger too closely, just in case it wasn't entirely anger. Fluster might come closer. "You have your head in the clouds. Fate and destiny... what a jest. You're no better than any skirt-chasing scoundrel, though your words might be prettier. My mother would have liked you."

"*You* like me," he pointed out. "Or else you would have thrown me out the second you saw me inside."

"I didn't wish to cause a scene in front of my father," she retorted. "That's the only reason you're still here. He believes in guest right still, and expects me to uphold it."

Rurik's biceps flexed. "You are a most vexatious female. Why can you not admit that you want me here?"

She refused to look at his bulging biceps. Simply refused. "My mother taught me never to utter a lie."

Slowly he prowled around her. "You liked my kiss. You begged me for more, and curled your fists in my hair. I do not understand what you find so distasteful about the idea. You wanted me. You still want me."

Every word drove straight through her abdomen, bringing little hammer-flashes of memory with it; the dance of raindrops on the roof; the feel of that hard body driving her into the wall; the lush stroke of his tongue against hers. "I often want things that are bad for me—ginger cakes, ale, books that I cannot afford…. It doesn't mean I give in to the feeling."

He took a step toward her.

She took one back.

Rurik froze.

"Perhaps I enjoyed your kiss, but that doesn't mean I will lie with you." She could see from his expression that he did not understand. But then, he wasn't the one who might risk being left behind with a bastard child and a ruined reputation—what little there was left of it. "You're persistent, I shall give you that, but all men want the same thing."

"Your heart?" he challenged.

"A swift tumble in the hay."

"I am not all men," he replied. The shadows around him seemed to lengthen. "And you know little of what I want, Freyja. The second I saw you, I wanted to possess you—body and soul."

"You're being ridiculous. All these words—"

"I am bound by every word I utter," he told her, and this time when he stepped toward her, she let him.

Treacherous heart, beating swiftly in her chest. Unfaithful body, wet with anticipation, and trembling with desire. Freyja swallowed hard and shut her eyes. All she had was her faltering will. Her steadfast nature.

"When have I ever lied to you?" Rurik whispered, as though sensing her hesitation. His fingertips skated over her cheeks again.

This time she let him.

This time her shoulders sank and she finally lifted her eyelashes to look him in the face. Some part of her wanted to believe him, to lift her mouth to his and offer herself up to him. But the warier part of her, the part that remembered Benedikt's subtle viciousness, stayed her hand. "Why *me*?"

"Oh, precious Freyja." His breath shivered over her skin. Rurik cupped her face, callused thumbs stroking gently against her cheeks. "You are a fascinating contradiction. Barely afraid of me when you should be, but frightened of me when I am at my least dangerous. Every second I see that flash of fire in your eyes ignites something within me that I have not felt for a long, long time. Your very contrariness captures me, your intelligence, your fierceness... and the gentle nature that hides within. Shall I go on?"

"You see this as a challenge." And she knew men played to win. "That is all."

"The fact that you challenge me *is* part of the attraction," he breathed. "I'll concede that point. What man or woman does not care to be challenged within a relationship? If you agreed with me all the time or kissed my shoes, then you would be quite uninteresting."

"I will *never* kiss your shoes." The very idea offended her.

A slow smile spread over his lips. "I know."

"I will rarely agree with you."

"Even better."

"I am stubborn, and angry, and not very good at conversation," she said, giving in to exasperation. "I am not beautiful—"

"There you are wrong." He cupped her cheeks in both hands and tilted her face to his. "Every inch of your skin pleases me. Every time our eyes meet, I want to consume you. You have lightning in your veins, precious Freyja. And when you kiss me it feels as though I can taste that lightning too. There is something between us that cannot be denied."

"Fate," Freyja whispered. She still didn't believe in the word, but there was... something there. In that he spoke the truth.

Her heart kicked a little faster behind her ribs, the treacherous organ. There was a part of her that knew he was going to kiss her again, and this time she didn't think she'd push him away. Even just the rasp of his thumb against her jaw felt so good, a renegade pleasure that she could barely admit to.

Just who was she lying to? Him? Or herself?

"I don't know if I believe you," she admitted.

"Then set me a challenge. How shall I prove my intentions are true? How shall I win the heart of fair maiden?"

He was mocking her.

"Give me my heart's greatest desire," she shot back, dashing his hands from her face and darting for the door, "and I shall give you my heart."

Rurik stilled. It felt almost as if an enormous tail lashed behind him suddenly, like a cat about to pounce, and then he smiled. "So be it."

CHAPTER EIGHT

DISCOVERING HER HEART'S greatest desire was proving to be more vexatious than Rurik had thought.

The next two days passed with little sight of her. Freyja was adept at maneuvering on silent feet, and spent countless hours tending to her home, or to the flock of animals that relied upon her. Every time he found her he was either handed a broom or a shovel and told to earn his keep, or several dozen bleating sheep rousing into a sudden panic sent him fleeing before Freyja could question their terror. Rurik himself was forced to keep an eye on the skies. There'd been no sign of the other *dreki* in the area when he arrived, but he knew they were out there somewhere. He strengthened the wards on his lair, watched curiously as Haakon led fruitless expeditions around the volcano, then subsided at Freyja's to wait the other *dreki* out.

Two could play at this game.

And he was patient, for a *dreki*.

Or at least, he thought he was, until he encountered the might of Freyja's will.

It didn't help matters that her father, Einar, insisted on sitting with him for hours, inadvertently playing the part of chaperone.

"You're distracted," her father said one afternoon, as they sat over the small chessboard he'd dusted off and brought out. The little fox that lived with them sat on the side of the armchair, his dark amber eyes unblinking. Loki knew what he was, and when he realized that Rurik watched him, he bared his teeth in a faint growl.

Fair enough. The little beast was only trying to protect his household. At least he didn't run and bleat like Freyja's sheep did whenever they saw him.

Rurik eyed the spread of ivory pieces. He enjoyed this game, and the old man had clever wits, despite his blindness. "I was thinking of the dragon hunters in the village. They seem to be making little progress."

"Is that why you watch the window so often?"

Caught. "No. I'm watching for your daughter. She is doing her best to avoid me." He didn't ask how the man had known. Einar seemed attuned to each rustle of cloth, and all of his other senses were exceptionally good.

"Ah." Einar coughed faintly into the stained handkerchief in his fist, then reached for his knight. His hand quivered. "You have an interest in Freyja."

The stale scent of encroaching death emanated from the old man. Rurik stilled. "She is intriguing," he admitted. "She is beautiful, and clever, and stubborn, and utterly relentless."

"I need not remind you that your intentions had best be pure? I might be old and blind, but I can still be a force to be reckoned with when it comes to the daughter I love."

Rurik respected the old man's position, though he could swat him like a fly if he wished. "You can remind me, but Freyja has already lain down her rules. You might be a force to be reckoned with, but she is a force of nature."

The old man chuckled, a sound that slowed, then died with a faint hush. "Aye, she's proud and wary." He scratched at his jaw, clearly upset by some thought. "It bothers me to see her so long unmarried. My health fades with each winter. I... I worry...."

Rurik surveyed the board, then moved his bishop and told the man what he'd done. "Freyja can survive without you, I assure you of that. She is independent and strong enough to rule her own life."

"I know," Einar replied. "But she has always been so isolated. You've seen her eyes?"

"They are beautiful eyes."

"Some claim they are sure sign of a witch."

"It's a small village," Rurik replied, lacing his hands across his middle. "I expect the people here to be sheltered."

"Unfortunately, others don't share your lack of qualms." Einar looked troubled. "I always sought to spare her from their censure, and so Helga and I kept her close, and rarely invited strangers to the house. Or even guests. Maybe that was a m-mistake—" He broke into another hacking fit of coughs.

Rurik fetched the old man a glass of water. "Here," he offered, sending a thin tendril of his power through his fingertips to energize the old man.

"My thanks." Einar slurped the water down, and settled back in his chair, but at least his skin bore some faint signs of color now.

"Has she never had a suitor before?" he asked, as he waited for the old man to recover.

"I keep pushing her toward that Benedikt boy," Einar admitted, "but she will have none of him."

Every hint of the predator within him arose at the name. *Benedikt.* He was the man who threatened Freyja. Rurik's voice turned silky. "He is local?"

"His father owns half the village." Einar coughed again. "He's not the sort of lad I'd normally choose for Freyja, but...."

He was the only man who showed interest in her. If only Einar understood what sort of interest Benedikt showed....

Not for him to mention. No. Rurik had other ways of confronting his rival. Still, he couldn't say nothing, "Sometimes it is better to live alone, than to wed someone unsuitable."

"Unless someone else who is suitable comes along?" Einar suggested unsubtly, his hand hovering over his rook. He moved it. "I believe that is check."

So it was. Rurik frowned. It was the first time the other man had beat him.

"Your attention has been elsewhere," Einar mused, even as the door to the kitchen creaked faintly.

Rurik was suddenly all senses. There was a light footstep in the kitchen. Then another.

"And now you are distracted again." Einar chuckled, clearly hearing Freyja's entrance too. "Go," he said, waving toward the kitchen. "You have my best wishes. I can tell that she likes you."

"I am not so certain of that. But we'll continue our game later," Rurik replied, pushing to his feet and moving after his fascinating adversary.

He had to move quickly. He could hear Freyja heading for the door again. The swing of her golden plait came into view, and Freyja snagged her shawl, reaching for the door handle with one guilty glance cast over her shoulder—

"Where are you going?" he demanded.

Freyja paused in the shadows of the kitchen doorway, her shawl in her hand. "For a walk."

Lie. It ignited every single one of his senses. "May I come with you?"

"It is rather boring," she said quickly, and he knew she was up to something. "You will not enjoy it. Muddy, smelly... I daresay it will ruin your boots."

He was inclined to argue, but merely smiled. "Not my boots. Whatever would I do?"

Freyja shot him a narrow-eyed look, as if she couldn't quite work out whether he was being sarcastic or not. She tucked the shawl over her honey-colored hair, then headed for the door. "I shall be back later."

"I can hardly wait."

That earned him one last twitch of the brow, before she vanished.

Troublesome female. If he were in his *dreki* form right now, his tail would be lashing. But then, if she thought to dissuade him from the chase, she thought wrong. Nothing stirred his interest more than a woman who refused to fall at his feet. And there was no reason for her to lie to him about where she was going, unless....

Rurik waited for all of two minutes, realizing that Loki had followed him and watched from the corner of the cupboard, like some small chaperone.

"I am not going to hurt her, little brother," he told the fox.

Those amber eyes narrowed.

Rurik reined in his predatory impulses, and headed out into the yard to see if his suspicions were correct.

That small light-footed figure headed out across the moors, her green shawl wrapped around her shoulders as she made her way directly toward the smoking volcano in the distance.

Easy enough to guess where she was going. What he didn't know was why, or what she was up to.

His blood was up. Perhaps she was wary of Rurik the man, but she seemed to have reached a truce in her mind with the *dreki*.

It seemed she would be meeting him sooner, rather than later.

Rurik paced along the stone fence that housed her sheep. They bleated and scurried out of his path, pressing in a frightened huddle against the far wall. Freyja might not recognize him in this form, but all of her animals did.

He sighed. "I'm not going to eat any of you," he pointed out. "She's barely forgiven me for the ram."

He'd never live it down if he sampled another of her delicious morsels.

His stomach chose that moment to growl. The bleating grew louder. Rurik bared his teeth at them, and then stomped around the corner of the stables. Idiot sheep. And frustrating shepherdess.

He'd given her more than enough time for a decent head start.

And the *dreki* itched within him, wanting to taste the wind on its face.

Plus there *were* his boots to think of....

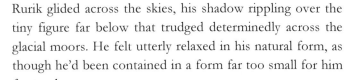

Rurik glided across the skies, his shadow rippling over the tiny figure far below that trudged determinedly across the glacial moors. He felt utterly relaxed in his natural form, as though he'd been contained in a form far too small for him for too long.

Wind whipped beneath his wings and he soared on the thermals, delighting in the warmth of the sunlight on his scales.

Not a sign of another *dreki* anywhere. He'd made careful forays over the past few nights, but there'd been no hint of them. Which suggested they'd taken to ground....

Where though? What was their game?

And who had his mother sent to challenge him?

Silver scales. That bothered him, because while the color was popular among his clan, there was one particular *dreki* who gleamed silver, and his mother knew Andri would be a weakness of his. A part of him hoped she hadn't sent his younger cousin on this mission, even as he knew better. Of course Amadea would exploit any weakness.

As for the bigger *dreki*, he hadn't gotten a good look, but thought he'd caught a glimpse of a dark shape. Darker *dreki* were more common than the lighter or jewel-tinted shades, and the bigger *dreki* could have been any one of his uncle's warriors.

He couldn't scent them around his territory. No, they'd glided on elsewhere, though he knew the foray into his domain could not been accidental. Every *dreki* male at court knew the territory lines. When a simple incursion might mean war and a battle to the death, it wasn't the sort of thing that *dreki* were careless with. Which meant they'd been looking for something—some mischief—and it bothered him that he could not figure it out.

Circling Krafla, Rurik caught sight of the determined figure crossing the moors far below. This was a terrible time to be seducing an obstinate woman, but he couldn't deny that he was enjoying the pursuit more than he'd imagined. Rurik banked with care, and alighted on the ledge outside the entrance to his cave.

Just what, precisely, did Freyja value most? Freedom? Gold? A crown, perhaps? A rich manor where she did not have to work all day merely to put food on the table? No. He didn't think so. She seemed to enjoy the work, speaking with fondness to the creatures that inhabited her small farmstead. It was only when he was around that her tone became more careful.

Rurik tapped his claws on the stone, one after the other, as he sunned himself. Her challenge presented an intriguing mystery.

"You are early." He sent the thought to her just as she locked eyes with him. *"You are not due for another three weeks."*

Freyja hauled herself up the last stone climb, her dark blonde hair glowing like spun gold in the sunlight. "I know."

"Why are you here then?" He stretched, and decided to tease her a little. *"Have you bought me dinner?"*

A scowl met the words. "You're big enough and scary enough to fetch your own dinner."

"Yes. But they frown upon that here. Something about rams and ownership, and tithes and not taking what is due to a creature of my magnificence...."

Definitely a scowl. "You think you are amusing."

"I think you are up to something. Why else would you be here, hmm?"

Freyja looked away, the wind snagging strands of her blonde hair and tugging it free from her tight braid. He'd love to see all of that hair unbound. It was her true wealth. She stared over the valley below them, and he realized she was focusing on her village.

"I came to warn you," she said at last. "Some of the villagers have pooled their money and hired a dragon hunter to rid themselves of you. Others don't wish such a thing."

He rested his chin on his claws, watching her sleepily. *"I know."*

Those mismatched eyes widened. "What? How?"

"I am not stupid, little mouse." Rurik snorted. *"What sort of* dreki *would I be, if I let your puny villagers thwart me?"*

Freyja's lips thinned. "They will not seem so puny and insignificant when they bring that ballista up here and spear you with it."

"I should like to see them haul their machines up through the boggy moors and along the cliff path. It should prove amusing. I might even drop a rock on it. Or perhaps I will merely pinwheel through the sky above them? I've seen the aim on that thing. The dragons they've hunted must stand very still for them." Rurik spread his wings with a flap, enjoying the warmth on them. Freyja gasped and staggered, her back plastered to the sheer cliff face. He paused, realizing he'd startled her, and slowly curled his wings up against his sides. *"You won't fall."*

Freyja eyed the drop carefully. "You're not the one who was nearly blown off this ledge."

"And if you did lose your footing, I would catch you," he continued. *"I am not done with you yet."*

This statement earned him a narrow glare. "Saying such things does not ease my nerves one whit. What do you intend to do with me?"

"I intend to hear your words," he replied. *"I am interested in conversation. One rarely finds humans brave enough to come into my den, especially those who have no designs for my gold."*

"A *dreki* who wants only to talk?" she countered. "I've never heard of such a thing."

"Surely you have heard the old tales?"

A snort. "Yes, I've heard the old tales. All of them. Including the ones where a capricious traveler ended up in a *dreki's* belly."

"I have no intentions of causing you harm," he replied. 'Dreki's *oath on that. I am merely curious about you. Most of your neighbors are fools. How did such a curious female come about, when most of the village flees at the sight of my shadow?"*

Freyja eyed him. There was wariness there still, but also a certain sort of interest. As if, so starved for company and derided by humans, she could overlook the fact that he was *dreki.*

"Stay," he cajoled. *"Talk with me."*

"Talk of what?" Freyja demanded, but the light in her eyes was back, her fear fading. Indeed, her tone had changed and she sounded more certain of herself when he was in this form.

Because you're no longer a threat to her as a dreki. *Only as a man.*

Which meant that someone else had *been* that threat.

The thought made all sorts of possessive, violent male impulses whirl within him. Rurik contained it. He already knew he felt protective toward her, but the idea that someone else had hurt her stirred the heart of the *dreki* spirit within him.

"Yourself. Tell me why Freyja Helgasdottir is no fool."

Freyja gathered her skirts primly, and settled on a jutting rock. The look she gave him was faintly cunning. "And what will you give me if I do?"

Oho. Delight ran rampant through his veins. *"For all your talk, you* have *heard stories of* dreki.*"*

"Bargain with them at your own risk," Freyja replied. "Keep your wits at all moments. And never, ever offer a truth for free, for they are curious creatures and cannot deny their interest. Next to their mortal form, their curiosity is their second major weakness. My mother told me many stories."

All of it was true. *"Did she also tell you that a* dreki's *second greatest strength is their patience?"*

"No." Freyja looked interested. "What is their greatest strength?"

"Now that *is a secret."*

"And if I'm counting correctly, you owe me one." Was that a smile that played around her stubborn lips?

"Perhaps. What do you want in exchange for your story? More gold?" He didn't know how he felt about that. His gold was *his* gold. But would it be worth it, to learn the heart of Freyja?

Yes. And not simply because he was failing in his efforts of seduction.

He wanted to know her. She would be his lover—that was a foregone conclusion in his mind—but the fascination for him extended beyond the physical.

"A truth for a truth," she told him.

Which was potentially dangerous. His eyes narrowed. Denial here could cost him any chance at bridging the chasm she'd set between them. *"A truth for a truth. So be it."*

Freyja held up a finger. "And not a random truth, but you must answer a question that I propose."

"What if I do not care to answer it?"

"Then I may feel free to ask another question," she countered. "Out of three questions, you *must* answer one."

Trouble. But damned if he did not wish to play this game with her. His *dreki* nature loved the challenge. *"Agreed. Now answer my question. Why is Freyja not afraid of me? Why did she dare confront me in my lair, when others would quail?"*

"You can see my eyes, no?"

"Such wondrous eyes."

Her smile stilled, but didn't entirely die as she gazed at her lap. "They call me elf-cursed," she admitted slowly, as if the weight of this secret weighed upon her somehow. "Or think I make deals with the devil. When I was a little girl, a priest came to our village, where my father was selling geese in the marketplace. I was playing and happened to look up, and the priest reared away from me and made a sign of the cross. He was horrified, and it scared me. It was the first time I ever realized that I was different.

"I don't fit in to my world, not very well. So perhaps that is the reason I am not scared of you, nor believe in provoking you. Because you are different and so am I, and maybe I understand what that feels like."

"You make no mention of magic."

Another of those slow, careful glances she was known for. "Is that another question?"

"Perhaps it is merely a challenge. For you gave half an answer. You know you have power, and that made you fearless when you came to confront me."

"I was scared," she admitted.

"But?"

"Mostly I was angry. And hopeless." She threw the smooth rock she'd been toying with. "There is a point one sometimes reaches that is beyond endurance, and I reached it the night you stole my ram. You are big and scary, and could have killed me. But a part of me simply didn't care."

He fell into those eyes. Freyja had such depths to her that he wondered if he'd ever see the entirety of them. *"Now that tastes more like truth. A full truth."*

Freyja sucked in a sharp breath, as if uncomfortable. "Which means it is time for my question."

"Proceed."

She frowned. "I intend to, but first I have to think of... the question that makes me most curious. I don't want to waste my chance."

Rurik laughed, a rumbling purr deep in his throat. *"So very female. Rest assured I have more questions for you. This doesn't end with one."*

"Oh." That little knot between her brows furrowed and she dragged her knees up to her chest, her skirts falling around her ankles. "Can you change shape?"

The one question he'd been dreading. *"What is wrong with this shape?"*

"Nothing."

"Yes," he conceded, scratching his head against a rock. *"I can change forms. It is part of the goddess's gift to us. But why would I? Humans are fools. They smell. And most of them are like brainless sheep. Then there are men here who wish to kill me, and I am slightly more vulnerable in human form—"*

"*More* vulnerable?" she broke in. "I thought it was one of a *dreki's* greatest weaknesses—the only time you can be easily killed."

"Easily is a matter of opinion," he growled. *"I am powerful beyond your comprehension, and my magic is available no matter what form I wear."*

"How often have you changed forms?"

He dipped a wing—the human equivalent of a shrug. *"That is like asking me, how many times have I eaten? I do not count such things. Often enough when I was younger, because I was curious, but not very often since. There is little reason to do so."*

"Have you ever seduced a human woman?"

"No." Not yet, anyway. *"And,"* he forestalled her, *"you now owe me three answers, for you asked four questions and I answered all of them."*

Freyja frowned. "You answered with some questions."

"But they were rhetorical, were they not?"

If he could smile, he would have, for she looked utterly captivating with frustration written all across her face. "I do not think that is entirely fair, but I'll allow it."

"How kind of you." Turnabout was fair play. His eyes narrowed. *"What type of creature are you? For it is clear you are not human."*

"Of course I am human," she shot back, opening her arms wide. "Do I not look human?"

"You look human," he admitted. *"You smell human, though you smell better than most of them. But you are not human. They have no powers, nor magic, unless it is god-given, and you do not bear the stamp of any gods."*

"You can sense that?"

"I once met a man in Norway," he admitted. *"He used to chew berries and send himself into a trance, where he could communicate with his god. The strain showed on his aura, and I was... wary of crossing him. He smelled wrong."*

"That is a very old practice."

"It is. But then, I encountered it when I was in my youth."

"How old are you?"

"Hundreds of years," he replied, with a faint shrug of his wing. *"Dreki think in terms of cycles, not years, so I am not entirely certain. I am in my tenth cycle, however. How old are you?"*

"Four-and-twenty."

"Where does your power come from?"

She paused.

"Did you think I had forgotten?"

"No." Freyja's lips twisted. "It's just... I don't know where it comes from."

Lie. It seared along his magic nerves, making him hiss.

"That's not the truth—"

But Freyja wasn't looking at him. Her gaze settled on a point behind him, her lips parting with a faint O.

Rurik craned his neck. And there, pinwheeling above the glaciers to the south, was the smaller silver dragon he'd sighted that night in Akureyri.

On the edges of his territory, practically *daring* him to retaliate.

"Go home," he growled to her, his claws digging into the rocks as he drew himself to his full height.

"Wait!" Freyja called.

But Rurik wasn't listening. Instead, he danced along the edge of the path, careful of her frail mortal body, and launched himself into the air with a powerful thrust of his wings.

"Go home, little mouse, while I take care of this visitor."

"Be careful!" she called.

"Always," he sent back. *"After all, you still owe me the answer to that question."*

It had to be a trap.

He knew this, and yet he went anyway, because to ignore intruders in his territory went against *dreki* nature. *His.* This land was his. Bought and bargained for with blood and death, and he could no sooner allow this transgression than he could roll over and submit.

Screeching a battle cry, Rurik roared through the skies. The power of the land shivered through him, until it felt like he'd captured the power of a storm, bottled lightning in his belly.

Ahead of him, the silver *dreki* spun, his wings stiff as he banked. There was the flash of a paler belly, and claw marks across the *dreki's* cheek, and then he withdrew in a dive that sent him fleeing.

"Andri." The unexpected sight made Rurik's wings skip a beat.

All of his earlier suspicions bore fruit. Of course his mother and uncle would send the kit he'd once considered a younger brother.

Rurik beat his wings as he dove after his younger cousin. Andri had been on the verge of adulthood, almost two cycles old, when Rurik left in exile. Now he was a *dreki* grown, though not quite as large as he himself was. A young warrior who would bear the mark of his father's temper on his face forever.

"Go home," he told his smaller cousin. *"And I shall forget this trespass."*

Andri hissed at him as Rurik fell in beside him. The smaller *dreki* was fast, but Rurik's strength and skill meant Andri would never lose him. *"My father sends his regards."*

"His regards? Or his son as a sacrifice?" Rurik spiraled in a slow circle around the other *dreki*. Together they began a dangerous dance. Airborne battles were brutal, and a fall could shatter wings and bones, but he'd been primed for this fight since the day he was born. *"Is Stellan so careless with his sons that he would send one into a fight that is not his own?"*

Andri refused to comment. And Rurik began to grow suspicious. Was Andri here on his father's terms—or did some part of the youth want to reach out to one he'd once trusted?

"I won't kill you," Rurik told his former squire, making a decision. *"Unlike others, I made an oath to protect you and I intend to keep it. You shouldn't be here. This is not your fight."*

"I have a duty to fulfill," his cousin replied.

"If you come against me and I am forced to protect myself, I'll knock you from the skies, but I won't kill you," Rurik warned.

Andri soared high over Krafla. *"You're a fool then. You're my clan's enemy."*

"You're my cousin," he shot back, *"And you were always mine, more than you were ever Stellan's. You're the one good thing he*

ever created, and you have more honor in you than any of your nestlings."

Andri broke the thought-thread between them, veering away. Rurik ignored his distress and went after him. There were only two reasons Andri could have sought him out today. Either the youth meant to lure him into a trap, or his guilt had driven him to make contact.

"And where's the other dreki?" Rurik caught up to his squire swiftly. *"Who did your father send? Vargur? Grimold? Magnus? T—"*

A shock of connection betrayed Andri's thoughts, and made Rurik's heart thud in his chest. *"Magnus,"* he repeated. *"Of course he sent his heir."*

He and Magnus were of an age. Kits raised together, but never friends. Never allies.

Magnus was everything that Stellan hoped to produce. A *dreki* with a heart as black as his hide. When Stellan and Amadea married into Iceland's *Zini* clan, they'd brought all of their Norwegian clan's prejudices with them. The intermarriage was meant to be a treaty between the *Zini* and *Zilittu* clans to broker peace, but all of Stellan's sons—bar Andri—thought of themselves more as *Zilittu* than *Zini*. And with Amadea sitting on the throne her husband, Reynar, once owned, it seemed the treaty had been more of a long-seeded plot than an honest reconciliation.

As Amadea and Reynar's eldest son, Rurik was the only *dreki* who could thwart their ambitions to rule both clans. His brother, Marduk, was too young to be a threat, and though Marduk was considered an adult, he wouldn't have the strength to combat Magnus. Would he?

"Tell your brother that I accept his challenge," Rurik said slowly, thinking of his brother. Magnus would want his path to the throne to be unhindered, regardless of whether or not Marduk could ever actually beat him. Then there was

Andri... *"We can settle this between us. You don't have to be involved."*

"He's not offering challenge."

Of course not. Magnus would consider himself the strongest male now, and hence the rightful heir, which meant Rurik was the one who had to offer. And he would let his cold dead body sink into the seas before he ever condescended to those who'd plotted against his father, then blamed Rurik for the king's death.

"Even if you offered, he would not accept it," Andri said quickly.

So this was not to be an honorable duel. *"Why are you here then? Does your brother know where you are?"*

"I wanted to warn you," Andri said, after a long hesitation. *"And no, he doesn't."*

There was the hint of his old squire: Andri, whose sense of honor would forbid an ambush.

"I knew you were here," he replied. *"But thank you. I had hoped they hadn't corrupted you completely."*

The skies gleamed blue around them as Andri broke the mental connection between them. Even so, Rurik caught the faint mournful taint of the younger *dreki's* emotions. This could not be easy for the youth. He'd followed Rurik around the court as a kit, like an enamored lass. The day Rurik took Andri as his squire had been the most joyful either of them shared.

The day that his young squire lied and said he'd seen his prince in the king's quarters the night the king was murdered, had been the worst.

"I don't hold you responsible for my exile," Rurik sent, in a thought-thread. He could almost feel Andri's guilt through the thread. *"You were never the sort to fall in line with your father's plots, nor were you ever interested in his bribes. I know he must have threatened you with something in order for you to betray my trust."*

Andri tried to shy away, but Rurik wouldn't let him break the thread. *"I forgive you,"* he told the youth. *"But you should have come to me the moment Stellan made his threat. I would have protected you."*

"You couldn't have," Andri whispered.

"I would have tried."

"I know."

The smaller *dreki* broke away, and this time Rurik let him go, hoping the words had been enough to sway Andri from this fight.

Because if Magnus was involved, then this only ended one way... with someone dying.

CHAPTER NINE

BY THE TIME Freyja returned home, Rurik was lying on a rug in the sun, reading a book. His shirtsleeves were rolled up to his elbows, revealing tanned forearms, and he clasped one hand behind his head, muscles shifting in his abdomen as he craned his neck to watch her walk into the yard.

It wasn't as though she'd suspected he was anything other than what he claimed, but a part of her had wondered.

He knew so much about *dreki*, after all.

But her *dreki* had thundered into the south, and that was the last she'd seen of him. He couldn't have beaten her back here, then changed form and waited for her, could he?

No. Not without Freyja seeing him in the skies.

She laid that faint suspicion to rest. She'd clearly listened to her mother's eddas too often as a girl. After all, what would a powerful creature ever want with the likes of her?

"Did you enjoy your walk?" Rurik graced her with a faint smile, taking in the state of her skirts. "Tsk. You've ruined your boots."

"Better mine than yours," she pointed out.

"True." Rurik rolled to his feet with fluid grace, setting the book upside down. "Where are you going?"

"Some of us do not have time to laze in the sun," Freyja shot over her shoulder as she headed to the barn. Thanks to her journey to warn the *dreki*, she was already behind in her day's work, and needed to see to dinner soon, if they were to dine at all.

Scrambling up the ladder into the loft, she glanced around, noting how much hay she needed to shift. Rurik's blankets lingered by the slatted window at the front of the barn, slashes of sunlight spilling over his makeshift bed. But she was not going to think of that.

"You look like you would enjoy an afternoon spent lazing in the sun." Rurik followed her up the ladder, looking far too male—a healthy one at that—as he hauled himself into the loft. There was a strength in his muscular frame that she could not match. "Maybe you should join me?"

"If you're only here to flirt with me, then I might as well put you to good use." She picked up the pitchfork and thrust it into his hands. "Here." She pointed to the pile of hay. "I need to shift that over there, so that I can drop it down into the stalls when I need to feed my animals. If you want to impress me, then you can help. I will be back to check on your work within the hour."

Rurik shot her a narrow-slitted gaze, then glanced at the pitchfork as if it was the first time he'd ever seen one.

"If the work is good enough for me," she pointed out, "then it is good enough for you, my lord."

And without waiting for a protest, she scurried down the ladder, and toward the door. She needed to fetch her small flock in, then set her stew on the stove. The clouds were brewing with all their spring glory, indicating a storm later that night.

It took longer than she'd expected—her small flock didn't want to go anywhere near the barn, the stupid beasts—but she finally managed to hunt them all inside their stalls, and swung the iron pot she'd prepared earlier over the stove, before she returned to the loft.

Climbing the ladder revealed no sign of Rurik.

Nor were there any sounds of labor in process. Typical. She was just about bristling by the time she reached the top of the ladder and—

—found herself staring at a pile of hay near the top.

"What? How—?" Freyja looked around her.

All the hay had been moved. The pitchfork rested against the nearest beam, and Rurik was stretched out upon his blankets in the corner, with his coat folded neatly beside him.

Rearing up onto his elbows, he sent her a heated smile. "You're back."

"You... finished." It usually took her at least an hour to do the same amount of work. Rurik didn't even seem to have raised a sweat, though his collar was undone now, revealing a healthy slice of chest.

"Would I have dared otherwise?" Slowly, he rolled to his feet.

She examined the hayloft. "There's no way you could have shifted so much hay in such a short time." The bare timber floorboards where the previous pile had rested were a mockery. Not even a single loose straw lay there.

"Do your eyes deceive you?"

"You cheated. Somehow." She simply couldn't accept that he could work swifter than she could.

"Aye." Rurik slowly crossed his arms, his eyelids heavy and his smile smug. "I called upon the *nisse* to help me impress you, and they answered my prayer."

Freyja set her hands on her hips. "*Nisse* are a fairy tale." The small wights were said to help take care of the house or the barn, but only when the farmer lay asleep, and only in exchange for milk.

"Do you believe in *dreki?*"

That was different. "I have seen *dreki* with my own eyes."

Freyja strode around him, trying to find some means for the almost miraculous feat. His shirt wasn't even damp with sweat. Rurik glanced behind as she circled him, and the muscles in his thighs and ass tightened behind his trousers.

"You won't find *nisse* there," he pointed out, and she realized he'd caught the direction of her gaze.

Insufferable, smug bastard. She was tired, frustrated, and struggling to resist him, and that did it. The impulse to tackle him to the ground suddenly hit her, but something told her he'd win any fight she started. After all, he dwarfed her by a good six or seven inches.

Grabbing a handful of hay, Freyja stuffed it down the back of his shirt then began to run.

She made it two steps before his strong arms caught her up. Her feet left the ground, and her back hit his chest. "Where do you think you're going? You owe me a debt now."

Freyja wriggled, but there was no denying him. He was simply too strong for her. Muscle-bound arms trapped her like a cage, and she felt like she wrestled a wall. "I don't owe you anything."

115

Rurik dumped her on the pile of blankets he was sleeping upon, and Freyja rolled onto her back breathlessly. Ripping his shirt from the waistband of his trousers, he shook himself with a growl. "This itches!"

"Perhaps *nisse* can help clean all the hay from your shirt?" she told him, innocently enough.

Oh, yes. That was definitely one irritated male shooting her a baleful look. Freyja couldn't stop herself from laughing. He looked like he couldn't believe she'd done it.

And then that devil's smile crept over his face. "Perhaps I won't need them. Perhaps you could assist?"

Reaching over his shoulder, Rurik grabbed the collar of his shirt and hauled it over his head. Pieces of hay dropped from his skin and shirt, leaving him bare chested above her. Freyja's mouth gaped. This was not what she'd planned. Not at all.

In the flesh, Rurik was breathtaking. Every inch of his skin was that sun-kissed color, and a taunting trail of golden hair edged all the way from his navel to where it disappeared into the waistband of his trousers. His chest seemed carved of heavy slabs of muscle, and he towered over her, perhaps six and a half feet tall of frustrated, dominant male.

He'd allowed her to set the pace in all of their previous encounters. For the first time, Freyja felt like she might have stirred him too far, and unleashed the predator within.

And, startlingly enough, she wasn't frightened of him.

Perhaps it was the smile, the one that said he knew just how much he affected her.

Or perhaps it was the fact that Rurik had never once taken what he'd wanted from her. Instead he'd allowed her to set the boundaries and he'd respected them, even as he flirted and teased her to the point where she wanted to growl in frustration.

She was the one who'd shoved a fistful of straw down his shirt.

Uh-oh.

"Indeed." His voice came out in a velvety growl. Rurik threw his shirt at her, and Freyja caught it, almost recoiling from the heat retained by the linen. His scent wove around her, spicy-hot and alluring.

No, no, no.

She might have started this game, but she had the bad feeling he was going to come out the winner. Freyja scrambled to escape, but Rurik was simply too big, too strong, and too fast. He covered her with ease, caging her from behind, so that his masculine scent enveloped her. Freyja locked an ankle around his leg and threw his weight over her shoulder, and somehow they went down in a sprawl. His skin was deliciously hot, and she didn't think she was fighting as hard as she could be.

When her back hit the blankets, he slammed his body over hers, one knee pinning her skirts between her legs. Freyja ceased trying to free herself, and slumped beneath him. She wasn't going to win her way free. And if she were being honest, she wasn't certain she wanted to.

"Just what do you think the penalty should be for such an infraction?" he asked her, pinning her wrists above her head and breathing hard.

Freyja gave an involuntary shiver. All of that hard, male body was pressed above her, though he didn't make contact. Not fully. There was just enough space between them for her to catch her breath. "What do you think I would be willing to pay?"

Those amber eyes flared with heat as they both realized she was flirting back. *Oh, God.* What was she doing?

Enjoying the moment, curse her. Both body and heart wanted to see where he'd take this, and her curious mind wasn't far behind.

"I will accept favors," Rurik replied softly, "as I don't think you want me trying to return the gesture."

It wasn't the hay down her dress that bothered her, more the thought of him getting his hands on her bare skin. Freyja wasn't certain she'd have the sense to stop him, if he did so.

"What type of favors?" she whispered back.

Rurik's face lowered, and she found herself tensing in anticipation, and—

Nothing.

Freyja glanced up beneath her lashes, only to find him staring down at her, an inch between their faces. She let out the breath she'd been holding, her chest heaving against his. What was he waiting for?

"If you think I am going to steal a kiss," Rurik said, in a voice turned molten with heat, "then you should think again."

Freyja wiggled a little beneath him, her body tight with thwarted anticipation. She ached, and it was a deliciously horrible feeling. "What do you mean? You didn't just wrestle me down onto your blankets for the sheer enjoyment of it."

"You don't know that. I was planning on tickling you into submission. Kissing you was not my intention," he admitted, rolling slightly to the side, so that he rested on one elbow. His right hand came up, brushing a strand of hair off her face in a gentle touch, and Freyja realized that he wasn't actually going to kiss her. "Though I might have thought about it, now we're here."

Soft fingers trailed down the sensitive skin of her throat.

Freyja sucked in a sharp breath, and became very still. Those fingers trailed lower, lower, then his knuckles brushed against the soft wool of her dress. Again she writhed, but it was a different feeling to when she'd wanted to escape. This felt like a silent demand, like her entire body wanted something her mouth couldn't articulate....

And he knew it, curse him.

"If you want a kiss, Freyja"—that smile turned utterly devilish—"then all you have to do is ask."

What? She froze. Her treacherous body was in utter rebellion against her common sense. Her body knew what it wanted. And she had to admit that her own desires were somewhat thwarted. She'd expected him to kiss her, damn him. Then she wouldn't have to admit to herself that she wanted him to.

"I thought you were here to seduce me," she said.

"I am."

"Then you're doing a rather poor job of it if you expect me to kiss *you.*" She took an unsteady breath.

"Am I?" There was that smile again. Rurik's thumb caressed her cheek, and his eyes grew heavy-lidded. "You want me to steal a kiss—"

"I don't *want* you to do anything of the sort."

"Then you expect it," he countered, his breath whispering over her skin. "Most likely so you can push me away and tell me that your hell hasn't frozen over yet."

Freyja swallowed. *Maybe.*

"I now realize," he continued, in that same silky-soft voice, "that the men you have known have not been the sort to take 'no' for an answer. You know nothing of seduction, *sarratum zamani*; and you fear that a single kiss will not end there."

"You've called me that before," she whispered.

"You're stalling," he replied, and tugged her braid over her shoulder. Rurik bought the end of her plait to his nose, and inhaled the scent of it, then those amber eyes locked on her again as the ends of her hair tickled across his lips. "Your choice, Freyja. All you have to do to receive a kiss is ask for one. If you want more, then you may take more. And if you want me to stop, then all you have to do is say so."

Her choice. Freyja turned the thought over in her head. It felt strange to consider such a thing, but... she was tempted. What would it feel like to have the reins in her hands? To be able to explore without fear that he would push her further than she was ready? "I'm not going to lie with you, so... if we start, then it will end with a kiss."

"Is that a yes?" he purred, and his thigh nudged between hers.

A thrill shot through her as his weight shifted over her again. She could control this. Her hands curled around his upper arms as he rested his forearms beside her head. Freyja slid a hand up his bare chest. The heat of his skin felt like some inner furnace burned within. "What did you mean by more?" she whispered.

Rurik lowered his mouth to hers, hovering there. "I could show you so much, Freyja. If you trusted me."

If she trusted him....

It was her choice to brush her mouth against his quivering lips. Hordes of butterflies took flight in her stomach. She didn't know how he did this to her. What was this odd connection between them? "Maybe a little more," she whispered, as she opened her mouth to his.

Rurik licked her tongue, his hips pressing flush against hers, and the hard length of his erection rubbing against her lower stomach. Each stroke of his mouth was an enticement, rather than a claim. Daring her to kiss him back, and letting her set the pace. Freyja's hands curled around his biceps, and she stroked his arms, her hands sliding up over his shoulders. All of that hot skin.... More. She wanted more. But Rurik held himself curiously apart from her, matching her kiss for kiss, and nothing else. Every time she touched him, he reciprocated. Every time her nails dug into his back, he grew a little more insistent, pressing his hips between her thighs and rubbing that heavy cock against her.

Her entire body ached, wetness dampening the skin between her thighs. An image of his hot mouth closing over her breast in Akureyri assaulted her, and Freyja moaned as she arched her back beneath him. She could almost feel his lips on her nipple, but the memory felt hollow, not quite substantial enough to satisfy her.

She didn't know how to ask for what she wanted.

Freyja curled her fists in his hair, and tugged. Hard lips captured hers, as if to encourage her. Not a sweet kiss now. This was messy. Pent-up frustration poured from him as his tongue tangled with hers, and his erection ground against the wet ache between her thighs.

More. Definitely more. That sweet friction made her body want to curl up on itself. She writhed against him, and her skirts rode up between them, leaving her legs bare. Then her greedy hands slid over his shoulders, exploring all of that smooth skin. She wanted to lick it and so she did, nipping at the muscle in his throat.

"Freyja." He sucked in a sharp breath as he turned his face to the side, muttering an unsteady curse under his breath. Hands trapped her wrists, and then Rurik pinned her hands above her head, leaving her utterly helpless beneath him. Those golden eyes locked on hers, and he shuddered, his voice turning all growly. "If you don't stop doing that, then this isn't going to end here."

"Doing what?" she whispered, cupping his hips with her thighs and rocking against him experimentally.

Rurik's lips parted, and his gaze became distant. It felt so, so good. But there was something *else* that beckoned and she couldn't quite understand what it was, or how to get there.

"You told me you didn't intend to lie with me," he growled, his lips curling back off his teeth. Utterly primitive expressions crossed his face. "Have you changed your mind? Or do you just want a little more?"

"I want...." She stalled there. And his body hovered over hers, his cock pressing with heated possession against her.

But he didn't make a single move, and it hurt to deny herself, and *oh, God....*

Those golden eyes darkened as if he understood what she wanted when she herself didn't. "Do you trust me?"

That was a dangerous question. Freyja's mind raced. "Yes." Barely a whisper.

"Good." He claimed her mouth in another heated kiss, even as his hands slid down her arms, setting her free.

Freyja's hands tangled in his golden hair. His found the laces on her dress. Suddenly she knew what he intended, and her eyes shot wide, even as his lips traced their way down her throat.

"Let me please you," he whispered, nuzzling aside her neckline. Sharp teeth nipped at the curve of her breast, and then he traced the sensitive area with his tongue.

Pleasure threatened to claim her. Freyja rolled her head to the side. *Yes. Yes.* "More," she breathed.

The rasp of his stubble grazed her sensitive breasts as Rurik rocked his hips against her. Somehow the steely length of his erection met the seat of her pleasure, and he rode over that delicate part of her, nearly sending her wild with need. Tugging her neckline open, he claimed her aching nipple with his hot mouth, and it was all she could do to stifle the cry that sprang from her lips.

"That's it, *ati me peta libbu*," he whispered. Teeth scraped her nipple, and then he was licking her there, that talented tongue driving every last thought out of her head.

All that remained was a creature of pleasure. She could feel the storm building within her, whipped to greater heights by that teasing tongue and the mocking rock of his hips.

Clasping her hips, Rurik slid his hand under the lengths of her skirt. The material rode up her thighs, leaving her in her drawers and stockings. Freyja wrapped her legs around his hips, even as his questing hand trailed between her thighs. Gentle fingers stroked her damp drawers, and a shudder went through her. Nobody had ever touched her there. Only herself, and she'd shied away from exploring too far.

This... this was like lightning coiling all the way through her.

Freyja cupped his face. Rurik stared down at her, lazy-lidded and curious, as if he wanted to see every single expression that crossed her face.

"Do you like that?" he whispered, as if his fingers hadn't just worked between the slit in her drawers and finally found her, damp and trembling.

"Oh." Her mouth fell open on a gasp as one finger stroked her in her most private place. Rurik traced tiny little circles there, seeming to find the secret heart of her, the place that seemed most sensitive.

"What are you *doing*?" she blurted.

"Want to ride the storm, Freyja?" He kissed the side of her jaw, his face nuzzling against hers, even as his fingers worked her with slow and patient circles.

Almost there. Freyja's eyes shot wide, and her fingernails turned into claws in the soft skin of his shoulders. There. *Yes.* Almost. Almost.

She shattered.

Her entire body clenched on a wave of pleasure, and somehow she threw her head back, crying out in soft abandon as Rurik pushed her over the edge. This time the lightning wasn't in the sky. She felt like a bolt of it struck her, and flash-burned all her nerves. Exquisite. Breathless. The fiercest ache she'd ever felt....

Then it was over, and she was collapsing into a gasping mess in his arms, her heart thundering in her chest.

"That's it," Rurik whispered, still tracing his fingers through the slick folds between her thighs. "That's it, my fierce, precious Freyja."

Somehow her mind caught up with what he was doing. She buried her burning face in his throat, her body quivering with aftershock. She couldn't take any more. Freyja shook her head and grabbed his wrist, pulling his hand away from her. Another shiver worked its way through her. So intense. She felt like the earth itself when something monumental shifted beneath the ground.

And maybe something monumental *had* shifted....

Rurik kissed her temples, then her closed eyes, then her nose. Somehow he found her mouth, and this kiss was another gentle one, as if he tried to calm her flighty heart.

Too late. She would never be the same again.

"*More*," Freyja whispered, tilting her face to present her throat to him.

Rurik stilled, and then something hard and predatory slid over his face. Something she didn't quite recognize. Then he shook his head, his expression tinged with regret. "As much as I would like to comply, you're not ready yet. And I have no wish to rush you."

"Am I not the judge of that?" Freyja clapped a hand over his, then urged it back beneath her skirts—

"Freyja!" Her father's voice cut through their reverie.

Freyja froze, her hand on Rurik's, even as her pulse beat out of control. Their eyes met, his dark and predatory.

"Looks like we have little choice," Rurik rasped, his head twisting toward the window. The sun was beginning to set. "Damn it."

"Freyja?" her father called again.

Freyja shoved Rurik off her and rolled out from beneath him, her cheeks so hot she could rival a sunset, she imagined. Oh, my goodness. What had she been about to do? Lose her virginity in the barn? She tugged hay from her hair and out of her dress, yanked her laces tight, then pulled the material over her bare breasts. Everything in her body trembled, including her knees.

What would her father think?

What had *she* been thinking?

Clearly, she had not been.

"Don't give me that look," Rurik growled, under his breath. He groaned, and then slumped back onto the blankets, rearranging the fierce erection in his trousers. "What we just shared was not wrong."

"Be silent!" she hissed, scurrying to the ladder. "He'll hear you."

"Freyja."

She paused at the top of the ladder, her knees still unsteady.

Rurik sprawled on his blankets, his chest bare, his golden hair tangled across his brow and his smile dangerous. "This isn't done."

"Oh, yes it is!" she shot back, and fled down the ladder.

CHAPTER TEN

RURIK CLASPED HIS hands under his head and stared at the shadows of the barn roof as night settled in. He'd dined with Freyja and her father, though Freyja barely looked at him. Every time she did, he could see thoughts racing through her eyes.

She'd let him touch her, please her... and now she was curious.

But the stubborn part of her nature had reared its head also. Freyja was not the sort to accept such a vital turning point in her seduction so sanguinely. She would turn herself in knots, no doubt all night, and in the morning their dance would begin again.

He could hardly wait.

Rurik could be patient, even as his body ached with the lack of release. Freyja was worth it, and today had been a concession he hadn't expected her to make just yet.

Closing his eyes slowly, he let his spirit hover just inside his body. Tonight he had another debt to repay, and if he felt perhaps a little frustration, then this would assuage the hunter within him.

A long time since he'd walked the dreams of man. A long time since he'd wanted to.

Rurik let his spirit separate from his mortal flesh, and rose high above the world. The little barn lay beneath him, and lights flickered merrily from the main house. He drifted above its grassed roof, and then turned his sight upon the nearby village.

One thought and he was there, the world rushing past him. Dozens of spirits flickered below him as men and women moved through the village, banking the fires for the night.

Rurik sorted through them, his predatory senses touching and discarding several souls before finally alighting on the one he sought. He circled the fine manor house, sensing the snoring pig that awaited him.

"Benedikt," Rurik whispered, feeling the other soul waken to his call, the man turning fitfully toward him in bed.

Not quite all the way awake, but not lost in sleep either.

Rurik formed within the room, staring balefully at his nemesis.

This man had hurt Freyja. Not physically, for she had her own defenses, but he'd struck at her where she was most vulnerable. Little whispers in the right ear, setting superstition against her, and threats to those villagers who might have helped her and bought her produce. Oh, yes. Rurik had offered good coin for that information, as he waited for Freyja to make her way home from Akureyri.

Benedikt wanted her weak, alienated and powerless. His intentions had never been about seduction, but ownership. He'd wanted her begging and on her knees, rather than meeting her on equal footing.

No man of honor would ever pursue such a course of action.

Crossing to the bed, Rurik looked down on his prey. Every inch of him wanted to spill blood, but that went against the code he lived by. No true *dreki* could ever commit murder, no matter the offence. You did not take human lives, unless they attacked you first. It was a treaty that went back hundreds of years to when the human Althing met with the *dreki* court and demanded a cease to hostilities between human and *dreki*.

He had never before felt the need to break one the *dreki's* greatest laws, but he came close now.

Killing this coward, however, would be too easy.

Rurik reached out with his spirit hand and clasped Benedikt's shoulder, plunging them both straight into the dream world.

Rurik manipulated the dream, twisting it to his liking. Taking his immortal form, he flapped high above the moors, where he set Benedikt to running. The man staggered and babbled with fright, finding himself in unfamiliar terrain. When Rurik's shadow rippled over him, Benedikt looked up, his face whitening with fear.

"Run," Rurik whispered.

Mist surrounded them, hot fumes bubbling from small crevices in the ground. Enjoying the mortal's staggering plight, Rurik flapped lazily above him, then suddenly cut his wings flat against his sides and plunged into a dive.

Benedikt bleated in fear, and splashed through a hot spring, his voice turning to a scream as the acid water burned him.

Swooping just short of him, Rurik climbed again as the man scrambled across moss-slick rocks.

"It is not fun to be prey, is it?" he taunted, diving again.

A wave of incoherent fear swept from the man. He pissed himself, and Rurik chose that moment to lash out with his claws, catching the man by the shirt. He hauled him into the air, wings beating as he climbed. The shirt ripped, jerking Benedikt in his grasp, and Rurik shook him a little, just to frighten him.

"Please!" Benedikt screamed, as the tear in his shirt began to jerk wider. "Please! I have gold—"

The shirt finally gave and Benedikt tumbled end over end with a high-pitched squeal as he plummeted through the air. Rurik waited until the last moment before he caught his blubbering prey. His claw locked around the man's ankle.

Now he had the peasant's attention.

"I don't want your gold. Nothing that you say can or will sway me. This is a warning."

Turning toward his dream-rendition of Krafla, he flapped lazily as Benedikt cried in his grasp.

"You have turned your village against Freyja Helgasdottir. You have threatened her, and threatened others so that they may not provide her aide or trade coin with her. You're not a man. You're a sniveling coward, and you know not who you provoke."

Circling the tip of the volcano, he pictured lava bubbling within the hollow of the caldera, flames licking up the sides as if they wanted to eat Benedikt alive.

"That bitch is lying! I never touched her. I never threatened her—"

"If you die here, then you'll never wake." Rurik bared his teeth as he circled above the volcano. *"If you so much as look in her direction ever again, I shall roast you alive,"* he snapped, and then finally let go. *"I know who the liar is."*

Benedikt slammed his hands out in front of him as the lava rushed up to meet him, only to realize there was something wrong, something…. He jerked awake from the dream and plunged upright in his bed, his skin clammy with sweat as his familiar room formed around him. The fire in the grate had died down, but lit enough of the furniture for him to grasp hold of his sheets in relief.

Not real. Just a nightmare. His lungs sucked in air and his heart raced as he groaned and sank his head into his hands. His nightshirt was wet with piss. The image of the caldera rushing up to meet him sprang sharply to mind, then he was crying and snot was bubbling out of his nose, and damn him, he was a man, not a child. Benedikt wiped the tears from his eyes furiously, sucking in enough oxygen to stem the flow of tears.

"Just a dream," he told himself hoarsely, even though it felt real.

Pain speared through his ankle as he twisted to right his sheets, and he dragged them up to see what the problem was—

There, against his skin, were the reddened claw marks of the dragon.

"Not a dream," something whispered in his head.

Benedikt's back hit the headboard as he scrambled up the bed, staring at his reddened skin. "Blessed father, watch over me," he whispered, his heart thumping like a rabbit's.

He scrambled for the chamber pot as his stomach suddenly heaved, too overwhelmed by the thought of what had happened. Real. Far too real. Benedikt vomited into the pot, piss splashing against his face. He was held captive by his stomach, however, until the wave of fear wrung everything from him.

Ripping his nightshirt off, he wiped his face and collapsed in a heap against the wall, shivering.

That bitch must have set the dragon upon him.

There was more than one way to answer *that* insult. He shoved to his feet, and reached for his clothes. He was halfway into them when the dream returned.

"If you so much as look in her direction, I shall roast you alive," the dragon had hissed.

Benedikt swallowed, then he slowly dragged his trousers up his legs. It wasn't as though *he* was going to do anything. Not overtly. That was what he was paying others for.

He considered the thought for a long moment, turning it over in his mind to find the flaw in his argument.

There was none. He couldn't just accept this threat.

And he had a dragon hunter up his sleeve.

The dragon had to be dealt with. And Benedikt knew just the way to do it.

The fire crackled as Haakon nursed his horn of ale in the village taproom. Another long, seemingly pointless day stretched behind him. The frustration ached, but he knew to be patient. Today they'd mapped Krafla, finding no sign of the *dreki* itself, but plotting where the best place to set the ballista lay.

Turning the silver pendant his wife had given him over in his fingers, Haakon rubbed the embossed metal. A hawk in full flight gleamed, its wings flared and its eyes seeming to stare right through him.

"A hawk for a hunter," Arja had teased as she lay beneath him the night of their wedding, and looped the chain around his neck.

He hated the fact that the memory had grown ragged around the edges. He knew her face, but when he pictured her, somehow the image wasn't quite fully formed, as if he was forgetting parts of her. Hair the color of spun gold crowned her face, and eyes like polished amber stared up at him.

Six years of misery. Six years since the *dreki* stole her from him.

Haakon's fist closed over the pendant. He could wait another night or two, so long as his patience gained him what he desired.

"Who are you looking at?" Rollo demanded with sneer, his loud voice cutting through the taproom laughter. "Don't think I won't ruin that pretty face of yours!"

The enormous man shoved to his feet, fist drawn back as he launched himself toward the youngest of their company, but before Haakon could move to restrain him, another was there.

One of his newest recruits, Magnus, caught the man's wrist and shoved Rollo against the wall as if he didn't weigh the same as a bear. His lips curled back from his teeth as Rollo's attention turned from the young hunter to this newest threat.

"Keep your hands off my brother," Magnus warned, and that voice sent a chill through Haakon.

He pushed to his feet, recognizing the danger signs. His men were hungry for a kill, and the careful planning and days of unsuccessful hunting were wearing at them all. If he didn't stop them, blood would be spilled. "That's enough."

Both Magnus and Rollo looked at him, though Magnus's expression didn't change. He and his brother, Andri, had joined Haakon's party in Akureyri, lured by the sound of plentiful coin. Though he had enough men, he'd taken one look at their hardened eyes and battle-ready frames and known warriors when he saw them.

Which was precisely what he'd need, where he was going.

"Focus on the *dreki*," he told the room of watchful men. "You'll get your blood soon enough."

"When?" Gunnar demanded.

"Aye," Jon snarled. "When do we take the dragon's lair?"

The rest of the men echoed him, thumping fists on table, and clapping their tankards on the trestle tables. Haakon held his hands up, the pendant chain curled around two fingers. "Tomorrow!"

A chorus of cheers went up.

But Haakon felt eyes on him, and noticed that Andri was staring at the pendant in his hand. Slowly the boy's eyes locked on his, a shock of black hair falling over the youth's forehead and highlighting those dangerous blue eyes.

Just a lad, barely past the threshold of youth. But Haakon felt something shift inside him as their eyes met.

Even a boy could be dangerous, and he almost wanted to demand to know what put *that* look in Andri's eyes—as if the sight of the pendant stirred something heated in the lad's chest.

A foolish thought, for the boy had no connection to Arja. He would have been in short pants when she first swept into Haakon's life and turned his world upside down.

"Tomorrow," Magnus echoed, slowly sinking onto the bench beside his brother, his hawk-like features sharp with some unfettered bloodlust. He had no love of dragons, or *dreki*, or whatever they bloody well were.

"I want to mount that dreki's head on a spike," the man had said the first time they met.

Andri's lips thinned, and then the boy looked away from the pendant that had held him captive for long moments.

Haakon curled his fist shut over it and sank onto his chair, just as the boy's head tilted toward the door. Sliding the pendant into his pocket, he picked up the sword he'd been polishing earlier.

The door to the tavern banged open and Benedikt appeared in the doorway, his plump cheeks full and his mouth turned upside down. He spilled inside from the night, as if Hel's three-legged horse, Helhest, were on his trail.

Something had upset the little farmer, Haakon thought, sliding an oiled rag along the length of his sword.

Conversations lagged as the mercenaries all noticed the pampered brat. Gunnar locked eyes with Haakon, and then spat in the reeds. He'd already voiced his thoughts on their benefactor and the way Benedikt seemed to think he'd bought them.

"I don't care what the little lordling thinks," Haakon had replied coldly. *"He's paying for the men and the ballista, and I need them to get my wife back."*

Looking the worse for wear, Benedikt slammed a pouchful of coin on the table in front of him. Haakon's gaze locked on it, then slowly lifted to the would-be lordling.

"I'm not paying you to sit on your ass and polish your sword," Benedikt snapped. "You've been here four days, and you've barely done a thing."

Gunnar lowered his tankard as Haakon shifted forward in his seat, putting both feet on the ground. Standing up, he loomed over the petulant man-child, then slid his sword into its sheath at his hip with a steely rasp.

Conversation died. His men shifted in their chairs as they craned their necks to watch.

They weren't the only ones who were hungry for blood.

And Benedikt might be paying them, but there were certain insolences Haakon wouldn't tolerate.

Haakon rested his knuckles on the table and loomed forward, so they were of a height. "You know nothing of hunting dragons," he said quietly. "And this is no ordinary dragon."

He'd seen it circling Krafla two days ago, sunlight gilding its golden hide.

His heart had caught in his throat at the sight, and every instinct within him urged him to scale the mount and launch a full-scale assault upon the *dreki's* lair. He'd thought of Arja in that moment, begging any god who listened for her to still be alive.

"The volcano seems empty and the entrance is barricaded by an invisible door, or perhaps magic," Haakon continued. "To scale the mountain, we must take a narrow route, which leaves us vulnerable. I'm not throwing men at the *dreki* needlessly until I can figure out how to get it to meet me on my terms."

"You want the dragon?" Benedikt snapped. "I know how you can lure it out."

Stillness slid through him, and his knuckles ached as he clenched his fist. "How?"

Benedikt stomped his boot on the trestle seat, then reached down to peel up his trousers. "It visited me in a dream." There, around his leg, were the unmistakable red marks of a set of claws.

No wonder the little bitch was bleating so hard.

"What did it want?" Haakon demanded. Here was his chance, he just knew it. He'd stared past that invisible barrier to the *dreki's* lair and called his wife's name in desperation, hoping she was inside.

If he could just break the spell on the door, or bring the *dreki* to him.... Maybe it was madness, but he *needed* to discover if Krafla's wyrm had stolen his wife. Being here, so close to the shadow of the mountain was sending him mad with pure want. Arja haunted his dreams all night, pleading for him to rescue her, until he didn't dare sleep.

Patience be damned, there was a feeling tingling through his veins as if fate rushed to meet him. This was it. This was the dragon who'd taken her. He knew it.

"It wanted to warn me," Benedikt said, smiling a little, as if he could see Haakon's need on his face. "It wanted me to stay away from Freyja Helgasdottir, or it would kill me."

The blood rushed from Haakon's face, leaving his cheeks cold. "Then Freyja is the key to luring it out."

CHAPTER ELEVEN

THE NEXT DAY, Rurik went in search of Freyja, feeling oddly restless. He'd taken care of the threat against her, now he just needed to charm the stubborn woman. At least he had yesterday's success still brewing in his mind.

And in his body.

He knew why he felt restless. Denying himself release yesterday during his encounter with Freyja had been sensible, as she wasn't quite ready for that. But it still ached.

And he was fairly certain yesterday's events would be lingering in her mind too. Which meant one step forward, no doubt two steps back. The bloody woman could give a rock lessons in stubbornness.

The faint scent of her captured his attention, and Rurik tilted his head toward the back of the house. There.

She was just lowering a wooden box into the dirt near the hot spring behind the house. Baking more of that bread he liked so much, by the look of it. Taking her pitchfork, she swept the heated earth back over the top of the cask, then brushed strands of damp hair from her forehead.

"Good morning," he called, striding down the slope toward her.

Freyja's shoulders stiffened faintly, but she nodded to him. "Morning? I've been up for almost six hours."

"So have I," he told her.

Freyja shot him a doubtful look. "Doing what?"

Flying halfway across Iceland, and paying a small fortune for things he thought she would like. "Preparing a surprise for you."

"A surprise? For *me*?"

"It's the sort of thing one does when one is wooing a young lady." Rurik crossed his arms over his chest, hoping that her curiosity was stronger than her wariness. "Or so I am told."

"I don't have time for surprises," she said, and he admitted that she did look tired. But Freyja also hesitated, and glanced at him from beneath those thick dark lashes.

Curiosity engaged. He smiled. "Give me an hour, and I will give you my afternoon's labor. After all, you do not know what I have in mind...."

"As long as it doesn't involve hay," she said.

"Nor stuffing it down someone's shirt."

Freyja tried to fight a smile, but couldn't seem to help herself. "Do you never cease? You're incorrigible and relentless and—"

"An excellent lover."

She shot him a swift glare. "What happened yesterday will not happen again."

Rurik brushed his hand against her hip as he moved past her; the lightest of caresses, as he murmured in her ear, "You shouldn't make promises you might not be able to keep."

"Do you think you're the first man who has set his sights on me?" Freyja looked dangerous as she turned to

139

follow him, pitchfork in hand. "Yes, you might own a silver tongue, and I'll admit that you intrigue me, but no man has won my heart before and I doubt one ever will."

"Perhaps. But then, you have never been wooed by one such as I."

A frustrated sound echoed in the back of her throat. Freyja stabbed the pitchfork into the ground.

"Spare me an hour, and I'll leave you alone," he said, taking pity on her and capturing her fingers. "One hour, Freyja. Do you not want to know what surprise I have in store for you?"

She was wavering. He saw it in her eyes. "One hour," she finally said, sighing. "It had better be worth it."

"Oh, it will be." Tucking her hand in the crook of his elbow, Rurik led her around the house, into the sunshine.

He'd spread the blanket within a circle of birches that guarded the hilltop overlooking Freyja's farm. The birches stood in a perfect circle around them, and though he remained wary about entering such a circle, he couldn't sense any magic within it. Freyja's interest was piqued when she saw the blanket and the basket he'd set out.

"A picnic," she exclaimed.

"You work too much," he replied. "You deserve a treat."

"Someone must," she replied, and folded her skirts neatly around her as she settled on the blanket. "Unlike others, I cannot rely on *nisse*."

"No one can," he replied, stretching out beside her. "They are unreliable little beasts, and if you don't leave enough milk out for them, they're liable to turn upon you."

A smile softened her face. "Do you know, sometimes I almost believe you when you speak of myths and fairy tales."

There was a hint of sadness around her eyes.

"Why would you not?" He stroked the edge of her skirts, fingers rubbing the soft wool between them.

"Because I know what hand of fate life deals," she admitted, opening the picnic basket. "*Nisse* and *huldufólk* and trolls are all well and good, but they are stories for children."

"You believed then, once upon a time."

She set out the breads and meats that he'd brought them, her face strangely devoid of any expression. "My mother believed. It was she who spoke of *dreki* and *huldufólk*."

He hesitated. "What happened to her?"

"Five years ago, she disappeared for several days. When we found her in the stone ring up near Krafla, she looked like she had aged a decade, and nothing seemed to satisfy her. She wouldn't say where she'd been, or what had happened, but she began to waste away," Freyja said gently. "She didn't want to eat our foods, nor drink, but she consumed just enough to live. Yet it was as though someone took the light from her life. It took her two years to die, and no one knew what was wrong with her. My father has not been the same ever since." Freyja sliced some of the soft cheese onto a piece of bread, and handed it to him.

"I'm sorry," he said, placing his hand over hers.

Freyja looked at him very steadily. "You remind me of her sometimes." She turned her hand beneath his, her fingers lacing through two of his. "She was a dreamer too, but... I don't think I have enough left within me to dream."

Dreams could be dangerous. He understood that. He'd spent thirty years hibernating within Krafla, trying not to think of the past, allowing the locals to bring him food so that he did not even have to hunt. Merely drifting with his mind entwined with the volcano beneath him, feeling the earth crack and groan as he tried not to think of all that he'd lost.

Rurik's thumb caressed the smooth skin of her hand. "I think... that I had stopped dreaming too," he admitted. "Until I met you."

That brought a blush to her cheeks. Freyja rolled her eyes. "Of course."

But she didn't understand. He watched as she devoured the small spread of cured meat and cheeses, mixed with fresh strawberry jam and white fluffy bread, the kind that Freyja had never eaten before.

The night he'd taken her ram, his entire life changed. Driven from Krafla by hunger, he'd thought little of the hunt behind the desire to fill his belly, but it had brought so much more into his life.

It had brought her.

He could still recall Freyja brandishing that sword at him, her face full of determination and weariness. Years of sleepy dullness sloughed away from him in that instant. He'd stepped aside from the world, turning his attention to the earth and fire beneath him, but she brought him back in a single moment, slamming into his life like a thunderstorm of epic proportions.

He felt alive, for the first time in years.

And he was starting to think of the future, of what part she would play in it. For he couldn't let her go, not now. Not when she was the catalyst for this new awakening within his heart.

"What are you thinking?" she asked, nibbling on one of the fat strawberries that he'd hunted high and low for.

"I am wondering: what is your greatest desire?"

"To finish my work swiftly, so that I may have an hour or two to myself tonight," she replied, red juice staining her lips.

He wanted to lick the taste of it from them. "That seems a small dream."

"You *would* say that, but just because it is a small dream, does not mean that it is not a joy to me." Freyja slowly rolled onto her back, resting on one elbow. Her braid slung over her shoulder, and she took her time with the last mouthful of strawberry, entirely innocent of what the sight of her eating it did to him.

"If you were not bound by time, nor money, nor any other mortal constraint, what do you wish you could do?"

Freyja gave him that serious look again. Rurik caught the end of her braid, toying with the ribbon that bound it. Her breath caught, and she tossed the stalk of the strawberry away.

Come on. Give me your heart. Tell me how to win it.

"Travel," she whispered, as he tugged the ribbon loose. "See these great cities that my books speak of. See this world."

There it was. He smiled and began to unravel the bottom of her braid. Silky hair curled around his fingers. He'd dreamed of it spread over his sheets, dreamed of running his hands through it. "You like my stories, because you dream of adventure."

"I like any story." She watched what he was doing. Not with trepidation, but almost as if she wondered what he intended. "It reminds me that there is something more out there, something beyond my day's worth of chores."

"And is this your greatest desire?"

"Why are you so insistent upon dreams?" she growled under her breath, capturing a handful of her unraveling braid. "They're little more than wistful thinking. Wonderful in the moment, but rather insubstantial, because nothing will come of it."

"To dream of something more is the greatest gift that one owns. Without them, there is nothing to strive for. No reason to continue breathing. We might as well become the rock and stone beneath our feet." Rurik brushed her hand aside and spread thick waves of golden hair across the picnic blanket, even as Freyja shifted as though she wasn't certain she should allow him to continue. "And because you have set me a challenge: to give you your greatest desire, in exchange for your heart."

Her heart began to beat a little quicker. He heard it. "That is not my heart's greatest desire."

"Then what is?"

Freyja suddenly smiled. "I'm not telling you. If you were paying attention, you should be able to work it out."

"Vexing woman." Rurik grabbed a fistful of her hair and tugged gently until she rolled onto her back. He came over her, shaking the last of her braid free. Thick strands of molten gold spread across the dark blanket, crinkled into loose waves. "I think you like being pursued."

"You're the mighty hunter," she teased. "You wouldn't enjoy the chase if it were too easy."

"True. But then I know what comes at the culmination of the chase," he replied, heat in his eyes. "And I enjoy that far more than chasing."

Bringing a handful of her hair up to his face, he rubbed it across his cheeks. She smelled like a summer breeze, like a wild storm. And her mismatched eyes watched his expression as though she saw something there that she didn't know how to interpret. "What are you doing?" Freyja whispered.

"I have dreamed of running my fingers through your hair like this." He rubbed a strand of it between forefinger and thumb, his eyelids lowering lazily. "You have beautiful hair and I want to see it down."

Those perfect lips were so close to his, still stained pink from strawberries. Sweet, and lush, and practically begging for his caress.

Rurik lowered his face to hers, his fists curling in handfuls of her hair. One taste and he was lost. He licked her slowly, teasing his way into her mouth as Freyja opened up to him, slowly, softly, as if she were testing the waters.

The thought of yesterday consumed him, setting him on fire. Or maybe that was Freyja. She was light, and brightness, a catalyst of pure fire that awoke every single one of his senses. Something was happening to him, and he didn't quite know what it was, nor what it meant. But she was the key to it.

Freyja put a firm hand against his chest. Not so much pushing him away, but asking for space, and perhaps time to gather her thoughts. Both of them were breathing hard.

"You make me feel alive," he whispered, somehow perplexed by the complex emotions swelling within him.

"You make me want things I shouldn't want," she whispered back, as if it were some secret confession.

Not ready. Not yet. For though she craved him, something still held her back. Shifting to the side of her, he rearranged the painful press of his erection, and then stroked the soft river of her hair.

"What do you dream of?" she suddenly asked, glancing up from beneath those thick golden lashes.

Me? He froze. Nobody had ever asked him that. Nor had he dwelled on the matter.

"I long for... home," he replied slowly, startled to realize that it was true. A sudden yearning filled him: the urge to drag his sister into his arms one more time, and to see his younger brother's smile. Just one more day at Hekla, where his people lived, and he could belong. Home. A sense of belonging, his father's voice echoing through the halls—

A dream dashed. There was no home for him there. Nothing more than memories of a time thirty years in the past, before he'd chosen exile. His father was long gone.

For all his power, he could never, ever relive that time again.

"What stops you from returning?" Freyja stroked his cheek, fingertips trailing over the roughened hairs that marked his jaw.

Restlessness edged through him, despite the tender touch. "Freyja, I can never go home."

Pushing away from her, he drew one knee up in front of him, his heart heavy. His erection was gone, thoughts of seduction fading away. Freyja dragged herself into a seated position, a thousand questions dancing in her eyes. "Do you wish to talk of it?"

"No."

She accepted that. Simply began to pack away the remains of their picnic. This wasn't what he'd intended when he set it out, the afternoon suddenly souring. And yet, he almost felt as though this was what he needed to broach the walls that guarded her heart.

"I am exiled from my clan," he admitted gently. "If I returned, my uncle would try to kill me."

Those witchy eyes locked on him with a dangerous intensity. "Why would he want you dead?"

Old wounds ached in his heart. "Stellan is my mother's brother. When my father died, Stellan took his place as..." How to say this? "...head of the clan. I believe... I believe he had something to do with my father's death, with my mother's help."

"You didn't fight him?"

Rurik felt his face shutter. "I was exiled, instead. Blamed for the murder of my father."

Freyja's mouth fell open. "But—"

"I didn't do it, Freyja. I loved my father. But I was the first on the scene, I found his heart pierced with a blade of pure iron. There was blood on my hands. And... a witness who claimed I did it. A witness whom no one disputed."

"Who?"

His heart sank like a stone in water. That betrayal was one he could never forgive. "My mother."

She reached out to stroke his face. "Why would she do that to her own son?"

Rurik pressed into the touch, capturing her hand in his and holding it there. The fury of the *dreki* within him melted at her touch. Only she could tame it. "She wanted power, most likely. She controls Stellan, and he comes from the same clan she did. She has never controlled me. You cannot think of her as you think of your own mother. She birthed the three of us into the world; Árdís, Marduk, and me. But she had not the raising of us. We were marks on a contract to her. A fulfillment of the oath she gave my father and his clan when she married him. A duty. It was my father who loved us and reared us."

And his heart ached in his chest at the mere thought that his own people could consider him the hand that murdered his father.

"I'm sorry," Freyja whispered on a thought-thread she didn't even know she sent.

And he could not link back with her, not when she thought he was merely human.

Rurik looked down, into her eyes. "I accepted the exile so that my brother and sister would not be drawn into a war. They weren't ready. Neither was I, to speak the truth. But this is not the first time my mother and uncle have tried to see me dead." He squeezed her hand. "It is the first time, however, that I have something more to lose than merely my life. My family are... a proud people. They would not accept you, nor any consummation between us."

Freyja drew her knees up to her chest, resting her chin upon them. "You miss your brother and sister?"

"Fiercely."

"Not so small a dream," Freyja whispered, as if cognizant of the turmoil within him.

"No." He met those beautiful eyes, aware that the ground beneath them both had shifted, and that he suddenly understood her own quiet yearning. "Not so small a dream."

There was a long moment of silence, each of them lost in their own thoughts. He ached to know hers. Instead, he lifted a hand and brushed the backs of his fingers down her pale cheek.

Freyja tilted into the touch, her lashes shuttering her eyes, and her lips slightly parted. In this moment she was without fear or thought, existing only to *feel*.

And he thought that he should kiss her again. The sudden urge to do so left him floundering as he realized that this urge had little to do with pressing her against the ground and plundering her sweet mouth, or even body. It wanted nothing more than to taste her mouth, to share in her moment of peace, of acceptance. He wanted to kiss her for the sake of the kiss itself, and because she... she meant something to him.

Rurik drew back. What was this? He didn't know what precisely he felt, but he knew that it was different.

There was no endless curiosity in this feeling. No desire to claim, or plunder. Merely... tenderness?

Freyja looked up. And the moment passed, and suddenly he became aware that he was staring at her as if she'd stolen his heart from his chest when he wasn't looking, and he didn't quite know what to do with that fact.

"The day is wasting," he said abruptly, drawing away from her. "If you want some time to yourself, then now is the time to steal it. I have promised you an afternoon's labor, so use my time wisely. We're done here."

We're done here.

The thought plagued her as she tried to read.

She'd purchased a new book in Akureyri, and normally such a thing as *Gulliver's Travels* would cause the room to vanish around her as she lost herself in the world within the covers.

Time to herself.... It seemed a dream, until one lived in the moment and realized that all she *had* was time to herself.

Freyja closed the book with a slap.

"What's wrong?" her father asked.

"Nothing." And everything. Freyja found her feet. "I just feel restless, that's all. I'm going out to check the fences."

"Restless, hmm?" Her father closed his eyes, drowsing in the sunlight that spilled through the window. "Wouldn't have anything to do with Master Rurik, would it?"

Freyja went still. "Why would you say that?"

"Because he is clearly interested in courting you, and you've been distracted ever since he arrived."

Freyja toyed with the edge of her skirt. "Don't get your hopes up," she said quietly, though she wasn't certain whether she was speaking to her father—or herself. "There is no future between Rurik and I." Snapping her fingers, she headed for the door. "Come, Loki."

The little fox sprang to her side, licking his lips, as they exited the small house. Freyja tidied her braid as she strode for the barn. Memories of his hands coursing through the silken waves of her hair heated her body. She had no intention of ensuring the fences were tidy. No. What she wanted was to find him. The earlier dismissal vexed her.

Rurik was the one who'd decided to chase her, wasn't he?

And now, *"we're done here...."* Just when she was starting to feel something for him. Just when she'd allowed him to take certain liberties.

Freyja knew she was being unfair. She'd kept him at arm's length, and insisted nothing was going to happen between them, so why should she be so upset when he turned the tables on her?

Because he'd let her into his life a little, with the talk of his exile and his home. For a second, she'd felt as though she knew him intimately.

Because I'm lonely too.

The small herd of ewes hovered against the stone fence outside the barn, eyeing her with wild eyes. Ever since that blasted *dreki* stole her ram, they'd been riding on the edge of their nerves. It was a wonder her goat was still producing any milk.

The barn lay empty, though Hanna snorted when she saw her, as if asking for reassurance. All the jobs she'd given Rurik were completed, though there was no sign of the man himself.

"Not you too," Freyja grumbled to Hanna as the mare whickered with nervousness. Sunlight spilled between cracks in the loft floorboards, and dust spiraled through each shaft.

Loki bumped into her ankles, almost tripping her.

"Rurik?" she called up into the loft.

A shadow moved up there. She hadn't seen him since they'd spoken of dreams, and a part of her felt sympathy for what he'd shared of his past. Enough sympathy that she'd brought out the *hangikjöt* and carved it, broiled some potatoes and set a loaf of *rúgbrauð* baking in the warm spring behind the house. It was the type of meal she might serve at Christmas, and the scent of smoked lamb already filled her small kitchen. The bread would almost be ready.

"I wanted to invite you in for dinner," she called, craning her neck. Floorboards in the loft creaked, but why hadn't he replied? "I made something special." Freyja hesitated. "To remind you of home, perhaps."

Still no answer.

All the hairs on the back of Freyja's neck rose. "Rurik?" she called, crossing toward the ladder to the loft.

Loki barked, and Freyja tried to hush him. Then he darted into the shadows, growling deep in his throat in a sound she'd never heard from him before.

"What is it?" she asked, taking a step back. There was something about the sullen silence in the barn that bothered her. Someone was there. And she didn't think it was Rurik.

A man cursed under his breath, and then Loki yelped and fled. "Little bastard."

"Who's there?" she demanded, peering into the shadows of the stall. "Loki?"

Noise whispered behind her. Freyja whirled, and another man stepped out of the shadows. Darting toward her pitchfork, she turned and almost ran him through, baring her teeth at him. "Rurik!"

"He's not here," someone said behind her. "Seems you ran him off."

Rurik was gone? The warmth drained out of her. What had she done or said to him? She didn't understand. He'd said that he... cared for her. Was it all just a jest? Or had Rurik merely been interested in bedding her, and given up?

That didn't make any sense. He could have had her yesterday afternoon if all he'd wanted was to bed her. If she were being honest with herself, she wasn't certain she would have said no.

Laughter spilled out of the shadows as another man appeared. "Can you blame him? Look at those eyes."

Three men circled her. The words shouldn't have hurt, but they did. The speaker made a vague sign of the cross.

"You," she said, recognizing one of them as Haakon's man, Gunnar. "Get off my property."

"Haakon wants a word with you," the man replied, holding his hands up in a placating manner. "We're not here to hurt you."

"If Haakon wants a word, then perhaps he should have asked nicely." Freyja made a feint toward the man on her right as he took a step toward her—the one who'd made comment on her eyes. Fear filled her chest, tightening her ribs around her lungs. What did they want of her? She'd thought Haakon was a man driven mad by loss, but he'd seemed to hold some common decency. Had she been wrong?

"Just grab her," the third man ordered. She still hadn't gotten a good look at his face, though he was taller than the others and something about his presence made her uncomfortable.

"Make one more move," Freyja told them, knowing she couldn't hold all three off with her pitchfork, "and I'll set my magic loose."

Silence fell. All three men froze. The only noise was Loki yipping and barking madly from where he seemed to be locked within a stall.

"You like my eyes?" she told the man who'd sneered at her and made a sign of the cross. "One of the *huldufólk* gave them to me, along with the gift of magic. I can manipulate storms, and throw lightning from my fingertips."

Two of the men exchanged a look.

"She's lying," said the taller one, the one who scared her a little. He snorted. "Why would one of the *álfar* gift her with magic?"

"Don't call them that," Freyja murmured. "They don't like that name."

Gunnar muttered something about "there are no hidden folk" under his breath, but it seemed her ruse had worked. He wasn't going to grab her.

Crossing to the stall, the sinister man reached down and hauled Loki up by the scruff of his neck. "I am done with talking." He reached for his knife—

Loki! "No!" The power seemed to flood up from somewhere within her, sending a whirlwind through the barn. Stalks of hay flew through the air, and both Gunnar and the superstitious man backed away from her, faces pale.

Freyja summoned heat into her hands, and turned on the man who'd grabbed Loki—

He hauled Loki against his chest, putting a razor-sharp blade to the little fox's neck. "Use your magic against me, and I'll cut his throat."

Freyja let the power spill through her fingers, her heart thumping wildly in her chest. She could feel Loki's terror and protective urges pushing against her mind. He wanted to rescue her, though he was frightened of whatever the tall man smelled like....

"Let him go," she whispered, swallowing hard.

"Easy, Magnus," the man with the enormous beard said. "We're not here to spill blood."

"We're getting nowhere without it," Magnus replied, and his eyes burned as they locked on her. "Release your power."

There was no choice. Her gaze met Loki's frightened amber eyes. Freyja let the wind and fire fade, the barn falling into silence. "If you hurt him," she said coldly, "then I will not rest until you are naught but ashes."

Gunnar and the other man grabbed her by the arms. Gunnar's grip was at least gentle. "You won't be hurt, I promise. Haakon just needs you for bait."

Bait? For what?

The other man plunged a hood over her head, and the world faded, her breath refracting back from the black wool and making her feel slightly claustrophobic. Tears pricked her eyes.

"Keep her eyes covered!" Magnus ordered. "If she cannot see, then she cannot work her magic."

And Freyja shivered, because how had he known that?

Rurik soared back to earth behind Freyja's barn, his form shrinking and power rushing through his veins as he made the change. A *dreki's* bugle to the south had sent him hunting, circling Krafla and looking for the challenger, only to find nothing.

Or maybe that was an excuse. He was still haunted by that moment during their picnic, when something monumental seemed to shift inside him.

Freyja.

Sighing, he found his clothes where he'd left them, and was about to pull on his trousers when Loki's terrified barking caught his ears. Rurik froze. It seemed to be coming from within the barn.

"Little brother?" he asked, his thought-thread tangling with the fox's.

—angry, snapping at air, took the mistress, hurt her, hurt her, let me out—

Rurik tried to sort his way through the terror and fury. *"Freyja? Someone took Freyja? Who?"*

Images assaulted him: the bearded giant who rode at Haakon's side, and a stranger he didn't recognize.

But it was the image of the third man that made him suck in a sharp breath. A man with sharp, predatory features, amber eyes, and raven-dark hair. A man who held a knife to the little fox's throat and used the threat to force Freyja to submit.

"Magnus," he whispered, turning his face toward the village.

His cousin had Freyja.

CHAPTER
TWELVE

THEY TIED HER to the village green, both of her hands bound and tethered by pegs they drove into the hard earth. A rough strip of black linen covered her eyes, leaving her blind to the nightmare about to befall her.

"Please," Freyja begged, but without her sight there was nothing for her to work with. She was blind to the world around her, and the ropes they used to tether her had been drenched in blessed water. It itched against her skin, resisting all her attempts to free herself.

The truth of it stung. They had planned this—no, Benedikt had planned it. He alone knew of the strength of her unnaturalness, and had worked to counter her.

Her heart thundered raggedly in her ears as the crowd fell silent. She could hear the harsh rasp of Benedikt's breath behind her. Excited. Enjoying her discomposure. *Be careful of a man's pride, my love,* her mother had whispered when they'd both noticed the way Benedikt began to watch her. *It is a dangerous thing, and unpredictable if rebuffed.*

"Blow the horn," he instructed.

The enormous bellow of the troll horn cut through the silence, rumbling across her skin and vibrating in her ears. Freyja flinched. She had never felt so helpless in her life. This was what her mother had warned her of. *Choose your battles wisely, Freyja… for you are not invulnerable.* Every creature of power had a weakness, even the mighty *dreki* they were summoning to claim her.

Where was Rurik? She didn't believe that he'd left her. She *couldn't* believe. But if he hadn't gone, then he would have heard the villagers take her. He wouldn't just let them do this to her. Would he?

The thought made her breath catch.

Unless he truly had gone. She shivered as her memory of their words that morning washed over her. "We're done here," he had said, a death knell of finality underscoring the statement. Stepping back, bowing his head politely to her.

Rurik! She threw the thought out into the world on an ache of despair. *I'm sorry!*

There was no answer but the wind swirling through her skirts. Then the thundering bellow of the troll horn again. The last time a man had blown that horn had been thirty years ago, when her father and the other villagers called the *dreki* forth to forge the treaty.

"Here he comes," Benedikt murmured with satisfaction. His voice dropped even lower as he stepped closer. "I'll see you when you return, my sweet."

No mistaking the dark intent behind those words. If he couldn't have her now, then he would take the scraps that were left once the *dreki* had finished with her.

Freyja strained at the ropes to no avail. Her shoulders sagged as she heard the villagers moving back, scurrying for the safety of their homes to watch.

She couldn't see. Yet she felt, more than anything, the mighty thrust of wings through an icy sky; the sudden ache of the pressure his immense presence wrought.

Wind beat down upon her as the *dreki* wheeled overhead. Freyja went to her knees, but there was no escape. She was almost flattened by the wind his mighty wings stirred, as the tether binding her left arm was tugged, then fell away.

The right snatched loose, the rope nearly jerking her arm from its socket. Free? She froze for one tremulous second, gathering her feet beneath her.

"Not free," the *dreki* whispered in her mind. *"Mine."*

Then its massive claws curled around her shoulders with a delicate gentleness, and with a mighty surge, he thrust into the sky.

"Now!" Benedict bellowed, as Freyja's feet left the ground.

She screamed and wrapped her arms around the scaled claws; terrified the *dreki* would drop her.

"Release!" That was Haakon's voice.

The world turned upside down as the *dreki's* war cry pierced the air and it threw itself into a tumble. Over and over and over, her body jerked around like a rag doll. Something screamed through the air as it tore past them, and Freyja suddenly realized what had happened.

They'd used her as bait. Something to lure the *dreki* from his lair so that they could kill him.

She ripped the blindfold from her eyes as the *dreki* righted himself, catching a glimpse of the tableau beneath them. Wind whipped at her skirts as little figures ran and screamed, pointing at the sky above them.

Haakon was clearly visible, the muscles in his biceps straining as he loaded the ballista and cranked the shaft back. The heavy steel cable tautened, the deadly sharp spear gleaming in the sunlight.

And Freyja felt a rage she'd rarely felt before.

Not powerless now. Not blinded, her magic muted within. She lashed out, her temper a whip she wielded with ruthless efficiency. She couldn't touch the iron cable—iron was one of the few things that refused her power—but the heavy wooden wheels of the ballista were made of the earth. As Haakon reached for the release, she smashed each wheel.

The ballista angled forward, its sharp steel point dropping as the handle tore through Haakon's grip. The cable let go, steel snapping with an audible twang as the javelin cut straight through cloth and flesh and buried itself in the stone wall of one of the houses, with Benedikt dangling from the end of it.

He squealed like a stuck pig as the *dreki* wheeled around curiously to watch.

"Remind me never to allow you near that thing," the *dreki* whispered in her mind with a laugh.

Then he angled sharply, his fluid shape cutting through the wind as he soared toward Krafla.

"What makes you think I need a ballista?" she replied.

The flight was barely ten minutes, but even Freyja was starting to shiver with cold by the time Krafla loomed in front of them. The sparse, barren fields that surrounded the volcano smoked and bubbled, but she could see the glittering white of the glacial fields further south, and her breath caught, even as the wind stole it from her.

She could scarce believe the sight before her. The entire world stretched out in miniature, like a map come to life.

The *dreki* touched her mind, as if wondering what had caught her attention so. A light caress against her senses, a sudden connection where she sensed his curiosity.

"You wish to see the glaciers? I will take you one day...."

And just like that her sense of wonder died, protective walls sliding into place between her mind and his. *"Put me down."* She eyed the sheer rock walls of the volcano's side. *"Gently, please."*

They wheeled lower, the sudden downthrust of his wings halting them mere feet above the ledge that led to the caves. His claws released her, and Freyja dropped. She landed on the ledge, her ankle giving way beneath her as she fell. Though his touch had been gentle, her shoulders ached from his grip, and for a moment she simply lay there, trying not to hurt.

The sinuous head was suddenly directly in her field of vision, and Freyja screamed despite herself, scrambling onto her back and away. The *dreki* froze, his golden eyes gleaming.

"Are you hurt?"

Freyja stared at him with the rock walls against her back, her breath coming hard and her skirts tumbled around her knees. "Am I hurt?" she gasped weakly, hot and sharp emotion dampening her eyes. She could barely hold it in anymore. The only creature that gave a damn about her was the *dreki*, and even he had ulterior motives, though what they were she couldn't even begin to guess.

"I have been kidnapped, tied down, and offered as sacrifice to... to you. Then dragged through the air, dropped, and—" She couldn't hold it in anymore. *Rurik, damn you.* "Nobody came to save me! They all just watched!

My father will be beside himself with worry! Who will care for him? What do you want with me? Damn you, what?"

She exploded into tears, angry, damning tears that blinded her to the world around her. The last thing she thought she saw was an expression on the *dreki's* face that could only be described as perplexed. And that set her off, laughing, crying, and hiccupping all at the same time.

"Why am I even telling you?" she whispered, scrubbing at her hot eyes. "You would not even begin to understand what is wrong with me. With the world."

"There are many things wrong with the world. These puny humans insist on marking it as theirs, even though it belongs to no one."

"Not even you?"

His glorious eyes narrowed. *"Only a fool thinks he owns such power. I may wield it, but I do not own it. And why would I wish to?"* Even she heard the hesitation. *"I admit I am not certain what is wrong with you, however. It is difficult to understand in this form. Where is your blindfold?"*

"M-my blindfold?" she stammered. "I tore it free."

"Make another."

Freyja's jaw dropped. "What for?"

"So you cannot see."

And blinded, she would be powerless again. "No."

"I will not hurt you, Freyja. I swear it."

As binding as a dreki's oath, the goodwives often said, to indicate manners of legal standing. No *dreki* would willingly break his word.

She had felt powerless when Benedikt jerked her out to the green, hooded and vulnerable. Powerless when she cowered beneath the unknown, wondering when the *dreki* would strike. She hated that feeling.

Yet her hands tugged at her hem, taking the small knife she wore secreted in her boot and slicing a strip of the black wool free. Shaking slightly, Freyja bound it over her eyes, the wool irritating her reddened skin. He was not taking her power away. He had asked, and she had complied. That gave her some illusion of control.

"Why?"

Power washed over her, hot and liquid, an enormous cascade of it. Every inch of her skin tingled, her stomach pooling with heat. Tidal waves of molten power. She wanted to reach out and drag her hands through it, but something warned her not to.

"Because I do not wish you to see me," a man's deep baritone voice said.

Freyja's jaw dropped open, her hands rising automatically to her blindfold.

"Don't," he warned.

Somehow she stopped herself, though she couldn't contain the shock. He'd said there was little reason to shift shape. And with that thought came another, unbidden. *Why do the dreki hunger for virgin flesh, Freyja? Not to eat, for a certainty. Which means....*

"Because we are jealous creatures," the *dreki* replied, his bare feet rasping over the stone as he stepped closer. She heard skin shivering over muscle as he knelt in front of her. "We do not like it when someone has touched what is ours."

Fingers came out of nowhere and stroked her cheek. Freyja jerked, her heart racing, but his touch was soft. Gentle. Like a man soothing a startled filly. Insanely hot, as though the volcano's fire burned beneath his skin.

And suddenly suspicion burned within her.

This wasn't the first time a man's skin burned with an unnatural heat. No. It couldn't be. Could it?

"What do you want of me?" she whispered. But she knew. Oh God, she knew. And even as she thought it, she suddenly started putting together the little puzzle pieces in her mind.

He hesitated, but not, she thought, for lack of courage. Gauging her reaction, most likely. "It is time, Freyja."

His warm hand cupped her cheek and she softened, leaning into it. Hungering for… something. Not want, not need. So desperately did she want to be touched as if someone cared.

And this fearsome creature had never hurt her, nor betrayed her.

But had he misled her? She didn't know the answer to that.

"Yes," she whispered, leaning into the *dreki*'s touch. There was only one sure way to find out if her suspicions were true.

Let me burn my fingers, just once….

His hand caught hers, drawing her fingers to his scalding lips. "You will not be burnt, Freyja, but you *will* burn, this I promise."

And a *dreki* never lied.

CHAPTER THIRTEEN

ARMS SWUNG BENEATH her and lifted her with appalling ease, swinging her against a chest that was chiseled with muscle and entirely hairless. Freyja pressed a palm over his heart, feeling the erratic thump of it deep within him. An almost purring sound echoed in his throat. Pleasure. As he swept her under the overhang of the cave into a blackness that she noticed even with her eyes bound, she slowly rested her head against his shoulder.

No sight. But she could smell him, that sweet cinnamon smell that seemed almost familiar, and she could hear the rapid thump of his heartbeat beneath the curl of her palm. Her fingers flexed, exploring the feel of him. She quite suspected he was completely naked, and despite everything that had happened to her today, she couldn't help feeling curious about this fact.

The only man she had ever come into such close contact with was Rurik, that night in Akureyri and again in the barn. Her cheeks flamed as a flash of memory struck her: gasping beneath his kiss, grinding her hips against the hard bulge of his erection, begging, her nails digging into the hard slab of his shoulders….

And again suspicion danced within her.

Perhaps it was the *dreki* she curled against. His voice was deeper than Rurik's, but something in the timbre of it reminded her of the man, and they were much of a build perhaps. Strong, sleek muscle slid beneath her fingers. She flexed again, tracing the harsh edge of his clavicle, dancing her fingers up the thick column of his throat as she explored. She couldn't deny how similar they seemed….

"If you keep petting me like that I shall not make the bed," he purred in her mind.

Instantly Freyja's curious touch froze. "The bed? You have a bed?"

What would he need such a thing for? Then her cheeks heated again. There was only one purpose she could think of….

"I created it for you, Freyja. The night you came here, hunting for your ram." His mind brushed against hers, a dark caress that made her gasp. A feeling of overwhelming satisfaction flooded through the link between them. *"Dreki can manipulate raw matter if they will it, and create small pockets of existence out of Chaos magic. The dreki court is one such place. A… sidestep into another world, if you will. Or a small pocket of existence within a bubble of Chaos. It's how Tiamat first created the universe, except her bubble expanded until it contained the entire world, and many others. You're about to enter one, so it may feel strange at first."*

"Why would you create it for me?" she whispered, though her heart ticked loudly in her chest.

"Would you prefer that we do this on the floor of the cave?"

This? Freyja swallowed.

"Because I want you," the *dreki* added in a quieter thought-thread. *"There have been no other women for me. Not for*

a long time. You are important to me, and I wanted us to have time alone, where we will not be interrupted."

"Why me?" She turned her face in the dark, feeling her breath refract off the skin of his throat.

Another low growl sounded deep in his chest. *"Vixen."* Then he laughed. *"Because nobody has ever challenged me the way you did."* And he sounded incredibly pleased with this fact. His arms tightened, possessive and strong. *"Fierce,"* he whispered in her mind.

And Freyja stilled.

Fierce. A word that another man had used for her. A man who hadn't been there today to rescue her.

She felt that soft brush against her senses and pulled everything about herself in tight, thrusting up her mental shields as she sorted through the sudden cacophony of thought. All her suspicions seemed to form into one loud voice.

Memories flooded through her:

Rurik suddenly turning up in Akureyri, a stranger the likes that even the local port town had never seen.

Rurik, with his deep knowledge of *dreki* culture, and the way he'd challenged Haakon about killing the *dreki*.

Rurik, kissing her in the barn, his touch setting her alight even as he proclaimed that fate had thrown her into his path.

Suddenly it all made a horrid kind of sense, like a dozen misshapen puzzle pieces abruptly fitting into place. And she didn't know how she felt about that. Angry that he'd lied to her. Relieved, that all the little things that hadn't quite added up finally made sense. And also a vague, choking sense of loss.

Because some part of her had begun to look at Rurik in a way that saw him in her life forever, and now there was no chance of that.

"I do not like it when you close yourself off," he growled.

"You may have my body, my lord," she responded tartly, even as she worked her way through her confusion, "but you do not have the right to all of me."

Tension radiated through his menacing build. Oh no, he did not like that at all, and now she had a powerful, irritated *dreki* to handle.

Strange, how fear was the last thing she felt. She knew this man—or creature. He wouldn't hurt her, of that she was certain.

No, not physically.

Freyja slid a hand down his chest, enjoying the soft feel of his skin and the power that she suddenly felt. He had the ability to take her mind, rip it apart, and steal any of her thoughts. But he wouldn't. She knew so little about this curious beast, but that was one truth. There was more honor in a single eyelash of this inhuman creature than in Benedikt's entire being.

"You think to taunt me?" He didn't sound irritated anymore. Intrigued, perhaps. *"You throw such challenges in my face without thought to consequences."*

"Consequences?"

"Yes," he hissed. "You'll let me in by the end of this night, Freyja. I swear you shall."

The *dreki* turned her sideways and Freyja clung to him, sliding her arms around his neck. A cool wash of power whispered over her skin like static, as though she'd stepped inside the heart of a storm itself. "What is that?"

"It's a portal to my Chaos bubble."

The static shot straight through her, current consuming her until she gasped. Whatever they stepped into, she could feel the immensity of his power riding through the walls and humming through the floors. The air was cooler here too, and something sweet lingered in the room like a scented oil. It wasn't painful, but she couldn't escape it.

"Here we are, Freyja." He let her slide slowly down his body, each glorious inch of him pressing against her. Freyja's feet landed on the floor with a small jolt, and she leaned against his chest to catch her balance.

Her hands fought to make sense of what her eyes could not tell her. Bare skin met her touch everywhere, and she could feel the heavy thrust of his cock against her stomach. Her first instinct was to step back, but as her fingernails raked over his abdomen, she found herself hovering in indecision.

And then an evil thought brewed.

It would serve him right for deceiving her. "I want you," Freyja whispered. "I've never before wanted a man like I want you."

Hands softened on her hips. "Never?"

"Never."

The *dreki* stilled. "Surely there has been one...."

"Not a single one." Let him chew on that.

A faint growl sounded in his throat. Then he moved past her, the brush of his skin against her sleeve turning her head. Fingers trailed over her hip. *"Let me close the portal so we won't be disturbed."*

Behind her she heard the soft swish of a rug—or carpets—parting beneath his heavy tread. Freyja's heart jumped into her throat as she lifted her hands. Dare she? A wave of resolve swept over her. Pandora... Psyche... she knew their weaknesses well. And the growing certainty in her heart made her fingers jerk to the blindfold and tug it free.

Freyja blinked as the room swam into view, the haze of candlelight melting over an enormous bed covered in decadent red sheets of some material she'd never seen before. Cushions spilled over the surface, white and gold and red. Her eyes couldn't quite take in all of the gilt. Mirrors clung to walls everywhere, sconces gleaming with candlelight. And small lashes of static lightning seemed to arc through the walls, as if they weren't quite solid.

Her eyes lifted to the arched stone ceilings far above. Columns of heavy rock supported the roof, craggy and unfinished, as though he'd hewn this bubble out of the heart of the volcano itself. The mixture of savage nature and human decadence suited him.

Freyja's breath caught as she took a step forward, toward the bed. A room fit for a prince.

The sudden loss of static alerted her to the fact that the bubble was now closed. She spun on her heel, the strip of black wool hanging from her fingertips as her gaze raked over him. One hand splayed against a stone circle in the wall as he whispered ancient words to the stone.

Golden windswept hair brushed against his nape, smooth amber skin sweeping all the way down.... Her ruthless gaze raked over the heavy muscle in his back and the taut globes of his buttocks. Her mouth dropped open, but it was too late. Something told him that she was watching him.

Rurik turned around sharply.

Amber eyes narrowed over that once-broken nose as he saw her glaring at him. Silence fell, and Rurik tilted his head curiously. "You don't seem surprised."

"I only just figured it out," Freyja snapped. "Fierce? That's a certain word that you use to describe me, in both forms."

"I see. You're angry."

Freyja set her hands on her hips. "I was starting to care for you. I trusted you, and you don't know how rare that is for me." There was a lump forming in her throat.

"You told me that 'we were done here.' And I felt bad about your history and what your family did to you. I even tried to cook something nice for you...."

Those eyes turned considering. "You thought that I had said we were done?"

Freyja stilled. "That's what you said."

There was a dangerous look in his eyes. "It was an uncomfortable conversation for me, one that brought up many old memories. I didn't mean...." He cursed. "And you: 'Not a single man has ever tempted me'?" he paraphrased her, crossing his arms over his broad chest, a move that highlighted everything else.

Do not *look down.* Too late. She could feel heat spilling into her cheeks. "You deserved that. You lied to me!"

"I never lied," he growled, taking a step toward her. The hard planes of his stomach were dusted with golden hair, and his cock bobbed against—

She jerked her gaze to his face, with its sensual mouth and cat-slit eyes. The *dreki* swelled within him. Not quite human, not quite her Rurik. But still there. "Not directly," she replied, recalling a half-dozen statements that, in hindsight, had revealed all. "That must have required some very careful wording."

"Oh, it did."

Anger swelled. "The whole time I was tied to that stake, I waited for you to come for me, but you—"

"I did come for you."

"For me?" she demanded. "Or to flaunt your might in front of Haakon and his men?"

"For you." Rurik's eyes shuttered, and he stepped toward her with dangerous allure. "Everything's been for you. Do you think that I would take human form for the sheer enjoyment of it? I told you this was fate, Freyja. The night you dared come into my lair was the moment that I knew you were the one. How could you doubt that I would come for you? You're mine, Freyja."

"Don't say that."

"Why?" he asked. "You know I cannot lie."

"I challenged you," she pointed out. "That's why you did this. And you might not lie, but your wording—"

"*You're mine*," he growled out, and there was nothing to say to that, no means with which to misunderstand him.

Freyja tilted her chin up stubbornly, aware that the ground was shifting beneath her.

"Of course it's because you challenged me." His voice turned gravelly. "You're beautiful, but I have seen beautiful women before. No, what captured my attention was your fierce pride and stubbornness. Your determination. The storm brought me a warrior in female flesh, and I knew then that I wanted you. You were utterly glorious that night. *Because* you challenged me. Because, in all my long years in exile, I have never met a woman who dared."

Freyja's gaze dropped, then she jerked her head away, the image of his nude body burned into her retinas. He was taller now than he'd ever been as Rurik, bristling with heavy muscle, the ripple of his abdomen giving way to the proud jut of his cock. A creature that sauntered toward her with unearthly grace, knowing that it alone was the ultimate predator.

She swallowed, her voice suddenly very small. "And what happens when you've conquered me?"

"How does one conquer a storm?"

That was not an answer. How typically *dreki* of him.

Freyja took a step back as he took one toward her. She had refused to allow Rurik to court her, knowing that she risked her heart. Yet a small part of her had begun to think that perhaps he might own some genuine feelings toward her. She liked his flirting. She liked having him chase her.

She'd even begun to think of him as perhaps something more: a potential husband, a lover, a friend. A whisper of a dream that she'd not even thought existed in her heart. And this time, it was no small dream.

An impossible one now.

The *dreki* did not fit into her future. Rurik had, but he did not.

"You do not seem pleased."

"You're not who I thought you were." None of this had turned out to be what she had thought it was, and a little part of her ached at the loss.

"You made your own assumptions and I didn't bother to correct them."

"Because it served your purpose!"

He took a dangerous step toward her. "And what do you think my purpose is?"

Freyja didn't look behind her, but she could almost feel the heavy presence of the bed at her back. Her fists clenched and she tipped her chin up, the scrap of wool still in her fingers. It was very clear what he had wanted of her now.

"If that was all I wanted, Freyja," he purred, "then I would have had you last night."

A smile curled over his made-for-kissing mouth. Dangerous. Despite everything, her heart started thumping faster, excitement flooding through her veins, as her body recognized that look.

"You've cornered the dreki in his den," Rurik whispered in her mind, the touch of it trailing over her heated skin. *"Now what do you think I should do to you for disobeying me?"*

"I didn't disobey you." Another step back. Then another. She dropped the blindfold, her chin tilting with the same stubborn arrogance he owned himself. "You told me to put the blindfold on, and I did. You never said I mustn't take it off."

"You argue like *dreki*." His hand reached out toward her, and Freyja's breath caught in her throat. "Or a solicitor."

"Considering the fact that you willfully deceived me, you have little ground to stand upon," she shot back.

"True. But now we're here, and you know the truth. What are you going to do now?" His burning gaze lit her blood on fire. "Always stubborn, my Freyja. I think that is what I like about you most. That you never fear what you probably should."

"Why should I fear you?" She took another step back, the backs of her knees hitting the bed. "After all, you're the one who warned me that you don't intend to harm me. No, what was it? You planned to *eat me all up*."

That smile turned dangerous. There was nowhere to go. "Perhaps I *still* plan to eat you all up."

Rurik took that last step between them and then she was tumbling onto a mattress so soft and fine that for a moment, she could only stroke the deliciously soft material that covered it.

"Silk," he murmured with amusement. That devilish light still lit his eyes. "Especially for you, Freyja. I have dreamed of you on my silk sheets. Dreamed of what I would do to you." That hot gaze scored her body. "Wondered how soft your skin would feel against the silk." He held his arms out, the thick muscle in them flexing as he gestured to the room. "All of this was for you, and you say that all I want from you is one night?"

Freyja swallowed hard. He didn't know what he did to her with those words, or how long she'd dreamed of someone saying that to her. Foolishness. She knew it, and still she'd dreamed about it.

"I do know." His eyelids hooded over dangerous eyes. *"I want to say them all to you—and more."*

Freyja slammed her shields back into place. He wanted her in his bed. He'd pursued her, tricked her, and finally resorted to taking what he wanted. Well, she would let him. He would have her body; he would never have her heart.

Rurik bared his teeth at her, swooping down to pick up the blindfold. Freyja scrambled back, her skirts slipping on the cursed sheets. Then his hand locked around her ankle, burning hot and immoveable. She squealed as he hauled her back toward him.

A hand slid behind the back of her knee, his callused flesh meeting hers as her skirts curled around her waist. The feel of his touch so intimately against her made a shiver run over her sensitive skin. Images from the night before drove into her brain, and she remembered *everything.*

"I want all of you, Freyja. Not just the parts you choose to share with me," he told her, the other hand capturing the back of her other thigh. He parted her legs as he stepped between them, and yanked her closer to the edge of the mattress.

The position put her aggressively in front of him. Freyja's hands pressed against his thighs as if to halt him, her fingers digging into the bare skin there. Deliciously soft skin rode over hard muscle. She looked down, unable to stop herself. A surge of *something* went through her at the sight of his arousal, leaving her frantically sucking in breath, her fingernails making small half-moon marks in his tanned flesh. She didn't understand any of this. How could she ache so at the sight of his desire for her? The sensitive skin between her thighs throbbed with it, even as fear circled through her.

He asked too much of her. For he asked not just for sex, or to take what he wanted from her, but to own her. To possess her heart entirely, and make her his.

And that terrified her.

"Well, you don't get to choose how much of me you get," she shot back.

"Don't tempt the *dreki*," he said. His hand caught her chin and lifted it, one of his knees pressing into the mattress between her spread legs as he leaned over her. "Or there will be hell to pay."

Freyja's fingers flexed against his chest. Heavens, but every inch of him was hard. "You don't scare me."

"Really? Then why is your heart beating so hard?"

"Because I'm arguing," she pointed out.

Rurik gave her a slow, hot smile, amber eyes flaring with golden heat. "You're always arguing."

"I wouldn't have to if you didn't think you ruled this part of the world... and me."

"You would argue until your face turned blue." He leaned over her, one hand beside her hip. "You would argue until the world turned to dust. It wouldn't matter what I said."

"Then why bother with me?"

"Maybe I like arguing with you." His cheek brushed against hers, his lips nuzzling her ear. "It gets me all hot under my skin. Makes me think of ways I could win the argument."

Heat crept up her throat. She felt like she was in his claws again, flying through the air with the wind whipping past her. Any moment he could drop her, and then she'd be freefalling through the air, and damn her beating heart, but the thought almost excited her. "Rurik."

"Like this...." His mouth trailed across her jawline.

Freyja's breath caught. His knee came down on the bed between her thighs, pressing her skirts beneath it. She was trapped. And all of this... predatory male heat was spilling over her.

"And this." Another kiss skated over her cheek, then her mouth. He nibbled at her lips, his tongue darting out to taste her.

Freyja tumbled onto her back as he followed her down, leaning on his elbows above her. That enormous weight came down upon her, pressing her hips into the mattress, and... oh, lord. Freyja's eyes shot wide, even as he claimed her mouth.

There was no denying him, nor herself. She didn't want to. She wanted to drink down this memory, to give herself something to sustain her in future days. One night with the man who made her heart leap in her chest.

"Am I winning the argument, Freyja?" he whisper-laughed against her lips.

Damn him. She curled her nails in his shoulder, and a soft groan escaped him. Freyja's fingers flexed as thought raced. Maybe there was more than one way to best him?

"I offer you this one night," she managed to say as his mouth brushed hers again.

Rurik's lips stilled, tension coiling through his shoulders. "I want all of them."

"We don't always get what we want." Some lick of anger stirred in her, and he drew back, hands fisted in the sheets beside her head, his eyes *glowing* with that strange light.

Freyja waited for him to deny her or demand more. Instead, a slow, wicked smile curled over his lips.

"Stubborn," he whispered, dropping his head to kiss her throat. His lips burned and Freyja writhed helplessly, a shiver running across her skin. "You throw challenges at me as if they were curses. Haven't you learned? There is no better way to capture my interest than to challenge me."

"I wasn't challenging you. I was setting the rules." She gasped as his wet tongue dipped into the hollow of her clavicle.

"I don't like your rules." As if to prove the point, his teeth dug into the tender skin of her shoulder. Shifting his weight to one side, he slid his roughened hand over the soft wool of her dress. Tracing her hips, her bottom. He thrust into the vee of her thighs, his cock riding over the wool. "There are no rules, Freyja. Not in this. You are mine. I'm not letting you go now."

She caught his shoulder, her breath catching as he rubbed against her. "You don't have a choice."

"No?" Rurik's lip curled back in a hiss as he lifted his head. "We'll see. Now you have the *dreki* to pay, my love. And he is much more dangerous than your devil."

Another kiss captured the protest on her lips. A kiss full of possession and ruthlessness, a kiss to drown in. It told her more than words precisely what was going through his mind. He staked his claim on her mouth, his tongue thrusting past her lips even as his hips slid against hers again. Somehow his hand slid down her leg, drawing her knee up so that he settled deep between her thighs. The position made her gasp, but there was no escaping him.

Even if she'd wanted to.

Freyja's fingers curled in the heated skin of his shoulders, her nails flexing against the heavy slabs of muscle. One night she would give him, and she would take everything he had to offer her. She began to kiss him back. Sweet goddess, why had she ever resisted?

"That's it," he whispered, locking her ankles behind his bottom. Her skirts bunched between them, and she could feel the rasp of the fine hairs on his legs against her inner thighs. "Kiss me, Freyja." His voice dropped into a series of words she didn't understand, yet somehow her body did. The whisper curled in her abdomen, pulling at her, wetting her, making her ache.

She rocked against him, hands sliding up his nape and locking in his hair. This time her mouth met his, cutting off those foreign words. Her tongue darted against his. The taste of him was as smoky as his scent. And by the gods, it felt good. So, so good.

Rurik growled deep in his throat as he caught her wrists and pinned her to the bed. He nipped at her lip. "You steal my intent," he rasped, "and make me forget to take this slowly."

"I don't want slow." A gasp stole from her lips. His erection slid against her inner thigh. "I want you to make me feel...."

She needed to surrender to the storm building between them. Every inch of her body ached in unfulfillment.

Rurik's gaze half shuttered. He lowered his head and bit the fleshy lobe of her ear. "But you forget," his whisper trailed down her throat, "that you are not in control here."

Pinned beneath him, her body spread in surrender, Freyja narrowed her eyes. "I could be." She slid the soles of her feet down the backs of his thighs, rubbing her hips against him right where it ached the fiercest.

And she felt the response shudder through him, his gasp wetting her skin. "Vixen." Rurik bit her chin, her lower lip, lifting his hips away from her. "It appears that I shall have to take a firmer hand with you."

Freyja's nipples hardened. "What does that mean?"

Rurik dragged the woolen blindfold up and tossed it on the bed beside her. Kneeling over her, he smiled darkly. "You're wearing far too many clothes."

Freyja rocked onto her elbows, eyeing the blindfold. "What did you mean?"

But Rurik urged her over onto her hands and knees, kissing the back of her neck and trailing his lips over the sensitive skin there as she straightened. A shiver of pure need lanced through her. He tugged at the buttons that ran down between her breasts, popping each free of its loop. The black wool sagged over her shoulders and he tugged it down to her hips, teeth sinking into the soft flesh of her shoulder.

Freyja lost herself in the sensation of his mouth. Rurik yanked the dress over her bottom and out from under her knees. Freyja shivered, practically naked. Suddenly a sense of shyness swept over her.

"And this," he murmured, starting to slide her chemise up.

Freyja flinched as the worn fabric slid over bare bottom, her cheeks heating. "Rurik—"

"Now this," he purred, "is better."

Lips traced the skin of her hip as he slid her chemise up her back. Freyja yelped as his teeth left a mark on the fleshy bottom. Then he was pushing the chemise over her head, tongue trailing up the indentation of her spine.

Blinded by the fabric, Freyja tried to fight her way free. His hair-roughened thighs pressed against hers, his cock dipping between her legs in a teasing movement that had her heart racing. Then she was free, and he was rolling her onto her back, one hand sliding up her throat to capture her jaw as he took her mouth fiercely.

Couldn't think with him kissing her like that, thrusting against her, dragging her hands up above her head. Stealing her breath until her head spun and she was pinned beneath him, something tightening around one wrist… then the other.

Rurik levered off her just enough for Freyja to catch her breath, and then she realized that she still couldn't move. She tugged at her bound wrists, craning her head back to make sure that, yes, he had tied her to the bed, and now she was naked and lushly spread before him like his own personal banquet. "What are you doing?"

"Taking my time." That wicked, self-satisfied look was back. Then his gaze locked on her body, and Freyja went still at the hungry look in his eyes. "You are so perfect." His hand skittered over her ribs as he knelt between her thighs.

Freyja squirmed as his gaze dropped to the thatch of blonde hair between her legs. No man had ever seen her like this.

"I could just eat you all up," he purred, leaning over her, kissing her breasts, his teeth rasping over her nipples. "After all, is that not what you claimed that *dreki* do? Devour innocent young maidens...." His breath stirred against her skin.

Suddenly it was all Freyja could do to stay still. "Please—oh, gods, oh!" How could a woman think like this? With his hands and mouth all over her, stroking her ribs, up under her breasts, plumping them up for the heat of his mouth. His tongue swirled teasing circles around each nipple, suckling them, making the ache fiercer.

The pressure in her body almost hurt. She could feel it building, a storm within. One of his palms pressed against her lower abdomen, as if sensing the power there.

"Yes," he whispered, and heat slid from his hand, sinking down into the molten core of her.

Then those lips were trailing lower, his tongue darting into her belly button. Freyja's eyes went wide. *He wasn't—?* Another kiss lower, as he nuzzled into the blonde hair between her thighs, sent a thrill of shock through her. *He was*. Suddenly she understood all of the "devouring her" references.

"Rurik!" His name stole from her lips in a gasp as those broad shoulders nudged her thighs wider. Freyja craned her neck, unable to look away. His honey-gold hair fell across her pale stomach, and then he glanced up with one last smoldering smile, before he lowered his face and licked her.

There.

Volcanic heat sent a rush of power flooding through her body. Freyja's spine arched at the lance of sensation, her feet digging into the bed. She couldn't think. Could barely breathe. Sweet goddess, but what was he doing to her? "*Oh, my God!*"

The wet lash of his tongue left her with nowhere to hide. He nuzzled her, suckling the small bud between her thighs gently, until she could do little more than pant helplessly, straining at the woolen tie around her wrists.

"Am I winning the argument now, Freyja?" he purred.

"What... argument...?"

A laugh, and then Rurik tongued her deeply.

Suddenly it became too much for her. She felt like she stood in the heart of a maelstrom, or as if her own lightning had struck her body. Freyja screamed, hips jerking beneath his tender ministrations as Rurik licked her with slow, purposeful intent, absorbing each and every aftershock until she felt wrung dry.

She didn't know if she could stand it any longer. Freyja gasped. "*Please*. Please... I can't...."

Then he was kissing his way up her smooth abdomen, while she shivered, her inner muscles clenching. Freyja realized the room around her trembled, and Rurik glanced up, then looked at her with a slight frown.

She could barely think, but something about his expression managed to penetrate the fogged state of bliss she existed in. "What's wrong?"

"You shouldn't be able to affect this place." Capturing her face in both hands, he rested between her thighs, the heaviness of his body so abruptly intimate that she sucked in a sharp breath. "What are you?" he whispered, and not for the first time.

"I don't know."

"I will find out."

"Good. Then maybe you can tell me?"

Freyja swallowed, glancing down between them. His skin rubbed against hers, hairs rasping between her slick thighs. She couldn't even contemplate what he'd just done to her. It seemed... indecent. Shocking. Wonderfully wicked. And she wanted more.

"I would love to know what you're thinking right now."

Not quite a question from her mighty *dreki*, yet nor was it a command. Freyja kissed his mouth gently. "Untie me. Please."

He smiled, and nuzzled her lips. She could taste the musk of her own body there. "Why should I? I like you like this. Splayed out like some treasure I'm about to plunder." The smooth rock of his hips showed her exactly what he meant by the word *plunder*. The heavy length of his cock slid slickly against her, riding over exactly the same spot he'd recently devoured.

"Because I want to touch you," she cried.

Those amber eyes shuttered. "Hmm," he said. But he reached up and tugged her wrists free.

Freyja slid her hands over his shoulders. She felt freedom in this moment, unfettered by so many of the unspoken rules that had governed her life. And she wanted to *take*, just as much as she wanted to be *taken*.

"Touch me then," Rurik whispered, and Freyja slid her hands down his chest, over the rock-hard ripple of his abdomen. Her finger tangled in the trail of blond hair that grazed his navel, then hovered there.

"You're not stopping there, are you?" purred her golden *dreki*. He clasped her hand, and drew it lower. "Not you, my ever-curious Freyja."

Curious, indeed.

Freyja locked eyes with him as he pressed her hungry touch over the heated steel of his erection. Time to throw caution to the wind. He felt enormous in her palm, and Freyja could barely wrap her fingers around him. Rurik shuddered, his lips parting as he curled her hand around the engorged width of him. "That's it," he whispered, eyelids lowering in sleepy abandon. The tip of his erection darted along the slit between her thighs. Freyja froze at the lash of sensation, then cupped him again, learning his most intimate secrets.

Rurik stole her mouth again, and something began to stretch her. She dragged her hand over his hip, curling her fingers in the flesh of his ass, not quite certain whether she could handle this.

"Fate, Freyja," Rurik breathed, and finally pushed inside her.

It was too much. And not enough. She wasn't sure what she wanted, but as he thrust inside her, she could feel that tremor building again. Her body pulsed at the ache of the invasion, even as it accommodated him.

Rurik groaned, his mouth slightly parted and his cock plunging within her. Freyja found herself lost to the storm building on the horizon. All she could feel was him. All she could breathe was him.

"More," he growled, and then he was rolling her over, shoving her onto her hands and knees. She'd barely had a chance to settle herself, when his thighs settled between hers and he was parting her once more, this time from behind.

Freyja cried out as Rurik buried himself to the hilt inside her. He felt deeper this way, and she didn't know how much of this she could stand, but she was more than willing to try. Power swept through her, threatening to consume her. How she had never tried this, she did not know. It felt utterly pagan, utterly sensual, and right in a way that she did not understand.

"Because you were waiting for me," Rurik growled, and he must have caught the edge of her thoughts. His hands clasped her hips, and he slammed into her again. "Mine, Freyja. Only mine."

Only yours. She arched her back as his hand slid along her spine, curling in her hair. Each thrust took her right to the edge again as he brushed over something deep inside her. That pressure was back, threatening to erupt through her skin. *Please. Yes.* And *more.*

Then it was shivering through her. Freyja screamed. This time she wasn't alone. Rurik growled, spilling words in that language he sometimes spoke, his thrusts coming faster and faster, his body plunging within hers—

He shuddered, body rocking with fainter motions, holding her tight, one fist closing in her hair, the other leaving marks on her hip. *"You belong to me,"* he growled in her mind, as their thoughts fused together, and then she was utterly shattered as he spilled his hot seed within her.

Together they collapsed, Freyja's entire body aching with the force of his claiming. The sweetest ache she'd ever felt.

Freyja lay panting on her stomach, Rurik's enormous body covering hers, and his seed wetting her thighs. This moment was a peaceful one, drifting on a wave of post-coital bliss.

One night. She didn't know how she'd survive it.

Her *dreki* curled around her, his long, lean body pressed against hers from behind. He stroked her hair across her shoulder, and Freyja glanced up at him as he nuzzled her neck, scattering dozens of little kisses there. She felt utterly lost in that moment. Gone was her Rurik. In his place was a rather satisfied-with-himself *dreki*. The two seemed to combine, and she realized that she'd only ever known half of their respective selves. This creature before her was a combination; the teasing man she'd kissed in the barn, and the powerful creature she'd met in a dark cave. A force of nature when he wanted to be, and a man who could be both warrior and scholar. His pupils seemed almost cat-slit, and golden light gleamed in his irises. Not human. Not now. If ever. And yet there was a sudden deep yearning in her heart, as they lay fused together, for she felt like she understood this creature in a way she'd never felt before. Lonely, he'd called himself once. Curious, somehow separated from the world, and hungry to reach out toward her. She could have been describing herself. Freyja stroked his hand where it rested on her shoulder. If only she could stay here forever, safe and secure, and utterly devastated with pleasure....

Rurik rubbed his cheek against her like a cat, his psychic touch brushing against her. *"I have never in my life wanted anything more than I want you, Freyja."*

She reached back to him: *"Neither have I."*

Her fingers paused on his hand, as she withdrew from the mental thread. She had promised herself one night. Nothing more. She didn't know if she dared accept anything else, for it was clear that it would be far too easy for Rurik to steal her heart.

Nobody had ever come close to scaling the walls she shielded herself with. He could destroy her, if she let him. There was no future here for them.

Freyja rolled onto her back, staring up at the rock ceiling. Then she reached up and kissed him, cupping the back of his neck and dragging him atop her again.

One night.

And only one night.

Best not to waste a single second of it on doubt.

She was gone.

Rurik raged as morning revealed an empty bed, tearing at the walls with his claws and scattering the piles of gold with the lash of his tail. It spilled everywhere, sparkling in the light reflecting off his scales, but for the first time in his life it failed to soothe him.

Like most *dreki*, he loved gold, loved its shiny allure and glittering beauty, craving its presence in an almost obsessive way; but it was cold and it had no light of its own and it could not give him what he wanted.

He screamed his rage into the skies, feeling the walls of the tunnels shake and tremble around him. Beneath him the volcano stirred, hot molten lava licking at the crust that covered it, and bubbling below. He felt its heat seep through his mind, answering the frustration in his roar.

To unleash its lava would sate him. To let it burn and explode into the air, like a *dreki's* rage, the earth's furious answer to a storm above.

But there was a little cottage out there on the moors, its lights flickering cheerfully in the night. To unleash the mighty fury of Krafla would bury that cottage in ash or lava, sweeping away the one thing that he wanted most.

Rurik let his head fall, his wings trembling with suppressed rage and pain. How could he win her back? Why would she not succumb to him? Why hold herself back?

And how had she stepped from this world, back into her own?

He had never felt this way before. The wyrm's form separated him from the emotion he felt in his human form, yet even now he felt thwarted. He ached, and it wasn't a pleasant ache.

He had to win her back.

Somehow.

CHAPTER FOURTEEN

FREYJA GRABBED THE milking bucket as she opened the front door, and nearly went head over heels. Dawn light silvered the sky in the east, gleaming on the thing at her feet.

An ancient Viking helmet sat on the stone step, the burnished brass filled to the brim with gold and gemstones. Freyja's heart dropped to her stomach and she stepped over it, staring around. A single day had passed without a sign of her lover. She'd spent most of it tending to the jobs at the farm, but she couldn't deny that every whisper of wind made her heart race a little faster, and every shadow that flitted over her made her shoulders slump when she looked up and found only clouds.

He hadn't pursued her.

He hadn't even reached out to her.

Until now.

And she didn't know how she felt about that.

The world was quiet. Freyja's gaze took to the skies, but there was no sign of him there either, curse him. "You cannot buy me," she whispered, glaring down at the treasure.

She stared so long at its gleam that the sun began to warm the back of her neck, the single milking goat they owned bleating at the fence. Freyja sighed. Would one of the *dreki* even think this was mercenary, or would he consider this a courting gift? She had no way of knowing. Not without confronting him in his lair, which she was loath to do.

But if she accepted the treasure—even for one day— then he would think he had won. Freyja grumbled under her breath, despite the way her body heated. Every moment she'd spent in his arms was imprinted on her skin like a sensory burn. "Cursed wyrm."

A part of her wanted to go back there.

A part of her didn't dare.

The jingle of tack caught her ear, and Freyja realized what she'd been hearing, but not acknowledging, for several minutes: the soft thud of hoof beats on the marshy ground. The blood drained out of her face and she swung her milking bucket over the helmet to cover it, turning just in time to see a threesome of riders trot around the end of her barn.

Freyja hurried forward, trying to draw their attention away from the house and what rested on the doorstep, tucking her hands in her apron.

"Good morning," she called in a barely civil tone, as Haakon rode into view through the morning mists.

He had some nerve in coming here.

His fur bristled over his shoulders, rimed with the morning's frost, and the rasp of stubble darkened his cheeks. Those cold blue eyes locked on her through thick dark lashes. "Good morn." He gave her a clipped nod, his gaze searching the yard as if looking for something.

Freyja's gaze slid past him to the two riders that followed silently at his heels. A chill ran through her, though she didn't know why. Magnus and another man, one she didn't recognize. Both were dressed in menacing black leathers, with a crossbow strapped to each of their backs.

Magnus and Haakon had been involved in her kidnapping. And if they'd returned to further their mischief, then she was going to unleash all of the rage and frustration she felt.

Magnus caught her eye and bared his teeth in a smile. She swallowed hard against the instinct to step back, toward the safety of her home. Something about him set her on edge. Bristling with weapons, he turned his huge black stallion in a circle, ignoring the creature's uncertain snort as he urged the beast closer to the barn. Steel spurs gleamed against the unrelieved black of Magnus's boots, and his fingers were bare as he gripped the reins negligently in one hand. The other hand rested on the powerful muscle of his thigh, a garnet ring winking on his finger in the soft light.

"What do you want?" Freyja asked coolly. "For I warn you that I am almost done with the three of you. If you have something further in mind than kidnapping, then we are going to have a serious disagreement."

No ambush this time. She was ready to make her point, as the thunder that suddenly rumbled on the horizon proved.

"You seem none the worse for wear," Magnus pointed out, and in that moment she hated him, he who had threatened her Loki.

"That's enough," Haakon warned him, and shot her an almost apologetic look. "We are not here to cause you further grief."

Civility held. One didn't speak of what happened when a *dreki* carried off a helpless young woman, though word of it was certain to be spreading around her small village.

None of her neighbors would ever receive her again. It was a curiously freeing realization.

The younger man swung down from his horse in a fluid movement, his raven-dark hair tumbling over his forehead. Those stunning blue eyes met hers and he smiled, white teeth dazzling. He'd not been involved in the kidnapping, and she hadn't seen him on the village green. "Mistress Helgasdottir. You might consider this early morning visit my fault." With a rueful smile, he slung his horse's reins over its glossy bay head and patted it absently. The gelding's nostrils flared, but he did not seem as unsettled as Magnus's black.

"Andri's horse threw a shoe some miles back," Haakon said. "He's beginning to favor his leg."

"I'm not surprised." Freyja reached out, offering her fingers to the bay to sniff. He snorted and danced at the end of the reins, not quite certain about her. Freyja stroked his velvety muzzle. "Hush, sweet boy," she whispered, reaching out to brush her senses against his, a touch full of warmth and gentleness. She'd always had more affinity for animals than she had for people. "I won't hurt you."

Pure foolishness to bring a horse like this out through the marshy terrain around Lake Mývatn. The lichen and moss concealed all manner of rocks and uncertain footing. A horse's leg could twist before the rider knew it.

It was one of the reasons she preferred the stocky ponies that seemed to thrive in Iceland's conditions. Poor Hanna might not be half as beautiful as these three beasts, but she would outlast them by miles.

Leaning down, Freyja ran her hand down the horse's foreleg, feeling the heat in the muscle. She tugged at his fetlock, and he lifted his hoof obediently as she examined the spongy sole, fishing out muck and stones from the arrow-shaped frog. One of the nails still clung to the walls of his hoof.

"You need to get that out," she pointed. "Why in heaven's name you would need to shoe a horse here is beyond me." There were barely any roads, and fewer tracks to follow.

Cornflower blue eyes danced into view, a crooked smile twitching over that devilish face. "Yes, mistress," Andri said.

And she realized that she was berating three powerful warriors.

Freyja let the hoof down and stepped back, brushing her hands against her hips. "Take him back to the village. Old Tóki will remove the nail, and then I suggest resting him. There's heat in the muscle. Is that all?"

Andri raked the yard with a hard glance, though his manner seemed apologetic. "We came to speak to the scholar." Those eyes locked on her with an intensity that made her shiver. "Master... what was his name again?"

"Rurik."

"Rurik," Andri repeated, as if it held some meaning to him.

Magnus shot them both a sharp look.

"I'm afraid you're too late. He's no longer plaguing my household." *Only my heart.* Freyja crossed her arms over her chest, a cold sweat springing up against her forehead. "I believe he took himself off that way." She pointed vaguely to the south, and the west. "Wants to see if the rumors of trolls are true."

Haakon dragged his gloves off reluctantly. "Mistress Helgasdottir. It pains me to mention what happened in the village—"

"You dare bring that up?" Rage erupted inside her, though she was doing her best to maintain her temper. "How is Benedikt faring this morning?" The last she'd seen of him, he'd been pinned to the wall and squealing.

"Better than my ballista," Haakon countered coolly.

Freyja crossed her arms. "A true shame."

"It was never my intention to lower myself to such a ploy," he replied, his gaze dropping and heat flushing against his sharp cheekbones. "I allowed the heat of the moment to sweep away my sense of decency." His lips thinned. "I will never forget my shame, and I apologize for the part I played, but I must ask… would you speak to us of the layout of the dragon's lair?"

Of all the nerve! "Get off my farmstead."

"It is not yours, is it?" Magnus spoke up, his horse dancing in slow circles. "But your father's. Perhaps we should take matters up with him?"

If her father heard of what had happened…. She couldn't imagine the shame on his face. Many years ago there had been no censure in being staked out for the *dreki*, but with even the crofters out here succumbing to religion…. And her father believed. Truly believed. Freyja stepped toward him, her fists clenched. "If you dare disturb my father—"

"You'll what? I would not be making threats if I were you, mistress." Magnus's gaze slid sinuously over her breasts, seeming to strip off each layer of clothing.

Magnus wasn't the first man to make her feel like this, and he wouldn't be the last. But she was so tired of being made to feel like an outsider, or a piece of cattle to be traded. If he weren't sitting on that horse, she might have lashed out with her power, but the poor creature snorted, as if sensing the slight shiver of her gifts across its skin.

Magnus's gaze sharpened and he urged the stallion closer, forcing her backward. "You—"

"That's enough!" Haakon snapped, grabbing his stirrup and yanking at it.

The two men locked gazes, something seeming to pass in the air between them.

"You're here at my discretion," Haakon challenged him. "Not yours."

"Magnus," Andri pleaded.

Magnus finally smiled, a chilling sight indeed. He bowed his head, though the gesture was barely a sign of submission, and more an indication that he would take up this fight at a later date. "As you wish."

Haakon let go of the stirrup and stepped back, turning on her with almost vicious intensity. Freyja drew back and he noticed it, his gaze flickering to hers. For the first time she saw the coldness in his expression melt, a sense of true shame creeping over his hard mouth.

"My apologies." He nodded to her, deeply. "We mean you no harm, you have my word."

Magnus glanced at her over Haakon's shoulder. Haakon might actually be speaking the truth, but the other mercenary had given no oath.

"Get off my land," she repeated quietly. "And don't ever come back. You've done enough."

Haakon opened his mouth as if to speak, then hesitated. He swung up onto his gray gelding and gathered the reins.

Andri swung the reins over his horse's head. Freyja licked her lips. He'd not done anything to her. "We use moss out here to make a poultice. He's strained the muscle in his foreleg, and you'll get few miles out of him today, if any. You'd be best to walk often, or you'll lose the use of him for several weeks."

Magnus snorted under his breath and kicked his black into a canter. Clods of dirt flew up as he rode directly past her. *Good riddance.*

"Thank you." Andri watched the bigger man go, then gave her a troubled look. "I won't let him trouble you again, mistress. My word on it."

"As much as your word is worth," she said pointedly.

He actually colored.

Haakon and Andri she could manage, for they were bound by some sense of common decency at least. But the look in Magnus's eyes left her cold, for he had seen her as nothing more than a common whore, a worm beneath his heel. Something to be used and discarded.

All of a sudden, she couldn't help the rise of shame that filled her. All three men knew what had happened to her in the *dreki's* lair. She had not felt shame until then. What had happened between her and Rurik had been both wondrous and private; a memory to last a lifetime and to warm her on cold, lonely nights.

For she knew now that she would never make such a choice again.

CHAPTER
FIFTEEN

FREYJA WOKE THE next morning to a rose on her pillow.

At midafternoon, she found a book on her windowsill, covered in red leather with gold embossed writing on the spine. It contained Scandinavian fairy tales, and reminded her of her mother. Freyja shut it with a snap and put it in the pile of gifts she was determined to return to her *dreki*, even as her heart gave an unexpected twinge. She'd been forced to sell most of her mother's books, and it had been years since she'd had the pleasure—or time—to read.

A bottle of wine greeted her at dinner. There was an extravagant ham waiting for her on the table for breakfast the next day. Freyja stared at it for a good ten minutes before deciding that there was no point in wasting it. Both she and her father were hungry. The ham would spoil if she took it back to Rurik, and she couldn't in good conscience allow a pig to die for nothing. So she made a thick and hearty soup with it, cursing him with every breath, even as she stirred the pot.

What did he want from her?

Forever, whispered his voice in her memories.

"Goodness, Freyja," her father exclaimed when he took his first taste. "This is absolutely delicious. Is that ham? I haven't tasted ham in years."

Freyja's eyes stung with tears as she watched him devour the bowl. Then another. How could she harden her heart to this? She wanted to thank Rurik for this gift, even as she knew that it took her down a dark road where she would only end with her heart broken.

Rurik had made it clear that he saw her as a conquest. He was *dreki,* and she was human. He wouldn't want her when she was old and gray, and she could not live in his world. There was no future for them. None. So she dried her tears, savored the soup, and then brushed off her apron to complete her afternoon's chores.

Only to find that the bloody stables were swept clean, her lambs were feasting on hay that she hadn't provided, and there was an enormous ram bleating in the spare pen, his horns magnificent and his wary eyes rolling as though he'd just had the shock of his life. He probably had. She could only imagine that flight. Freyja stood stock-still in shock. A ram. A cursed ram. She was right back where all of this mess had started.

If only I didn't go after my ram that night....

And the dratted man—*dreki*—was nowhere to be seen. She never heard him in the house, nor did she ever see him.

"Stop it!" she called, turning in circles in her empty barn after she found a necklace of extravagant emeralds that she barely dared touch. "I promised you one night. Nothing more!"

Silence remained her only answer.

Freyja snatched up the necklace and shook it, suddenly furious. "You will not charm me, you arrogant beast! There is nothing more I can offer you! Stop this foolish game!"

"They were your rules, dearest Freyja."

She spun in circles. Not a hint of him. "My rules? I promised you one night, nothing else."

"You promised me your heart, if I could give you your most secret desire."

Everything stilled within her. "I didn't mean it."

"Are you saying that you lied to me?"

"No!" She bit her lip. All she'd meant was to put him off and grant herself space. "I just.... It was a jest, nothing else."

"I am dreki, *Freyja. Our word means everything, or else we'd have brought war to this world long ago. It is all that keeps us from chaos and we must abide by our promises."*

She turned. "Where are you? Show yourself."

A caress stroked her back. Freyja spun, but she was all alone in the barn. *"Why should I? Unless you plan to thank me properly for my gifts."*

"Thank you?" she growled. "I want to give them back. I'm not keeping them."

"I'm not accepting them back."

"Damn you—"

"Throw them in the bog for all I care. They were gifts, Freyja. Courting gifts. You may do with them as you like. I daresay your father is enjoying his new boots, however."

Her heart plummeted through her stomach. "You leave my father out of this."

"Very well."

"And you are *not* courting me. Stop this madness. I won't abide by it. There is no future between us. Nothing but misery. You got what you wanted, so let me be."

Another gentle caress cupped her face. *"Stubborn, Freyja. I have barely begun, and you know nothing of what I want from you."*

"That's not fair. I don't want this."

Silence.

She turned, feeling utterly wretched for the words that spilled from her lips.

"You wanted me the other night," he finally replied, and she had the feeling that she'd almost hurt him. He, with his unshakeable sense of pride and place in the world.

"That's not—" She broke off with a curse. "Yes, I wanted it. Once. Something to remember you by. But we have no future, Rurik, and I am sensible enough to admit it. This might be a game to you, but it is very real to me. You will ruin me, if you haven't already. And... I might have given up on the idea of marriage and children, but I should still like to hold my head up high when I walk into town. You don't understand what you cost me.

"Besides"—her voice quavered—"I'm not the only one who might lose something here. You have dragon hunters searching for you. They know you took me. Haakon and his friends, Magnus and Andri, visited yesterday. They'll be keeping watch for—"

"Friends?" A dark shiver rolled through her at the sudden pressure that pushed at her mental shields.

Freyja clutched her temples. "You're hurting me."

Instantly the pressure was gone. *"I'm sorry. But I know those names, Freyja. And they want me to know them. They're not dragon hunters. They're dreki, in mortal form."*

"Dreki?" She knew she'd sensed something strange from Magnus, a predatory intensity that made her feel uneasy.

"Don't go near them," he suddenly warned, and all of his courtly charm evaporated. *"Don't welcome them into your house,*

nor challenge them. They're not like me. Or Magnus certainly isn't, and if he thinks you have my interest he'll hurt you to get at me."

"I have no intention of drawing his ire. What are you going to do?"

Silence.

"Rurik!" She took a step toward the barn doors. "Rurik, you're not going after them, are you?"

It was a long time before he answered, and she felt the distance between them, as though he was flying away from her. *"Would you care if I did?"*

She knew what the sensible answer ought to be. But she couldn't for the life of her utter it. *"Yes!"* Freyja threw the thought back at him. *"Please be careful. I don't want to see you hurt, even though I cannot allow this to continue between us."*

There was only a grim sense of acceptance in the link between them. *"I'll be careful. After all, I am not finished with you yet. I will see you later. You can thank me for my gifts then."*

And then he cut the connection and she found herself alone in the barn, her heart thundering in her chest as she wondered what he was doing now.

Courting aside, nothing could chill her more than the thought of Rurik in danger.

Rurik melted into mortal form in the small village near Freyja's homestead. Picking up the bag that he'd dropped, he shook out his clothes and put them on, then he went hunting.

A forlorn shape sat in the taproom, holding his head in his hands. From the smell of him, Haakon had finished several ales, and possibly more.

Rage smoldered in his heart, rage at all that Freyja had endured. Rurik let the door shut behind him with an audible click, grateful that the dragon hunter was alone.

Haakon's head jerked up, and weary blue eyes met his, devoid of emotion. Shadows bruised the man's eyes, and his face looked gaunt, as though something had stripped him of the vitality he'd worn on the docks in Akureyri.

"You," Haakon said in a toneless voice. "I thought you'd headed south."

"I heard what happened," he growled. "I know what you did to her. What type of man can you call yourself?"

He stalked the man through the warm shadows. Haakon's breath caught as Rurik prowled closer, but he moved before the man could even blink.

Shoving Haakon against the wall as he tried to stand, Rurik pinned him there, one hand around the man's throat. Haakon tried to break his hold, but Rurik simply lifted him higher, until the man's boots dangled off the ground. Haakon gasped.

"I can abide challenges to my territory," Rurik admitted, feeling heat fill his eyes as he let the *dreki* slip its skin, just for a moment. Haakon kicked dramatically as he no doubt saw the cat-slit pupils and the golden haze of the *dreki* in Rurik's irises. "I even find myself feeling sympathetic for your foolish quest to hunt and kill me. But still, that does not give me an excuse to swat you like the fly you are...." His grip tightened until Haakon's face began to mottle. Rurik leaned closer, until their noses almost touched. "But if you ever go near Freyja again, or threaten her, or let her be tied to a fucking stake like you did, then I will make your death a slow one, do you understand me?"

Releasing the man, he stepped back as Haakon sagged against the wall, clutching at his throat and coughing air back into his lungs. Haakon's eyes were wide with fright. "*You*," he sputtered, finally understanding what he faced.

"Yes, me," Rurik replied, stepping back out of reach before the hunter did something stupid, like reach for his knife.

Haakon lurched to his feet, and then stayed there, shaking against the wall. "You were there all along," he rasped. "Right under my nose."

"For a man who hunts *dreki*, you are quite terrible at spotting them."

Haakon threw himself at Rurik, his fist swinging. Rurik sidestepped, and then flipped the hunter onto the table, slamming him flat on his back on the timber. The breath whooshed out of Haakon, and Rurik stepped away, the muscle in his jaw ticking. "Don't make me kill you."

Haakon rolled upright, his eyes bloodshot and swollen. "Why don't you?"

He came again, and again Rurik drove him down, hammering an elbow between his shoulder blades. Haakon grunted on the floor, trying to rise, but his arms gave out, and he slowly rolled onto his back. A bitter laugh exploded from his lungs. It sounded like it came from a man who'd lost all trace of himself, and it stopped Rurik from making another move.

"I won't kill you," he said slowly. "I think you're punishing yourself enough. Killing you would be too easy."

"Did you know that I see her every night in my dreams?" Haakon whispered, hauling himself slowly into a sitting position. "Every night since I've been here. Begging me to rescue her. And these cursed storms don't help. They only serve to remind me of the night I first met her, when she was lost in the rain outside my village."

"I never had her," Rurik pointed out, squatting in front of the man. They stared at each other, and he realized what he hadn't seen before. This man was broken. And all it would take to drive him off the edge of the cliff would be a slight nudge.

After all, he wasn't the only one who could enter dreams.

"The dreams started the night Magnus joined your party, didn't they?" he mused.

Haakon flinched, then frowned. "Yes."

Rurik reached out a hand and hauled the dragon hunter to his feet. "Your friends are not human, Haakon. Nor are they your friends. Magnus and Andri belong to the *dreki* court, and they're here to kill me on their queen's whim. You're a tool to them, nothing else, and if you aren't careful, then you'll end up buried six feet under. Magnus is not the type of *dreki* to care for human foibles, nor share any hint of sentiment, not like I do. I'm sure you've had doubts. I'm sure you tried to test them the same way you did me that night we dined, but flinching at the feel of iron is an old wives' tale, nothing more. Magnus has been sending you the dreams."

A new fury roused in Haakon's eyes. "Why?"

"Because he wants me dead," Rurik replied, turning for the door. "But he won't confront me directly, not until he's certain he can beat me. No doubt you're a distraction, one meant to wear me down."

Haakon followed him out onto the village green. "Then this was all a wild goose chase."

Sympathy stirred through him. *Don't meddle....* "Maybe. Maybe not. You saw a golden *dreki* steal your wife—or thought you did—and I am quite clearly a golden *dreki*, though I had nothing to do with what happened to your wife." He paused. Árdís must have had her reasons. "But there is one truth I know, that you do not. Your wife is still alive."

"You said you didn't take her." Haakon's face paled. "How do you know that?"

"I am *dreki*. You know I cannot lie."

"Where *is* she?"

Rurik paused. He had little reason to give this man any hope, beyond a vague shared sentiment. He knew little of human emotion, but if that were Freyja.... There was nowhere on this earth that she could be taken where he would not hunt for her.

Fool of a dreki. He closed his eyes. He finally understood what was happening to him, and why he could not simply leave this quest to win her heart alone. Perhaps he and Haakon shared more than they knew?

"I don't think you're ready to know the truth," he said slowly, trying to sort through his thoughts of Freyja. "But you will be. Soon. And when you are," he smiled, "come and find me."

Spreading his arms, he felt them lengthen into wings as the *dreki* took shape with a burst of volcanic heat. Haakon stumbled back, shielding his eyes and face from the wash of power that erupted.

When it was done, Rurik smiled a particularly *dreki* smile. *"Let us hope that I am still alive to tell you the tale of your missing wife."*

Then he launched himself into the skies.

CHAPTER SIXTEEN

RURIK RETURNED TO the house. There was no sign of Freyja, though her scent lingered all over the place, ingrained in the homestead. A scent that filled his heart with joy.

There was an old *dreki* tale that spoke of *kataru libbu*, an alliance of the heart. *Dreki* were the half-souled, and he'd always felt somehow incomplete. When the great goddess tore her soul to pieces to share it with her new *dreki* offspring, she had left them vulnerable, always hungering for the other half of their soul.

A myth of the *dreki* court. Some *dreki* found other halves, the twin flame to their soul. Some did not. But all hungered for them. It was a concept beyond that of the mates they took, the lovers they consumed.

The second he saw Freyja, he'd known there was something different about her. He'd been unable to deny his yearning for her, and even now her distance from his side ached within him.

Was she the other half of him?

Was that why he was so helpless to walk away from her, so determined to claim her?

Some instinct stirred in his chest. He could not walk away from her. It would be like cutting out his heart. *Freyja.* Fierce, stubborn Freyja, who had brought him out into the light, brought him back to life. Without her, all he faced was an eternity of hibernation.

A *dreki* bugled, somewhere far to the south of him, reminding him that this was not the time for such speculation. His enemy was still out there, somewhere.

Rurik turned to face the brewing storm on the horizon, looking for Magnus.

The bastard had used Haakon and his men to test Rurik, but why? Why not face him? He remembered battles between them as youths, where they'd tested their strengths against each other. Battles that he'd won every single time.

There was a reason he'd been his father's heir. A reason his uncle and mother plotted for his exile, rather than outright killing him. If Stellan or any of his sons had challenged Rurik, then there was a possibility that he would have defeated them.

"Are you frightened to confront me?" he whispered, sending the thought-thread lancing through the skies as he searched for his cousin.

Magnus's awareness linked with his, the other *dreki's* fury searing his mind. *"Frightened?"* Magnus spat. *"How dare you?"*

"What else am I to think, when you hide behind the plots of puny humans?"

Days ago, he'd refused to offer challenge to Magnus, his pride standing between him and the thought of openly acknowledging that Magnus was ranked above him. But that was before he'd come to realize what Freyja meant to him. There was no moving forward until he defeated this threat.

"I offer challenge," he called, feeling the heat of his cousin's surprise. *"You and me. No mercy. Let us settle this once and for all."*

Magnus could *choose* not to accept.

"Unless you are wary of battling me?" Rurik added. *"I always won, did I not?"*

There was a long moment of silence. He almost didn't think his cousin would accept.

"That was a long time ago. Come and fight, you filthy cur. I am not frightened of you." Magnus's thought-thread linked with his, and for a second Rurik saw more than Magnus expected him to. Always a problem when two *dreki* linked. Magnus swiftly hid his thoughts, but there was enough there to cause Rurik to falter.

Magnus did not intend for this to be a fair fight.

"One hour," Rurik whispered, knowing that he would be facing two *dreki*, and not one. Sympathy for Andri's dilemma stirred through him, even as a hint of doubt assailed him.

Could he defeat both of them? Knowing that he would not—could not—harm the cousin that he loved?

Magnus faded from his consciousness. And Rurik was left standing there, gripped by indecision.

What if he did not win? He was relying on Andri's honor to stay out of this, even though he knew that some hidden pressure forced the youth to join Magnus in this plot.

If he didn't win, then what did that mean for Freyja?

She had not accepted him, not completely.

And he wanted so much more from her than merely a conquest, but how could he tell her that? He did not have the time.

Except... there was one last gift he could give her.

One last way to prove his intentions toward her were serious, and one way he could offer her protection, if Magnus defeated him.

Rurik slowly turned and looked at the house.

"You... you get out of here!" Freyja's father snapped as Rurik entered, maneuvering with wicked speed around the dining table. "Benedikt told me what you are, and what you intend with my daughter! You leave her alone, you foul beast!" He snatched up a cross and started praying in Latin. "*Our father who art in Heaven....*"

Rurik's temper flared. He had no time for this. "Did Benedikt also mention precisely what he's threatened her with over the past few years? The coin he's offered for her if she allowed herself to become his mistress? Or the threats he made when she would not?"

The prayer faded as Einar gasped. "*What?*"

It dampened Rurik's temper to a smoldering coal, but the heat remained. Freyja had refused to allow her father to share her burden out of some misguided attempt to protect him, but in doing so, she'd not allowed *him* to protect his daughter. "Your precious Benedikt threatened to name her a witch if she'd not lie with him. Who do you think tied your daughter to a stake and offered her up to me? Who do you think has been stealing your sheep over the years, and whispering in local villagers' ears so that they would not buy your daughter's barley when she tried to trade it? I have been talking to many of the locals. Some spit on your daughter's name for dealing with the devil—which you and I both know she has not done—but others admit that they were afraid Benedikt would turn his wrath on them if they traded with Freyja, or tried to help her. She's slowly starving because of Benedikt, and you cannot see it. He wanted to cut off all of her resources so that the only person she could turn to was him, when she was finally desperate enough. That is the snake whose words you listen to."

His words took all the wind out of Einar's sails. The old man slumped against the table, his mouth agape in shock. "She never said a word."

"Knowing Freyja as you do, did you think that she would?"

"But he... he said you had taken her."

"And so I did," Rurik replied. His temper got the best of him. "They'd tied her to a stake in the village green, and threw rotten food at her. What would you have me do? Leave her there?"

"Did you...."

He grasped what the old man wanted to know. "What happened between us is a matter purely for us."

The old man was gasping quite hard now. "No. No." He shook his head. "She is a good girl." His gnarled hands curled into fists. "Both Benedikt and you have ruined her!"

Rurik knelt in front of him. "You know that *dreki* cannot lie. You said so yourself. So, know this... I love your daughter and I wish, in another world, that she could be mine. I would not abandon her, not willingly, not if I had a choice. And I will never harm her, or place her in danger, which is why I cannot marry her. If I could—" His voice broke a little. "If Freyja would accept such a thing... then I would do so in a heartbeat. But to mate with Freyja is to place her in danger. I finally understand that. I cannot have her, not without bringing darkness into her life, no matter how much I wish to. But I also cannot leave her defenseless, and as much as she could bring this small village to its knees if she wished to, she is also remarkably vulnerable against those threats she has no power to control."

Rurik captured Einar's face in between his hands. "She needs you to protect her. And she needs you to be well, because she loves you. She will accept no other gift from me, but perhaps she will accept this...."

Power welled within him. Einar gasped as that honey-trickle of it slid through his skin.

"My cousin Magnus has accepted my challenge. I go now to face him." He let his power threaten to brim over, finding the shadow in the old man's chest, the one that was slowly killing him. "Think of me as the devil, or think of me as a monster, but the truth remains that I might not vanquish two *dreki*. I would not leave your daughter unprotected in the wake of my death."

Healing was not his greatest strength, but he knew well how to manipulate flesh and bone, and shift the core of the body. The shadow sat there, resisting him, a cancerous growth within the old man's lungs. Rurik poured more power into the working, using lashes of fire to burn away the shadow, then sweeping the cobwebs from the old man's vision, until Einar gasped, slumping against the table as though he breathed hot ash.

"Done," Rurik gasped, and took a shuddering step sideways.

Something was wrong. He felt hollow and empty; his bones curiously light, as though he'd expended too much raw power.

Einar clapped a hand to his chest, his skin glowing with health and vitality. "You... healed me."

Rurik could barely acknowledge him. "For Freyja," he said, then staggered outside.

The storm battered at him. He'd cost himself a great deal of power in healing Freyja's father, but it was worth it if by doing so, he could protect her. Rurik spread his arms wide, fanning the kernel of golden heat deep within him to flames. The change lashed through him, shockingly slow. By the time his wings unfurled, he felt almost breathless and a faint hint of nervousness lit his stomach.

Had he expended too much energy in healing Freyja's father?

No. Of course not. He was a prince of his people, not a weakling. Magnus had dared to challenge his territorial claim, and such needed to be answered. He'd beaten his cousin before. He would not fail this time.

But as he launched himself into the air, wings thrusting down in furious beats, he couldn't hide the hint of doubt in his heart.

CHAPTER
SEVENTEEN

HOOF BEATS DRUMMED across the rocky soil. Freyja drew to a halt, tugging her shawl tight around her shoulders and sucking in a shattered breath. Loki caught up to her, circling her skirts with a desperate yip.

Not now, she told him, brushing the hair from her eyes as Haakon reined in his enormous stallion. She'd been trying to take a walk to clear her mind, dwelling on Rurik. She couldn't escape the memories of their night together, and he'd come for her, courting her with gifts that she could not avoid. This was not done between them, no matter how many times she told herself it was, but she couldn't quite work out what the decision meant. She wanted a future with him. She wanted him. If she swept aside all her doubts and misgivings, that was the one fact she kept returning to.

But did she have a place in his future?

"Mistress Helgasdottir." Haakon seemed just as surprised to see her as she was to see him. The stallion beneath him sawed at the reins, sweat darkening its flanks as it danced in small impatient circles. Bruises darkened his skin, and blood had dried on his eyebrow.

"What do you want now?" she demanded, though his injuries bothered her.

"I came to find you, actually."

"Oh?" Thunder echoed in the distance.

The stallion's eyes rolled, and Haakon brought him back under control. "I came to apologize, and to warn you—"

"Apologize? For what?" Lightning split the skies, far too swiftly on the heels of Thor's thunder to be entirely natural. Freyja could feel her fury spitting beneath her skin, and curled her fingers into fists. She was so angry, and she didn't know if it was at Haakon, the world—or herself. She took a step closer to him. "For bringing your hatred to my village? For destroying the village's treaty with the *dreki*, the consequences of which could rain down upon innocent people? For tying me to a stake and using me as bait? For ruining any reputation I ever had, and stealing away any chance that I might ever make a good match?"

She saw her words strike him. He flinched, but Freyja was merciless. "I know that what you lost was not insignificant. I know that you can never get your wife back. But did you ever once consider what you were doing to the people around you? What do your family think? How many other villages have you brought your hatred to?" She paused. "How many innocent dragons did you kill, who had no hand in what was done to you?"

"Freyja." His voice came hoarsely. "You don't—"

"Perhaps the *dreki* stole your wife, but you are your own worst consequence. All you are is hatred and ruin, and while I might pity you for what happened, I cannot forgive you for allowing your hatred to consume you. What would your wife think of you now, if she could see you?"

"What would you not do to bring your lover back to you, Freyja, if the shoe were on the other foot? What would you do if it were *your fault* that she'd been taken?" His eyes begged her for understanding.

"I would do anything that would not harm another person," she admitted.

"Pray that you don't have to find out just where that line stands...." And she saw that guilt and loss had flayed the humanity from him, pushed him into making decisions that he might never come back from.

Just as she might never come back from the harsh words she'd offered to the *dreki* who challenged her. Her shawl flapped in the wind and Freyja caught it, but she shot Haakon a fierce look. *What would she not do if there was a threat against the man—or* dreki—*that she loved?*

Another shock of thunder rumbled across the horizon, and it felt almost as if it shook the earth itself. The clouds boiled now, seething masses of stormy white that threatened a dangerous storm.

"Another of those unnatural bloody storms," Haakon swore under his breath, circling his horse.

She'd thought it an extension of her own fury, but as she looked up she realized that she felt vaguely hollow and disconnected from the storm. This was not of her making.

The blood ran from her face.

"It's a *dreki* storm," she breathed, feeling the wash of power through her veins, but knowing that she was not the cause of it. No. She was merely a bystander, swept along in the current of its power.

But what was causing it? A glance back at the valley showed the lights gleaming in her father's homestead. As she watched, a dark shape came to the door and stared into the skies. Even from this distance she saw his golden hair, and felt that same twist around her heart.

214

She needed to tell him the truth about how she felt—and to apologize. Fear had driven her. Fear of the future, fear of handing him her heart on a platter and having him shred it—even fear of finally, irrevocably being cast from her community. Every time she'd been frightened of his intentions, he'd let her make her own choices. How could she refuse to allow him the same courtesy?

Fear had been her cage, and it was time to set it aside. Time to shed her skin and bloom into the creature that she'd always been meant to be. One that accepted her dangerous powers. One that knew she was different from the mortal world, and could never fit in. One that was not frightened of love, or rejection.

Daughter of the Storm, her mother had called her once, and it was time for her to accept her true self, and cast aside everything that held her back.

But even as she took a step toward Rurik, he spread his arms and began to shift. Wings formed, long and elegant. Golden scales erupted with slow grace, and then he took a belabored lunge into the sky that was less graceful than any she'd ever seen from him.

Something was wrong with him.

"Rurik," she whispered, her heart thudding dully in her chest.

He wrenched himself into the sky, and she had this horrible, impending sense of doom as she took a step toward him.

Too late.

The heat drained from her face. "Rurik!" she yelled, running toward him and waving her arms. "Rurik!"

"Freyja!" Haakon cut in front of her, his stallion's hooves churning up the sod. He thrust a hand in her direction.

"Get out my way." She couldn't see Rurik anymore, but she knew she had to get to him.

Something bad is coming, whispered the earth beneath her feet, and the sky around her.

And all she could hear were her parting words as she denied Rurik. *You don't understand what you cost me.*

Fate, Rurik had once told her. But she had spat in fate's face, and now... now that miserable wretch seemed to be warning her that once again, something was afoot.

"Freyja, here." Haakon offered her his arm as icy raindrops stung her face, and she realized he meant to sit her behind him.

Freyja drew her hand back.

Haakon's face twisted. "I know what I have done, Freyja. I know the damage I have caused, but you didn't let me finish. I came here to warn you. Magnus and Andri are not what they seem."

"What do you mean?"

"They're both *dreki*," he told her. "Rurik warned me about them an hour ago. I confronted Magnus and we fought. He couldn't entirely control himself." Haakon shook his head, horror lighting his expression. "I saw it in his face. For a second his eyes were gold and reptilian, and his skin seemed almost covered in scales. That was when I knew." His shoulders slumped. "They were using me to get to Krafla's *dreki*. Andri wouldn't let Magnus kill me, said it went against their oath—whatever that means—but I overheard them after they threw me in the cellar of the house I was leasing. They're here for Krafla's *dreki*, and they mean to kill him. They were using me to distract him and draw him out."

She gasped, but he wasn't finished.

"Freyja, this was all planned, and not by Benedikt. After I broke out of the cellar and found them gone, I went to him and demanded some answers. He didn't even know what he was dealing with, and had never seen Magnus nor Andri before in his life... but someone met him in Akureryi six months ago when he was trading, and offered him enough gold to sink a ship if he used half of it to offer a warrant for Krafla's *dreki*."

"Rurik," she whispered in horror, before realizing what she revealed.

"Rurik," Haakon confirmed, a knowing look on his face.

Freyja held herself between him and the house. "He's not the golden *dreki* who stole your wife. I know he's not!"

"I know." Haakon's stallion pawed the ground. He looked faintly disgusted with himself. "But he knows who did. Freyja, get out of the way—"

"I won't let you hurt him," she held her arms wide, and a tremor leapt from the ground at her feet, sending the stallion into a screaming whirl of fear.

Control it. Freyja grit her teeth and reined her temper in. She couldn't afford to give in to the power that was trickling through her veins. The storm pushed her in its wake, filling her with power she'd never felt before.

It had never been this difficult to control herself before. Nor had she ever slid so fully into that golden pool of molten power deep within her. Freyja saw the world through a haze of amber, before her vision suddenly cleared and the earth stilled.

Haakon stared at her, white-faced. Froth foamed at the stallion's mouth and its eyes rolled, but it was obeying him. Barely.

"I'm sorry," she whispered.

"The rumors are true then." It was not a question.

"That depends upon which rumor you listen to," she shot back.

217

"I don't intend to hurt him." Haakon hesitated. "It is clear that Magnus and Andri were using me for their own purposes, and I now know what that purpose is. They mean to challenge him and kill him. It's a trap, Freyja. But if we get to him first, perhaps we could warn him? Or help him?"

Her eyebrows shot up. "And why would you help him?"

"To make amends." He clearly saw her disbelief. "And because he has the information that I need to find the *dreki* who took my wife."

They stared at each other for a long moment.

"You'll get there quicker." Haakon's eyes seemed to soften, turning very blue. "You were right, Freyja. All I've done is cause harm here. Let me help. Please. Let me try and find my way back to the man I once was."

Logic dictated that she accept his hand. He was right. Speed was of the essence right now. Freyja jammed her foot into the stirrup he'd slid his boot from, and used his hand to haul herself up behind him.

"Hurry!" she yelled, wrapping her arms around his waist as he heeled the stallion with boots.

Freyja burst through the door of her house, her skirts flapping around her ankles. Time was of the essence right now, but she needed to make sure her father was all right.

"Father!" she called, dragging on his old oilskin coat, and reaching for his stout staff. Any weapon was better than none, and if Rurik thought she was going to allow him to face two treacherous *dreki* alone, then he had another think coming. "I have to go out this night. I need—"

"You're not going anywhere." Her father appeared in the doorway, blinking and rubbing at his eyes. He lowered his hands, revealing clear blue eyes that locked on her face. "Rurik told me everything. And he... he has given me a gift, in exchange for promising to keep you safe."

Those eyes. She hadn't seen him look at her like that in years.

The floor felt like it swayed. "Father," she whispered in disbelief, waving a hand in front of his face.

"Yes, I can see." Pressing a hand to his chest, his face lit up briefly. "It feels like such a weight has lifted off me, like my veins are filled with pure fire. I haven't felt his way in years."

Blood warmed his skin, breathing new life into it. Her father's spine had straightened, and he resembled the tundra in spring as winter finally sloughed away, revealing new growth. She felt like she might almost choke on her heart. His condition had weighed heavily on her too, and heat flooded her eyes as she realized that her father's long illness had vanished.

Freyja slid a hand over his paper-thin cheek in wondering fashion. "But... how?"

"The *dreki*," he said. "He gave me a gift."

Rurik had done this? Given her father new life? It struck her then, like an arrow to the heart. All along she'd been wary of him, holding him at arm's length even as she submitted to his touch. Guarding herself for the betrayal she knew would come.

She'd been wrong.

He'd given her more than she could ever repay, and her words bit through her: *Give me a gift beyond any worth, and I shall give you my heart.*

This was that gift. One last attempt to prove his sincerity when she had doubted it. Freyja clapped a hand to her mouth. Her heart beat a little faster, a little louder, as the world swam around her, shifting on its axis of what she knew to be true and what she'd feared to accept.

She'd not dared love him. Yet it had crept over her night by night, stealing through her intentions as if they were mist with every smile he gave her, every little argument, and every determined quirk of his brow when she refused to fall into place. She'd known it and worried over the sensation late at night. Locked it up tight within her so that he could never know, as if that could somehow protect her.

And now it left her utterly bereft.

"Oh no," Freyja whispered.

Tears blurred her vision. He'd gone off to fight two *dreki* alone, believing that she would refuse to let him court her. And he'd weakened himself, curse him, in healing her father so that she would not be alone.

That thought, more than anything, sent steel straight down her spine.

"Rurik visited me and told me everything. About Benedikt and what he had threatened you with. About him tying you to a stake." Her father's lips thinned. "Freyja, why did you not tell me all your worries? You know I would have protected you."

But how sprang to her tongue, where she managed to catch it in time. Her father had his pride. "I know."

She needed to thank Rurik. She needed to... God. To apologize for all she'd said to him. To make it right. It seemed her father wasn't the only one who had to account for pride.

"Freyja," her father warned, seeing the look on her face and interpreting it correctly. "Where are you going? Rurik wanted you to be safe. He doesn't want you involved."

She did not argue, or shout her sudden fury to the world. Instead she fetched the kitchen knife from its block. An odd sense of calm descended over her. "And what about him?"

"He's a *dreki*," her father said. "You cannot fight this battle for him."

"No," she whispered, "but I *can* stand at his side and give him a reason to fight."

"Freyja!" Her father caught her arm as she moved to the door.

Freyja eased his grip from her arm. "No, Father. I know you want to protect me, but that time is done." She hesitated. "And you should know that I am quite capable of protecting myself, even against *dreki*."

For the first time she let the storm show in her eyes. Her father's mouth parted, but no words came out. He'd always known she had power—*how could you not, when your child tore the earth apart with a thought?*—but he'd always pretended that she wasn't different. It had been her secret to keep for far too many years, something her mother warned her to hide, and her father pretended not to see.

Freyja gently let his hand go. "I cannot deny what I am anymore, Father. And I know this upsets your beliefs, but there is something within me that is not human. And I don't know what it is or where it came from, but I know my mother knew of it too. And I have to save the man I love."

"Your mother's powers are what stole her away," her father whispered. "Please don't ask this of me."

Freyja's eyes narrowed. "What do you mean?"

"She never breathed a word of where she'd come from," he admitted, "but she always feared certain things: circles of stone, or birch; All Hallow's Eve. I don't know why she entered that circle that last time, but when she came back, she was never the same. It killed her. They killed her."

"They?"

Her father shook his head and made a sign of the cross, and she knew he would not speak of it.

Freyja's heart ached in her chest. "I love him," she whispered. "He needs me. I know you're frightened to lose me, but I promise I will come back. Would you have let her go, if you could have saved her?"

Her father's hand curled into a gnarled fist. Then he finally broke down with a sob. "Be safe."

"Always," she said with a parting smile, and opened the door to step into her destiny.

Outside in the yard, Haakon waited impatiently. Time was running out, but she'd needed to ensure her father was all right before she went into battle.

"You want to make amends?" she asked him grimly.

"Yes."

"Then you can start now." She gestured to the south. "If Rurik dies, then you'll never find out what happened to your wife."

And she would never get to tell Rurik the truth—that she'd been such a fearful fool that she'd run away from the best thing that had ever happened to her....

Oh, Rurik. Heat slid through her eyes, but Freyja was determined. She was not going to lose him, nor her chance to tell him the truth she nursed deep in her heart.

"What can we do?" Haakon demanded, bringing her back into the present. "They're in *dreki* form, Freyja. Immortal, powerful, and impervious to harm. We are but human, and they could crush us like gnats."

"Almost impervious," she said darkly, picturing Magnus's face in her mind. "You have a ballista...."

"A crippled ballista," he countered.

"Then put it on a wagon. I only destroyed the wheels."

Haakon dwelled on the thought. "And you?"

"Well, you've caught a glimpse of what I can do, but that's not important. What I have is a burning desire to save the man I love," she said grimly, turning toward the stables to fetch Hanna. "Go and fetch your ballista, and I will meet you at Krafla. We don't have much time."

CHAPTER EIGHTEEN

RURIK SOARED IN slow circles around Krafla's smoldering peak, riding the thermals and the heated edge of his fury.

There was no sign of the other *dreki*, but he'd expected that.

"Come out, you cowards." He bellowed a challenge into the air, and it echoed like the thunder that was brewing on the horizon. Weakness stole through his veins, a little whisper that wore away at his confidence. Healing Freyja's father had taken more out of him than he'd expected, but the heaviness in his heart was the true weakness.

I should have told her how I feel about her.

Maybe then she wouldn't have run from him.

Rurik poured all of his world-weary pain into another bellow. *"You want your throne? Then come out and take it from me!"*

This entire plot had Stellan's hand all over it. His uncle, the *dreki* queen's brother, always liked to tie up any loose ends, and while Rurik and his brother were still alive, the queen's control over her throne was not complete.

Amadea could keep Árdís in check, but not her male progeny.

As if exiling him for a crime he didn't commit hadn't been bad enough.

Pain bled through him. He'd lost every *dreki* he ever loved by choosing exile over a challenge to his uncle and mother, but he'd made that choice to protect them. Challenging Stellan would have dragged his younger brother and sister into the war, and they hadn't been strong enough then to survive. He had little doubt his mother and uncle would cut their own blood down in a heartbeat.

After all, his uncle had murdered his father and his mother hadn't blinked at blaming Rurik.

He let the rage of his loss fuel his strength. *"Come out!"* he roared as he overshot Krafla and went south in a swoop over the glaciers.

"You're not fit to rule these lands," came Magnus's thought-whisper. *"And who are you to call us cowards? You, who tucked tail and fled when your mother took the throne?"*

"When your father stole it for her," he shot back. *"By plotting to murder his king."*

"My father didn't kill yours." It echoed with truth, and Rurik gritted his teeth together.

"Maybe it wasn't his hand that ripped my father's heart out of his chest," Rurik shot back, *"but his was the hand behind the murder."*

"You stupid fool." Magnus's laugh echoed through the link. *"My father had nothing to do with the death of yours. You did that yourself."*

Truth again. The rage that filled Rurik almost threatened to obliterate rational thought, but he couldn't afford to lose his mind now. Not when there was so much at stake.

But the answer still ached within him. All he could remember was blood slick on his hands, and his father's ribs spread wide, the heart torn from within. And the thought that he'd pushed this death upon his king, because he hadn't known enough to back down when he overheard his mother and uncle plotting a coup. In an act of mercy, an attempt to reach the *dreki* who'd birthed him, he'd actually warned her that he knew what she was up to. *No.*

"Come out, you coward! Where are you?"

"Here."

Rurik wheeled in a fury, sighting his opponent rising from a valley near Krafla. Bat-like black wings thrust Magnus into the skies, and his lip was drawn back from his fierce fangs. Twenty tons of fury struck through the air toward him, but Rurik was fueled by vengeance and rage.

Storm clouds brewed on the horizon, and he was riding his own storm now. The black *dreki* pinwheeled through the skies ahead of him, banking just enough to flash his claws at him.

"Rules?" Rurik demanded.

"There are no rules."

So be it. *"Killing you will be my pleasure."*

With a twist of his body, he plummeted toward Magnus, claws spread for a strike.

He had the better position and the weight advantage here, plus years of experience battling other *dreki*, but Magnus was no stranger to battle himself. They called him the Black Prince in the *dreki* court, for his cunning and deviousness, and Rurik was weighted down by the exhaustion that had stolen through his veins the second he healed Freyja's father. Magnus was completely fresh.

Which meant that he needed to finish this battle as swiftly as possible.

At the last second, Rurik flattened his wings against his body and dove straight down toward the other *dreki*, knowing that his claws could not pierce Magnus's black hide. Not from above.

Magnus's wings flared wide in surprise, and then he tilted sideways to avoid the clash in a defensive maneuver. Which was exactly what Rurik wanted. Ignoring Magnus's wings—the most obvious target—he caught his cousin's claws in his and then rolled and flung them both into a pinwheel of violence. The world blurred around him, sky then ground then sky flashing through his vision, and just as the ground grew dangerously close, he let go, flinging his cousin toward the jagged rocks below.

Perfectly timed. Perfectly executed. *"You're getting slow in your old age, cousin,"* he taunted, as Magnus used sheer strength to haul himself out of the dangerous dive in an inelegant maneuver.

"And you're still brimming with false nobility," Magnus spat back. *"No rules, Rurik. Remember?"*

A flash of shadow in the corner of Rurik's eyes alerted him a split second before claws raked his unprotected flank. Pain seared his nerves, but he'd twisted in time to prevent the second *dreki* from opening up his abdomen. Lashing out with his whip-like tail, he scored a cut along the silver *dreki's* snout, and it wheeled away in a spiraling pirouette that hurt his heart.

"Andri. Stay out of this."

His former page banked in an eerie glide. *"I have my orders."* Regret laced Andri's mental touch.

"You bring a dreki *youth to this battle?"* he demanded of Magnus.

"He was my brother before he was ever your page," Magnus spat back, *"and it is his turn to prove his loyalty to his blood kin."*

The betrayal would be tearing Andri apart. He knew the lad. Andri was the one shining branch in his uncle's family, the one son who remained uncorrupted. Rurik dove for Magnus, using his larger form to batter at the black. Claws slashed and tore, and wings thrust in midair to hold them locked against each other. *If he could get the bastard's throat....*

A body battered against his, knocking him aside a second before his razor-sharp teeth locked around Magnus's neck.

Andri, forced into this conflict against his will.

The three of them spiraled apart.

"This is not your fight," he shot toward Andri. *"Remember who you are. Remember what I tried to instill in you. You're better than this."*

The silver *dreki* drew back from his touch, rejecting the attempt to reach out to him. But guilt laced Andri's withdrawal, and Rurik had to cling to that.

Two against one. He'd had worse odds, when he fled the *dreki* court. But this was different. He wouldn't—he *couldn't*—strike down the younger *dreki* he loved like his own brother.

And Magnus knew that.

Time to play dirty. There was no honor in fighting a battle against these odds, and the last thing he wanted was for Andri to be forced to do something he'd never forgive himself for.

Battered on both sides, Rurik fought and slashed, smashing his body back against Andri's to force the youth out of the way, even as he tried to slash open Magnus's belly. The ground was getting dangerously close. Lightning stabbed through the air, but so far neither of them had brought their powers to bear in this duel.

Can't afford to.... Not with Andri hampering both of us.

228

Rurik's lungs strained. Care for the younger *dreki* was possibly the only similarity both he and Magnus shared.

Again they came for him. This time they were fighting in unison. And Rurik felt a crucial claw scrape against his belly, igniting a line of fire along his flank. Panic surged through him as Magnus's teeth scraped across his shoulder, and shuddered free. Close. Too close. For the first time, he felt the tides of the battle changing. A shiver of cold knowing ran through him.

He couldn't defeat both of them.

Filling his lungs, in desperation he vomited a gush of white-hot fire toward the fierce black dragon, and Magnus screeched and dove out of the way in frantic haste.

It was the one true advantage he had here.

"You're no true heir," Rurik shot at his cousin. *"I see fire still eludes you."*

Only the most powerful bloodlines still had access to Tiamat's gift.

Banking, he began to climb, his weary wings sweeping through the air so he could get some height. A silver wisp trailed him. Andri was far lighter than either of them, and moved through the air like a bullet.

"You don't have to do this." He tried once again to connect with Andri. *"I know you. I know this is not you. You have more loyalty in your littlest claw than either of your brothers, or your father."*

A mournful hesitation. *"It's been different since you left. You don't understand."*

But he did, oh, he did. Stellan had always wanted to drive the gentleness from his son, and he would have ruled the *dreki* court with an iron fist.

One last thought-whisper from the boy. *"I have to protect my mother, Rurik. Please understand."*

229

And then the silver *dreki* came after him with pure, bloody-minded vengeance.

No way out without hurting him. Rurik knew Andri's mental defenses, could have smashed through his psychic shields and knocked him from the skies with barely a thought. But the same mind that'd conjured this ploy knew his weakness well, and knew that Rurik could no more hurt the boy than he could lift a hand against his own brother or sister.

Someone else didn't have the same conflict. Andri flinched as he came after Rurik, shaking his head, and Rurik saw the golden dancing lights of Freyja's touch strike the youth.

Freyja. Intense terror suddenly struck him, straight through the heart. She shouldn't be here. She *couldn't* be here.

But he also knew that the stubborn woman would have come after him, if she'd caught any hint of what was going to happen here.

"No! Freyja, stop! Go home!" He threw the thought at her, losing track of what was going on around him for a split second.

And it was in that split second that Magnus attacked.

The furious black *dreki* came out of nowhere, slamming into him. Rurik staggered sideways, his right wing momentarily locking with Andri's. The smaller *dreki* lashed out, trying to catch his balance and stop himself from plummeting, and Rurik caught him with a claw around his shoulder, helping the boy stabilize—

Pain smashed through him, razor-sharp claws shredding through his left wing. Magnus saw only the win, not the risk to his brother.

Rurik flapped desperately, trying to get out of Andri's path, but something was wrong. His wing wasn't working properly, and as he plummeted between them, he clipped Andri, sending the youth into a spin.

One last thought speared through him. Rurik caught at Andri's mind, even as his crippled wing began to scream in pain as he fell. *"I forgive you,"* he whispered, and then lost the connection.

Air whipped past him. Panic. Fear. His claws scrabbled to right him as he tried to haul out of the dangerous plummet with his one good wing, knowing, *knowing* that it was too late.

Freyja! He saw her face in that moment, as if she stood there watching him, her hands clapped to her mouth and her eyes wide in horror. The only true regret he had was not knowing her love. And not telling her how much she meant to him. Capturing her mind in a caress of golden thread, he sent that last thought to her before it was too late.

"Rurik!" Andri cut through their connection as Rurik fought the air... and lost.

"Hurry!" Freyja screamed, urging Haakon and the rest of his men up the rough road that cut through the landscape. She could see the three *dreki* fighting in the air above him, and every harsh bellow and dive stole her breath, as the three clashed again and again.

The bloody wagon with the ballista was too slow. They'd never get there in time.

And Rurik was being hit from both sides.

It was also clear that though he attacked the black *dreki*, he merely avoided the silver one, when he could so easily clip him from the skies with one hard slam.

Something was wrong. Why wasn't he fighting back? He couldn't win against those odds. She could see it in the oddly reluctant way he tried to duel.

Her heart stayed in her throat as she belted her heels into Hanna's flanks and urged the small pony into a gallop. Everything that had never been said welled up between them, and for one ridiculous moment, her eyes were blurry with tears.

I never told him how I feel. I never told him that I love him.

Pure stubborn pride and a healthy dose of fear had stopped her from letting him inside her guarded heart, and she had the horrible suspicion that now she was going to be too late.

"*Freyja!*" Haakon bellowed behind her, but Freyja leaned low over Hanna's shoulder and urged the startled mare on.

Blow after blow was rained upon Rurik. Hanna balked at the top of the hill, nearly throwing Freyja over her shoulder. Three dueling *dreki* were probably more than the mare could handle.

Freyja wasted no time. Slinging her leg over the mare's back, she landed on her feet and let the mare flee. Then she was running, her skirts flapping around her calves as she hauled herself across the barren terrain.

The earth rumbled beneath her feet. Freyja's lightning flickered in the southern skies, but it wasn't anger she felt now, not when Rurik's was so hard-pressed, but fear. And fear kept her thunder quiet.

"Rurik!" she screamed, hitting the crest of the hill.

Freyja spread her feet, grinding her teeth together as she locked eyes on the silver *dreki*. Magnus and Rurik were too close together for her to attempt to take the black, but the silver *dreki* was like a dart in the skies, hammering at Rurik's golden back. She lifted her arms and felt the rush of lightning begin to skitter along her nerves. She'd never attempted something so powerful or focused before. The very air felt like it grew thick and static with electricity. Freyja unleashed everything she had in her toward the silver *dreki*.

And then it happened.

Rurik must have felt it, for he lurched into Andri's path, knocking the young *dreki* just enough to take the brunt of her energy upon himself.

She almost thought the silver *dreki* was going to overshoot Rurik, but then Magnus slammed into his golden body, just enough to send him straight in to the path of Andri. It happened in an instant that felt like an hour. Rurik's wing tore under Magnus's second strike, and those deadly claws went straight through his precious wings.

"Rurik!" she screamed, and scrambled down the rocky path, cutting hands and fingers as she ran for him. "Rurik!"

A flood of golden heat swept her up as he plummeted, and for a second she was seeing through his eyes as they linked. Warmth surrounded her in a golden haze. An absolute rightness of being that felt like she walked with her power braced against his. There was no him and her in this moment. No secrets, no lies. And she knew instantly what he was trying to tell her. What he'd been trying to tell her all along.

"I'm sorry, Freyja. My fierce, beloved mouse." And the feel of it was like liquid gold bursting over her skin, like molten warmth rushing through her veins. A feeling so pure and strong that she knew she could never feel alone again.

Then something cut the link.

No! She tried to grab hold of him, but the feel of Rurik's touch slipped from her grasp like mist dissolving in her hands.

233

Suddenly she was alone and falling to her knees, the pain of the blow shocking her back into her own skin, her own mind.

Just in time to watch her beloved *dreki* plummet from the skies in front of her.

CHAPTER
NINETEEN

"NO!" HER SCREAM seemed to echo in the air, in her mind, and even in others. She felt Haakon and his men fall to their knees behind her, and realized that she'd somehow extended her horror beyond herself and connected with other minds in the vicinity.

The silver *dreki* plummeted after Rurik, cutting through the air like a knife. Freyja slammed her hands over mouth in horror as the silver *dreki* attacked.

She had never, in her life, felt so helpless.

Rurik fell backward through the air, his claws scrabbling for purchase and his wings splayed flat. Andri almost caught him, claws reaching for him. And just when she thought he would cut her *dreki's* unprotected belly to pieces, he tried to catch Rurik's talons in his.

Andri's left talon caught Rurik's right, and it was just enough to turn him so that he was no longer flat on his back. Rurik slammed into the shale-covered side of the mountain with his left side. Andri tried to let go at the last minute, but it was too late. He crumpled atop Rurik, then flung apart when they both rolled and tumbled down the slope. Wings flashed and rock flew as both of them vanished.

"Rurik!" She was running before she knew it, watching hopelessly as he bounced and jolted down the shale, his wings held clear. Andri hit with a jarring thud, and slid past Rurik, sending a rain of shale down the hillside.

Freyja found herself caught in it, her boots finding little purchase beneath her. She reached out and the earth slowed beneath her feet as she manipulated it, letting her ride a flat piece of shale to a safe plateau. Freyja grabbed at a boulder and hauled herself to a halt as the avalanche swept past her.

Dust obliterated her vision and settled thickly in her throat. Freyja coughed, trying to sweep it from her eyes. Where was he? *"Rurik?"* She threw the thought into the void around her.

She couldn't see him. But she could feel his touch flicker against her own, a smoldering ember against the rush of heat it usually was. Their minds meshed again, just for a second.

"...so tired...."

"Hold on, you stubborn male! I am not done with you yet."

"Andri...?" She could almost feel him struggle to lift himself. He was protecting her from most of the pain he felt, but the searing edge of it made her head ache.

"I'm not sure where he is."

The dust began to clear. Freyja glanced around her. The shale had settled, but who knew what would set it off again?

You rode it last time. She wondered if she could do that again, and as she lost her connection to Rurik for the second time, she knew she didn't have the time to worry about herself anymore.

Freyja's gaze settled on a flat piece of shale and she hauled herself up, examined the distance between her and Rurik's crushed form, and then stepped onto it. Steering the earth beneath her feet, she whizzed down the slope again. Her passage set off another minor rockfall, but she managed to reach the bottom in one piece and jumped off, staggering at the sudden loss of velocity.

"Rurik!"

The enormous *dreki* lay crushed and broken. He struggled to lift his head and she simply couldn't look at that wing. One section of it was completely shredded.

"Rurik, you have to get up! Why did you take my wave of force upon yourself?" Her skirt tore, and her palms were grazed as she slipped and skidded on the uneven surface. "Damn you, I hurt you!"

"Andri is my... kin. I swore an oath to protect him when he was a boy, and a dreki's *oath is binding, or he may no longer call himself dreki."* Rurik's golden flanks heaved. The bone in his left wing sheered straight through the skin, making her feel sick.

"He was trying to kill you!" She finally reached his side and hesitated there, not quite certain where to begin. Bloodied gashes marked his flanks, and he wasn't moving very much, his wings curled in against his sides as though something hurt. Tears heated her eyes, turning her vision to a blur.

"If he'd truly wanted me dead, then he had at least three chances at my wings," Rurik gasped. The link between them seemed thin and faded, almost like a knot that was unraveling. *"He's as caught in this as I am. Freyja, get out of here."*

"No! I won't leave you." She put her hands against his golden scales, trying desperately to hold on to the link between them.

"Freyja." He managed to haul himself up onto his belly and she saw that the wing wasn't the worst of his hurt. Mottled dark veins bruised his left shoulder, and bloodied muscle protruded through his scales. *"This is... not done. Get out of here before Magnus hurts you."*

As if he knew that they spoke of him, a *dreki's* scream pierced the skies above them, and wind whipped as the black *dreki* sailed above them.

A fire began to burn in her heart. Her nostrils flared with anger. That treacherous snake had lured Rurik into an unfair fight. And it wouldn't end here.

"Will he try to kill you?" she whispered.

"He'll not stop... until this is done." Her Rurik sounded absolutely exhausted.

And the logical part of her brain said that Rurik had no more fight left in him. He couldn't handle a twenty-ton *dreki* like Magnus, not in this condition.

There was no one who could stop the fierce beast.

No one but her.

Cold slid down her spine and sweat broke out on her temples. She had some defenses, but not enough to take on a creature a thousand times the size of her.

But the alternative was to walk away as Magnus assassinated her lover, and that was something Freyja couldn't do. Something she wouldn't do.

Shale slid down the harsh slope. Magnus appeared at the top of the ravine, his dark wings spread in a victorious fashion.

"Freyja," Rurik pleaded, finally moving. But not to flee. No, instead he tried to shield her with his own ruined body.

"You should know better than to argue with me," she told him, stepping over his tail and facing the black *dreki*. Her heart pounded in her chest, but she'd felt the earth rouse to her call and she'd wielded lightning before. She was not helpless, and she wouldn't abandon Rurik. "Don't come any closer, you mangy cur, or I'll shred your wings!"

A wave of psychic force lashed down upon her, like a fist slamming into her mind. Freyja screamed and clenched her fists against her temples, but it wouldn't stop. Her vision blurred and something warm wet her top lip. Just as she thought that she could no longer withstand the onslaught, it suddenly vanished.

She came to pressed against Rurik's flank. Her nose was bleeding and he was shockingly still, but she could sense the warm cocoon of his own mind shielding hers.

"Run, Freyja," came the whisper, and that link between them seemed so thin now that she feared it would snap. *"I can shield your mind, but... not much more than that."*

He was dying. She could feel the heat of Magnus's psychic attack slamming against Rurik's shields, and knew that he was too weak to withstand them.

Too weak because he'd risked everything in order to heal her father.

Risked it for her.

"I love you," she whispered, running a hand over his flank. "Keep him out of my mind."

And then she stepped forward.

The earth began to tremble beneath her as Freyja reached for it. She held her hands out as shale began to skitter across the slopes. Magnus hissed as the ground beneath him began to move. Freyja could feel the currents of it rising to her call. She knew this land. She knew the feel of it, the weight of it, the immense power of it. Rurik might have claimed these lands as lord and master, but she was mistress of it.

"Shift," she whispered, tearing the earth apart with but a thought.

Magnus danced uneasily as a furrow ploughed its way through the rock beneath them, toward his feet. A thrust of his wings sent him into the sky, but there was no refuge there.

The sky belonged to her too, and the wind that whipped her hair behind her answered her call. For the first time in her life, Freyja lost herself to the power swimming through her veins. No more hiding, or trying to quash her own powers. She flung a hand toward the airborne *dreki,* and a whip of wind sent him scrambling for the ground again, landing on the haphazard slope. Magnus's claws scrabbled frantically, but there was no escape into the air, nor any shelter on the ground. As if he realized it, he turned and those vicious green eyes locked on her. He stopped fighting against the slide of shale beneath him, and rode it down into the ravine where she protected her *dreki.*

Thunder grumbled in the distance. Clouds swam against each other, brewing darkly as she called the winds to her and split the sky with lightning. Its electric lash ran through her veins and when Freyja opened her eyes, she knew they gleamed.

"You foolish girl," the *dreki* hissed as it alighted on flat ground. *"You think you can turn my own skies against me?"*

"They're not your skies," she told him in a hollow voice. "And they're not the only thing I control."

Freyja flung a fist into the air, and the ground erupted around the *dreki* in a whirlwind of shale and rock that cut and slashed at him. He screamed in fury, lashing out with his claws, but there was no way to fight a thousand shards of rock.

She caught a glimpse of narrow green eyes and then he lashed out, sending an enormous shard of shale directly toward her.

Freyja jerked her hands up. The shard stopped in midair, then dropped to the ground. So did all of the razor-sharp pieces that surrounded Magnus. She lost control of the whirlwind and it petered out, letting her skirts falls against her stockinged calves.

Freyja gasped, her knees trembling. Wielding so much current was taking its toll on her. She'd never mastered so many different elements at once. Only the storm, and she'd been angry then, the night she went after her ram.

"A child," Magnus chuckled, in a murderous voice that echoed in her mind thanks to the protective shield Rurik encased her in. *"Who does not know what she plays with."*

"Play with this," Freyja spat, and a strike of lightning speared through the skies toward him.

"Freyja, no!" Rurik screamed, and something seemed to encase her. A protective dome of... nothingness.

The lightning hit the ground where Magnus had stood an instant beforehand. The black *dreki* vanished as light obliterated her vision, and the world clapped around her in a sudden fierce explosion of heat. She realized her mistake almost instantly. She might wield the lightning, but she was not entirely impervious to it. Small fragments of rock cut against the dome around her and as she blinked, still half-blinded, she realized that Rurik had probably saved her life.

Between one blink and the other, an enormous shadow reared above her. Magnus. She'd missed him. Magnus began to strike toward her, his razor-sharp claws gleaming in the light above her, and his wings flared as though he were some demon from hell. Freyja suffered a moment where she saw her own death striking toward her with absolute inevitability.

"Fire!" someone bellowed.

Haakon. Freyja glanced up from beneath the arm she'd thrown above her head, and saw iron flash in the shaft of sunlight that suddenly split the clouds. Then the enormous bolt from the ballista sunk into the enraged *dreki's* chest, right where his black heart lay.

Magnus screamed, and the sound cut through her like a knife. Freyja slammed her hands over her ears, her blood seeming to vibrate within her veins as the earth had done at her call. She went to her knees and was grateful when Magnus hit the earth in front of her. His wings flapped like a downed bat's, and he clawed at the rocks, his tongue protruding from his gaping maw. Freyja slowly took her hands from her ears as Rurik stumbled into her, wrapping his right wing around her in a move too slow to prevent the previous strike. He made a mournful sound in his chest, one that sounded akin to a whale's bellow, and Freyja pressed her hand against his neck.

"I'm fine," she whispered. "Fine."

Stepping out from under his protective touch, she saw the light go out of Magnus's eyes. A green glow began to emanate from deep within his chest, and then it hovered in the air above his fallen form, an enormous wraith of electric green that flapped faint wings at them before it began to fly into the sky above them.

She'd seen those lights before, when the night skies darkened, and the flicker of green and pink began to dance across the Arctic. But she'd never before understood what they were. Freyja watched in wonder as Magnus's actinic form vanished over the horizon.

A mournful sound echoed behind her, and then a second joined it, as both *dreki* lifted their heads and wailed.

Andri appeared in a flap of wings, alighting with a limp beside her. Freyja barely had time to step back before Rurik's growl filled the air, and he somehow hauled himself up onto his feet, and hissed at the smaller *dreki*.

Those violet eyes blinked at her, then Andri bowed his head before his cousin. Rurik snapped at his cheek, almost in chastisement. *"Freyja is mine. If you touch her I will kill you."*

"You're barely in any condition to swat a fly," she snapped back, hurrying back to his side and pressing her hands against the hollow of his chest. "You stupid *dreki.*"

"You foolish mouse."

"Fierce," she corrected, stroking his muzzle. Her heart wrenched in her chest. "Don't ever frighten me like that again."

And suddenly tears spilled from her eyes down her hot cheeks. Freyja flung her arms around his neck, but could barely reach halfway around. She couldn't believe he'd survived. *I promise you I will never turn from my fate again, if only you heal,* she thought, hoping that any gods who were listening might hear her.

Heat shimmered beneath her touch. Power flushed and ebbed. Then her arms clung to the bare, naked shoulders of the man she loved so much. He winced and took a step to catch himself. Freyja clung tightly. "Rurik?" she blurted.

"Take me into the volcano," Rurik gasped, his left arm curled against his side and his skin mottled with bruises.

"What are you doing?" she demanded. There were *dreki* hunters here. Men she didn't trust, not with her *dreki's* life.

"Got to... protect my wings," he replied, and his face blanched of color.

Freyja turned, her gaze locking on Haakon's. He and his men stood at the top of the ravine, the ballista glaring dangerously down at them. His face remained implacable, but he nodded, once, toward her. An apology, and an offer of amends.

That didn't mean she trusted him an inch.

Freyja's eyes narrowed. She reached out and swatted the ballista with her power, and the hauling mechanism cracked and split in half.

"Just in case you have any foolish ideas before my *dreki* has a chance to heal," she called up to him.

"Damn it, Freyja." Haakon curled his fists at his sides. "That's twice you've broken my ballista."

"Which makes us even," she shot back, before Rurik groaned and slumped against her. "Now get out of here, before I really lose my temper."

CHAPTER TWENTY

"ONE MORE STEP," Freyja gasped, helping Rurik toward the steaming pool within one of his caves. Steam whispered from its surface, and the heat almost blistered her skin.

But Rurik stepped into the water with a sigh of relief, and lowered himself into the sulfurous liquid. He almost completely submerged, water turning his golden hair dark.

Freyja knelt beside him, though she didn't dare touch. Would it be enough? He'd said that the waters would heal him and that he could drain energy directly from the elements around him—fire, water, and earth—but she couldn't shake the horrible suspicion that his wings would never be the same again.

"He'll heal," Andri said, stepping up beside her. The youth had helped her haul Rurik into his caves. Black curls raked over his face, and his eyes were the same unearthly violet color that he wore in *dreki* form.

She wasn't quite certain she trusted him—but Rurik evidently did. And she had no one else to turn to, who might know how to help Rurik.

"Will he fly again?" she whispered.

Andri looked down at his cousin, his face devoid of all emotion. "If he allows himself time to rest, then yes. He's of the First Line. A pureblood."

The *dreki* saw her confused expression, and interpreted it. "His line descends directly from the goddess, and his blood has been kept pure. Within his line, *dreki* have only mated with *dreki*. They have not mixed their blood with dragons or serpents, or even humans. He has powers that very few *dreki* own, including the ability to directly channel fire. He can manipulate the damage to his body if he regains his energy. In fact, he should have been able to heal himself out there. He was dangerously overtaxed for some reason."

Her father. Freyja's nostrils flared.

"I understand why he helped you, but I do not understand why you helped him," Freyja murmured. She had no intentions of leaving Rurik behind, nor of turning her back on Andri even for a second. "You came here to kill him, and I won't forget that."

For the first time, conflicted emotion showed on Andri's face. He looked down at his cousin. "I came here because I was ordered to. My father wanted him dead and promised his lands to my brother." For a moment, he seemed more of a boy than a man. "You do not argue with my father. I am not the son he would choose," Andri replied, and lowered his gaze. "My father thinks my weakness is my mother's fault. She's his second mate, and he's never thought highly of her. I was given a choice: prove that I can be a son he is proud of, or watch her suffer. I had to come. I had to... to protect her. But being here... seeing Rurik again. It reminds me of everything I once was."

A hush fell.

246

"What will your father do when he hears you failed and watched your older brother die?"

More emotion in those dangerous eyes. Andri blinked through long lashes. "I do not know. His heir is dead. Some within the court will say that Magnus earned his death for daring to trespass on Rurik's lands, but... my father's loyal companions will take offense at this death."

A chill ran through her. "They'll come for him again."

"Maybe." The word echoed in the hollow chamber. "Some will be wary to rise against their prince. Magnus was one of the best, and Rurik defeated him. They'll—"

"Their what?" she broke in.

The *dreki* met her gaze. "He did not tell you?"

"He did not tell me quite a few things, from the sounds of it," she said angrily. *A prince.*

"Rurik was his father's heir," Andri said. "Which makes him a prince of our people. When his father was killed, Rurik was offered the means to fight for the throne or to go into exile. He chose exile.

"So not only is he their prince, but he is more powerful than most of the entire court. If my father's *dreki* come again, they'll come in force."

"I *won't* let them hurt him," she whispered fiercely.

"What are you?"

She'd been asked that question so many times. Circles, circles, what did the damned circles have to do with her and her mother? Freyja rested her elbows on her knees, next to where Rurik rested his head on the edge. A golden gleam seemed to emanate from his body, highlighting the dark waters, but he seemed quite oblivious to the world around him. "I don't know," she admitted. "My mother called me a Daughter of the Storm, and I think she knew some lore that gave rise to me, but... I don't entirely understand how it all works."

For so many years she'd been trying to hide from her nature, to suppress the unnaturalness within her. Every time the locals crossed themselves, she'd looked away and locked her true nature deep within her, but the past few weeks had pushed her to accept truths she'd long turned away from.

There was power within her.

Immense power.

And it seemed both tied to the elements as Rurik's magic was, but also somehow separate.

Andri squatted down beside her. He was naked, but until that moment she hadn't truly noticed it. He eyed Rurik with a faint frown. "Whatever you are, you're a threat to him, because you're the one person who could stop his people from accepting him. Without allies, Rurik has no hope against Stellan, regardless of your powers. And his people will never accept you, or any children you might bear."

A stark chill ran through her. "His people exiled him."

"He is beloved among those who were his *dreki*. I hear their mutters, their whispers that things would be better if Rurik were king. There is no love for my father, Stellan, but none are strong enough to challenge him."

"Except for Rurik," she said, finally understanding.

"Except for Rurik. But you're human and he is *dreki*. It's the one thing that could turn those who are loyal to him, against him. You're not *dreki*. Mating with you goes against the creed, and his people will consider this an act of defilement of his pure blood. We can take humans as lovers, but they are never accepted as our consorts, and their children are bastards. They will never accept you as his mate, and he can never come home again."

Home. The blood ran from her face. Home. Rurik's greatest dream, the one that had put shadows of loss in his eyes. His sister, his brother, his people... all things he could never have if he tried to stay with her.

A cold knot seemed to settle in her chest. "Rurik and I never had a future," she said quietly. "I have always known that."

"And yet you fought for him?"

"I love him," she whispered.

"Love." Andri seemed to consider the word. He frowned.

"Rest," she whispered, brushing a strand of wet hair from Rurik's temples, knowing she could not explain. "Rest and heal."

CHAPTER TWENTY-ONE

A WEEK LATER, Rurik awoke.

He was still submerged in the pool, and the waters were finally cool against his skin, as though he'd adsorbed all of the heat within the volcanic waters. Vague memories returned: of a hand cupping his forehead as though checking for a fever, and a pair of lips pressing gently against his cheek. Of words whispered in his ear that stole straight to the heart of him, even through his protective coma.

"I love you, Rurik. And so I must set you free."

"Freyja?" Rurik staggered to his feet, his knees still shaky, though his body finally felt whole. *"Freyja?"*

"She's gone," Andri said, stepping out of the shadows and staring at him.

No! He bared his teeth, primitive urges arising within him and shaking the volcano around them. His *dreki* heart ached, hollow once more, as though it had lost something far more precious than just love. "Where is she?"

"She's gone," Andri repeated, stepping between him and the exit to the cave. "I explained what would happen to you if she accepted your mating bond."

Rurik's head swiveled toward the youth, and he forced his fingers to curl into fists, rather than smashing him flat. "You explained *what*, precisely?"

"The truth." The words came out of Andri in a rush. "She's human and you're not. You cannot mate with her, or the entire court will turn against you. You can't defeat them all, and they'll destroy you for daring to pollute your bloodline."

"They can try." He shoved past the lad, but Andri slammed both hands against his chest.

"No!" the boy burst out. "No. I won't let you do this. Your people need you. They need their prince. You're our only hope."

Stillness slid through him. "You have a queen."

"We have a monster." The words tore from Andri in an almost sob. "You don't understand what has changed. Your mother doesn't believe in honor, or in *dreki* code. The strong make their own rules, and only the strong survive Hekla. I didn't even believe in the power of right, until I saw you again. Until you made me believe that it doesn't have to be this way anymore." The youth's eyes filled with tears. "I lost my way, Rurik. Everything that you taught me had been ground to dust under the never-ending erosion of my father's will. I stopped believing. I have *done* things that I will regret forever, but it wasn't until I saw you again that hope gleamed. You tried to save me. You wouldn't hurt me even when I worked against you because you *gave your word*. You don't know what that means to me."

Rurik's heart thudded dully in his chest. "If I'd stayed, I would have plunged the entire court into a war it couldn't cope with. *Dreki* would have had to choose sides."

"Father killed Áki, Príor, and Sámaur." All of them powerful warriors who might have swayed the court, and stood against Stellan and Amadea. "Marduk fled, and no one has seen him since. The court's already at war, and no *dreki* trusts another, for fear their words will reach Amadea's ears."

Marduk, the little brother who was named after a god-killer. Rurik froze, turning all his predatory attention upon Andri. Marduk and Árdís were the reason he'd accepted exile, rather than fight. His little brother had been barely across the threshold of adulthood, and no match for Stellan and his sons. Not yet, anyway. "Are you certain he's still alive?"

"Árdís seems to think he is." Andri hesitated though. "She doesn't say much, and told Amadea that she didn't know where Marduk has gone, but I've heard whisper among your father's *dreki* that his heart still beats. As for your sister, my father's promised Árdís's hand to Sirius."

Andri's other black-hearted brother. "What does Árdís think of this?"

"What do you think?"

Árdís would be furious, but with her uncle's *dreki* around her and no allies, there might not be much choice. Rurik paced, his knuckles cracking. He'd only ever intended to protect those he loved.

Could he kill his uncle? Could he challenge him?

Stellan's not the dangerous one.

Truth, said his *dreki* magic.

Amadea was only queen with Stellan's backing. As a female *dreki* she wasn't powerful enough to face challenges herself, but with her brother standing at her side, who could unseat her?

And could Rurik honestly kill his own mother?

"I'll think about it," he said hollowly. This was no small cause that he had to commit himself to. And Andri spoke part of the truth. Those who might be his allies at court would balk at seeing Freyja by his side.

How could he make that choice? He'd only just found her, and she was *everything* to him. Only with her at his side did he feel whole. *Dreki* spent their entire lives searching for their twin flame, the one lover who completed them.

And he knew now that she was it.

But as prince of his people, he owed them more than he'd given them. How could he stand aside and see his sister forcibly mated, and his brother hunted down and killed? How could he speak of duty and law and right to Andri, when he would not even accept the duty that his people needed from him?

"My father's been in contact with me." Andri hesitated. "I have to return."

"What did he say?" Rurik demanded, in a chilled voice.

The lad was young, but his eyes were ancient as their gazes met. "Someone must be punished for this failure, and for Magnus's death."

"He'll kill you." Rurik stepped forward, trying to catch his cousin's arm.

Andri backed away, his lips pressed together in suppressed emotion. "Maybe. Maybe not." Andri shuddered. "There is a great deal that I could survive, and he has already lost one son. Only Sirius and I remain, and Stellan likes having a spare in the wings. If I do not go, then he'll choose another to take my place." Thick lashes swept down over his eyes. "He'll choose my mother to submit to my punishment."

No. Rurik bared his teeth. "And the court allows this?"

There was no honor in punishing females or kits. And *dreki* youths were to be cherished, because they were so rare.

"Who can stand against him?" Andri asked simply.

Damn him. Turmoil turned Rurik inside out. He needed Freyja. This was no simple choice his cousin asked of him, but... this was wrong. And he was the only one who might stand a chance at uniting his clan and casting out the usurpers.

"I need to speak to Freyja," he said, because this was not a choice he could make alone. "And maybe you're wrong.... I don't think she's entirely human." Some part of his subconscious had been dwelling upon what he'd seen when she confronted Magnus. "I knew she could shift the earth and touch the storm, but what she did during that fight was more than simply open herself to the elements. She controlled them. She more than matched a *dreki*, especially one of Magnus's power."

"Only *dreki* control the elements," Andri said softly. "She's not *dreki*."

Did they? There was one other, but he'd barely seen fragments of that myth long ago in his youth, and he'd not studied enough to remember what it was. More a glancing recollection. But *Daughter of the Storm*. He'd heard that name before. Somewhere. "She might have some *dreki* blood within her," he argued, though he wasn't entirely convinced. "In the Dark Ages, when our numbers were dwindling, some *dreki* took humans for mates."

"And when it became clear that the progeny of such couplings could not fully control the powers they'd been gifted from their *dreki* side, the clans set to hunting down their descendants and killing them," Andri said incredulously. "That's why it's forbidden."

"Maybe they didn't find all of them," Rurik countered. "Maybe some of them could learn to control their magic?"

"And maybe her powers will spiral out of control—"

"If anyone thinks to move against her, then they will deal with me," he snapped. That was one decision that could be easily made. "Stay here, and wait for me. I will speak to her." He turned to leave.

"Rurik!"

He shot his cousin one more glance.

"Even if she isn't entirely human, you still can't have her. You're of the First Bloodline. Your children would lose the gift of fire, and no *dreki* would follow you. It's forbidden. It's been that way since the courts first formed."

"She is my twin flame," he said gently, seeing the boy flinch. "The other half of my soul. And I cannot walk away from her." His heart grew heavy. "I will think on what you have told me about the court. Don't make any rash decisions. I will need you if I decide to face your father."

There were debts to be paid before he could seek out his mate.

Rurik stopped in the village, following the scent of his old enemy—the man who'd saved his and Freyja's lives. Haakon could finally add a *dreki* to his dragon-killing tally, and Rurik hoped that none of Stellan's men ever discovered how their leader had died.

Haakon jerked upright as Rurik's hand clasped over his shoulder. He'd been slumped over the table in the taproom, staring so intently at nothing that he hadn't even heard Rurik enter.

"You again," Haakon slurred, then wiped a tired hand over his face.

"Me," Rurik said, surveying the room. Only one of Haakon's men lingered there, keeping careful watch over his leader, and sharpening his blade. "Out."

The man arched a brow, and looked to Haakon. "Go," Haakon said, slinging his leg over the bench so that he straddled it. "He's not here to kill me, Gunnar."

Gunnar hauled his enormous bulk to his feet and left—but not after shooting Rurik one last threatening glance.

"You survived," Haakon said, the second the door shut behind his man.

"It would take a great deal more than my cousin's assault to kill me—so don't go getting any ideas."

"What do you want?" the man growled.

Rurik stared down at his nemesis. There were a pair of coins in his hand, and he turned them over and under his fingers, moving with dexterous grace. They reminded him of what he owed this man. He bared his teeth. "Every move you have made since you arrived has been against me, but you also saved Freyja's life. I owe you nothing, for we are even now. But another of my kind does, another of my... line. And *dreki* always pay their debts."

While Haakon might have hurt Freyja, he had done so for a reason, and that reason was a lie. How many other innocents had been swept up in this mess?

"You hunt the *dreki* who took your wife," Rurik said, and Haakon sat up straighter. "This truth will cost you," he warned.

"Then I'll pay it. What do you want?" The man stood, yellow bruises splayed all up his face, as though he'd gotten in some fight. "I have gold! I have—"

"It will gain me nothing," Rurik interrupted, holding his hand up in the air. "But it will cost *you*. Cost you the depths of the lie you have been telling yourself ever since your wife vanished."

"Curse you!" Haakon suddenly roared. "Do not toy with me!" He kicked over a chair, then turned and upended the bench. "Tell me where she is!"

As the other man subsided into a pulsing heap of fury, Rurik closed his fist around the coins, his choice made. "There is only one golden *dreki* beside myself," he said. "Her name is Árdís, and she is my younger sister. She resides in the *dreki* court below Hekla."

As Haakon strode toward his bag, Rurik stepped in front of him, shoving him to a halt. "You will never get into the court. It was built with magic and resides between this realm and the next, created out of pure Chaos magic. A realm within a bubble of power. Over a hundred *dreki* live there. Perhaps you could kill one, but they will chew you up and spit you out before you even set foot in the place."

"I don't care." Haakon tried to shove past him. "That *dreki* took my wife!"

"She did not steal your wife, you fool," Rurik hissed. "She *was* your wife."

"What?" Haakon slammed to a halt, the breath hissing out of him.

"Think about it," Rurik warned. "*Dreki* do not eat humans, unless provoked. And what need would Árdís have to steal away your wife, when she has no interest in mating with her or eating her? You said yourself that your wife—*Arja*—had eyes like polished amber. You describe my sister's mortal form. Her coloring. Tell me this, did she like berries? They were Árdís's favorite too. And she despises smoked cod with a passion. She loves to lie in the grass, warming herself in the sun, and she has an obsession with jewelry, particularly emeralds." He saw the other man flinch. "I don't know if your wife had a temper, but Árdís does. She is petulant and spoiled, but when she laughs she could light the entire room."

The color drained out of Haakon's face. "*No*," he whispered, but it was with the tone of a man who knew he was wrong.

"Yes," Rurik corrected, righting the chair. "Your wife was a stranger to your village, one caught out in a wild storm one night, a storm the likes of which you've never seen before. Those are the kinds of storms that *dreki* ride upon. None of you knew her, you said."

Haakon's knees gave way beneath him as he sank onto the bench. "But... how? Why?"

"Ten years ago, my sister went abroad in the world. I heard the ripples of her passing in the wind, and she is the only *dreki* I've connected with since I was exiled. There would have been... pressure on her to breed, and Árdís has always disliked pressure. She wanted to see more of the world before she was old enough to accept a mate. Perhaps she came upon you. Perhaps you pleased her... for a time. But my uncle would have been pushing her to return, and she could never take you with her. I'm sorry. I don't know her reasons for marrying you when she knew it could never last, and I can only suspect why she left. But I do know that you deserve the truth."

Haakon scraped a hand over his face, reeling from the news. For a second, Rurik almost felt sorry for the man, and didn't understand why. One did not feel pity for one's enemies. But...

Haakon had based his entire life on a lie, and had killed three dragons and chased Árdís halfway across the seas in an attempt to find her.

Perhaps Rurik understood what would drive a man to do such a thing, for he felt the same need in his heart when he thought of Freyja.

"That lying bitch," Haakon whispered. He looked up, heat returning to her face. "Everything we had was a lie. What the hell do I do?"

"Go home," Rurik said gently. "Go back to your family. And bury your memories of your wife."

The other man's nostrils flared. "*No*. She owes me the truth from her own lips."

"The truth will get you killed."

"You don't know that."

"My mother believes that *dreki* blood should remain pure. The second she sees you, she will kill you for daring to touch immortal flesh. Perhaps the reason Árdís left you is because she sought to save your life. Doing this will only guarantee your death."

"I don't care," Haakon croaked. "What would you do if that were Freyja?"

Burn the world to ashes to confront her, and demand the truth. Rurik's lips twisted.

"You cannot change my mind," Haakon declared, and Rurik saw the truth of it in the other man's eyes.

"Dig your own grave then. I'll be no more a part of this insane quest."

He had paid the debt Árdís owed the man, and fate would work what it intended.

It was time to find Freyja.

CHAPTER TWENTY-TWO

RURIK FOUND FREYJA in the barn, pitching hay into the stalls where her lambs rested.

After all that was said and done, everything they'd been through, she was back to acting as though she had nothing else to do right now.

Doubt filled him as he watched her silently from the shadows. Light pierced a hole in the ceiling, highlighting the gilt in her dark blonde hair. She muttered to herself, cursing under her breath as she finished her task and leaned on the pitchfork to rest. His heart twisted in his chest at the sight.

Let her go, said logic. *Your uncle will kill her if he hears of her existence.*

But there was a part of him that was not so rational. A part of him that curled its lip and growled deep within at the mere thought of surrendering what was his. It burned within him like the molten heart of a volcano, threatening to erupt through his veins.

He could no more deny himself than deny the truth. Freyja was the other half of his soul.

The connection that burned between them from the start was finally one he understood. Here was his other half, the one spirit who could match him. All he had to do was claim her as his and bond with her, for the link between them to be complete.

Freyja's head lifted, almost as if she heard him, which was ridiculous.

Or was it? He still did not understand her powers.

"Rurik?" she whispered, turning around to search for him in the shadows.

Their eyes locked.

And he was done.

Fever danced within his blood, a primal need surging through him, driving him to claim her. Arguments whirled through his head, all the reasons that he should not do this. But there was such a sense of rightness within him too. His wildness ached for something more.

Rurik stepped out of the shadows. Freyja's face lit up hungrily, as if she too shared the wildness that lit him on fire, before she swiftly shuttered her expression. Her eyelashes swept down, hiding those magnificent eyes, sunlight staining the tips of them.

"You're well again," she finally said, and her chest heaved as she let out a relieved breath. She hovered on the balls of her feet as though she wanted to go to him, then stopped herself, brushing a strand of hair behind her ear.

Precious Freyja. More beautiful than a storm itself and almost as dangerous. Still a mystery, though he vowed he would unearth the secrets of her power. One day. If she'd let him.

"Thanks to you."

Color darkened her cheeks, and she finally met his gaze. This was when she was at her most beautiful. Both defiant and yet opening herself up to him. No longer holding him at arm's length.

"You weren't there when I awoke," he said, taking a step toward her.

"Your cousin said you were a prince," Freyja whispered, her hands turning white as she gripped the pitchfork. "Your people will not accept me, and I know you would stand between me and them to protect me. I cannot do that to you. You long for home, Rurik, and I will keep you from it. You long for your people, and I cannot join you there. I left as soon as I knew you were healing and that your cousin was no longer a threat to you."

"Is that not my choice?" he demanded, taking another step toward her. "I know the risks, and the dangers. And I accept them, for if I cannot have you, then what is the point in living? At every moment in our journey together, I have taken no more than you would allow. You wanted everything that happened between us to be your choice, and it was. So how can you deny me my right to make that choice now?"

"I love you, Rurik. And so, I must set you free." He drew the memory from his subconscious and shared it with her, letting her feel all of the hurt he'd felt at such a decision.

"Do you know what it felt like to wake alone, without my Freyja?"

Freyja swallowed, and a single tear slid down her cheek. "I watched you almost die," she croaked. "Because of me. You weakened yourself for me."

"And I would do it all again, because you mean everything to me, Freyja. Everything."

A look came over her face, as if the weight of his words finally sank in, as if Freyja finally accepted the inevitable truth. Their gazes clashed, and suddenly he knew that he wasn't the only one who felt that fire in his blood.

Capturing her face in his hands, he pressed a kiss to her lips. Then another. The desire to claim her was nearly overwhelming, especially when she slid her hands up and down his chest, kneading the muscles there, then slowly filtering lower.

But she needed to know what the mating bond meant for her.

He'd promised her a choice in everything he did to her.

With a groan, Rurik withdrew from her, clasping her wrist and drawing her hand away from its devastating work before he could no longer think. He pressed his forehead to hers, breathing hard. "Freyja, Freyja, stop. Wait."

"I don't want to wait." Her breath caressed his lips. "If I stop, I'll start thinking, and I don't want to think of all the reason this can't work."

Neither do I. Rurik bared his teeth in a snarl. "There's something you need to know first."

Those mismatched eyes opened and locked on his.

"This time will be different. There's no coming back from this. I mean to claim you and take you as my mate," he told her bluntly, breathing in her sweet, wild scent. His fingers brushed her cheeks, his body firm against hers as he pressed her against the stall door. "I've never felt this way before. You make me weak and mortal, and every instinct tells me that you will be my undoing, but I can't give you up. I can't. I need to claim you."

"Your undoing?" Freyja pushed past him, earning some breathing room. Her eyes spat sparks as she stood in the center of the aisle, facing him down with her hands fisted at her sides. Tendrils of golden hair snaked around her face, tugged free from her braid.

And something sang within him. The same sensation he'd felt when she entered his lair that first time and faced him down. A pure exhilaration unlike any he'd ever known.

He'd known then that she belonged to him, and that he would have her. He'd thought he could burn the feeling out of his blood once he slaked this reckless thirst on her flesh.

What he hadn't understood then was that reaching out and merely tasting her fury would never be enough. He could *never* slake this thirst.

But the cost would be tremendous. Freyja weakened him, for suddenly, he had far too much to lose. Not himself. Not his people, or his court. But her. The one being who owned his heart.

"Yes," he breathed, taking a step toward her. "My undoing."

"And you're mine," she shot back, no longer retreating. "I am mortal. And this... whatever this is between us... has an expiration date." Her expression suddenly turned entreating. "I have made some decisions in the last few days. I am no longer ashamed of what I am, nor will I ever hide from myself again. I am powerful and dangerous, and I... I love you. I know this now, but the practical side of my nature understands that loving you does not mean there are no more obstacles to surmount. You will not age, Rurik. And I will. Will you still love me when I am an old woman, and you are a young man? What of children? I've always yearned for them, deep in my secret heart, but your people will not accept my mating with you."

Rurik reached for her, but she darted under his arm again, igniting all of his predatory impulses. "I speak of love, and she throws logic in my face."

"One of us must be practical," Freyja whispered, wrapping her arms around herself.

Rurik cupped her cheek, caressing her silken skin. "I used to think that we had an ending too," he whispered, sensing how much she wanted him to convince her that there was a chance. "But I was wrong. There is no beginning or ending when it comes to us. The *dreki* speak of the other half of their soul, a being so twined together with theirs that when they find them, it is like realizing how empty you have always felt, and staring at the one being who completes you. You're my twin flame, Freyja. You're my forever. And I will rail against the stars themselves if they seek to part us."

"I think the stars might be your undoing."

He gave her a sleek, predatory smile. "Then you know nothing, little mouse. A *dreki's* lifespan is tied to their twin flame. We will age together if you accept this mating bond. And as for children, if anyone dared touch ours then they would face my wrath. Perhaps the *dreki* need to accept a new world order. But lying with you tonight changes everything, Freyja. The last time our bodies met, I was not entirely certain what was happening to me. Now I do. I'm mating with you. Claiming you again completes that bond, and there is no going back from this point." His voice dropped to a whisper. "It's your choice."

Questions danced in her mismatched eyes, making her gaze distant. Rurik bit her lip. "What was that?"

"What was what?"

"That doubt in your eyes."

Freyja swallowed, her eyes wary, as if he suddenly had the power to destroy her. "If I am your forever, then why would you call me your undoing?"

He brushed a strand of wheat-gold hair from her eyes, stroking it with a tenderness he'd never felt before he met her. It was a curious sensation. "Freyja, Magnus, and Andri didn't just come here of their own accord. They were sent here by my mother to kill me. I told you once about my exile, and my mother." A shudder ran through him. "Loving you weakens me. If my mother wants to strike at me, then now she has a means to do it. I would rip her throat out if she dared to harm you, but I don't know if I can protect you. Not from an entire court of *dreki* who are loyal to my mother." He finally exhaled, "You are my undoing, Freyja, but I am your destruction. They will kill you for loving me. You must know this."

He could not keep the truth from her.

Even if it destroyed this fledgling hope that beat in his chest. A dream of a better existence. A promise that he had been searching for, all his life.

Freyja frowned up at him. "They can try."

"Freyja—"

"No," she told him fiercely, pressing two fingers to his lips. "All my life I never dared yearn for more. And the one time when I could see my heart's true desire was when you walked into my life, and I pushed you away because I feared the way you made me feel. You nearly died, Rurik. Because of me. But you didn't. And in that moment I swore an oath to the gods, both old and new, that I would never turn my back on my fate ever again."

"I owe my people a chance at freedom," he said. "Andri wants me to challenge Stellan, and take my mother's throne."

"Do you want your throne?"

His heart seized in his chest. It had been all his father ever dreamed of. Everything he'd been raised to reach for. But matched against Freyja, it was little more than a cold, stone throne, and a heartless court. "Not if I cannot have you. I love you." His voice dropped to a whisper. "And I understand little the emotions that rage within me, but... I cannot give you up."

"Then let them come," she breathed. "I am not without my defenses, *dreki*-mine."

His heart skipped a beat in his chest. "There are others who can take the throne. Others I trust." His thumbs caressed her mouth. "But Andri is right. I cannot walk away from my people. I want to mate with you, but duty compels me to go to war for my people."

"I love you," she breathed, her eyes shining with unshed tears. "And your words terrify me. But I am done with fear. I am done with regret. And if your mother, or your uncle, or your fellow *dreki* try to come between us, then I will face them at your side."

"Freyja." He shuddered.

"I accept your bond," she whispered. "Forever and ever, no matter who tries to tear us apart."

A distant rumble of thunder echoed and he glanced to the walls, before looking back at her. Lightning danced in her eyes, the hum of power whispering through her veins.

Yes. His heart soared. This was just the beginning, and yet it was their beginning. He captured her mouth, his thumb stroking that wet tear from her cheek as he kissed her. "Everything and forever," he breathed, tracing the corner of her mouth, his fingers delving into her silky hair.

Freyja's tongue tangled with his. Fearless. Fierce. All of the things that first ignited his curiosity. Her mouth brushed against his, and he tasted the violence of her power on her tongue. *Mine.* Rurik fought free of her hands and captured her around the waist, drawing her into his embrace. This woman could be a queen, if only his people could see the same things he did when he looked at her.

Breathing hard, with her breasts crushed against his chest, she let him plunder her mouth. Rurik felt his hard body melting into her soft curves. It was a kiss to tell her everything that he felt in his heart. He wasn't letting her go. Maybe he hadn't been entirely certain of that when he came here, duty to his people warring within his breast, but seeing her now, having her skin beneath his, cemented his desire.

The court could wait. His uncle could wait. Freyja was his to claim, and without her there was no point in existing.

Suddenly, he could no longer withhold the heat of his need. The world reeled around them as he pushed her backward, hand sliding down her hips, then up, to the curve of her breasts, as if to make sure she was real. That she was really there, in his arms. He couldn't get enough of her. Freyja's back met the barn wall, and her mouth tilted to his as she claimed him with her hungry lips, her hand still fisted in his shirt.

Rurik dragged a handful of her skirts up between them, even as her hand slid down to caress his erection through the thin fabric of his trousers. Cupping her thigh, he dragged it up to nestle around his hip, thrusting into her hand. The shock of that touch lanced through him. *Sweet goddess*, but he'd yearned for this. To see Freyja boldly take what she wanted from his body, as if there was no longer any barrier between her heart and his. To curl those fingers around his hard length and work him, as if she wanted to imprint the feel of him on her skin.

Biting back a gasp, Rurik thrust his cock into her hand, rubbing against her touch. A desperate ache filled him. He wanted to be inside her. Now. To claim her and fulfill their mating bond, so that she could never, ever be taken from him.

His fingers found her, wet and slick. He didn't know if it was his hands that freed his cock from his trousers—or hers. But he grabbed her under the ass and lifted her, impaling her with a single thrust.

"*Mine.*"

Her thought-thread connected with his. "*I claim you, Rurik, prince of my heart.*"

"*And I claim you.*"

Power spilled between them as the mating bond roared to life. A strangled sound tore from his throat as the heat within him suddenly flared volcanic. The world faded. All that remained was him and Freyja, and her tight little body clutching at his as he thrust home. One. Last. Time.

Pleasure roared through him, and he could feel her match him as the mating bond took them both over the edge. Freyja cried out, throwing her head back as they rode the storm. *Sweet Goddess.* Rurik sank his teeth into her throat, rocking into her hard, grinding his hips against hers as his seed flooded within her.

Their minds danced against each other, until he no longer existed as Rurik, nor she as Freyja, but both blended as one. White-hot pleasure obliterated all else, until slowly sensation began to return; Freyja's hand cradling his nape, her face nuzzling against his throat as little aftershocks ran through her. Rurik turned his face and found her mouth, kissing her with slow affection. *His.* Finally his. Utterly and irrevocably. He gasped against her lips, completely spent.

Freyja's skirts fell around her thighs. Slowly looked up, her eyes heavy-lidded and a lazy, satisfied smile on her face. "*Everything and forever.*"

Her mind touched his, locked together in a thought-thread that could never be broken. She could never hide anything from him ever again. Nor he her. The feeling might have left him slightly exposed once upon a time, but this was Freyja. His mate. His twin flame. He could feel the sated ache in her body where they joined, as if her body was merely an extension of his own, and it felt like coming home. Like finally feeling complete in himself.

"Everything and forever," Rurik whispered, and lost himself in the sensation of loving her.

STORM OF DESIRE

BOOK TWO: LEGENDS OF THE STORM

Long ago, Haakon thought a *dreki* stole his beloved wife. He has sacrificed everything to gain revenge for her loss— including his own honor—but now Haakon knows the truth. His entire marriage was a lie. The woman he knew as his wife was a *dreki* princess named Árdís, in mortal form.

And when he finally tracks down the deceitful *dreki* princess, there will be a reckoning of passion and glory....

Want to know more about Storm of Desire? Make sure you sign up to my newsletter at www.becmcmaster.com to be the first to know its release date, read exclusive excerpts, and see cover reveals. When you subscribe, you will receive a link to the first two chapters!

Dear Readers,

Thank you so much for reading Heart Of Fire! If you enjoyed it, please consider leaving a review online. Rurik and Freyja have just begun their journey, but first there's a little tale of love and loss and revenge to deal with in book two, Storm of Desire, when Haakon finally finds his elusive wife...

I like to put my own spin on mythology, so you may note that some of the creatures and mythology presented within this series is not 'technically correct'. AKA I took the mythology and ran with it.

Why Tiamat? As you can probably see from the glossary, there are many different courts, and each region will have it's own mythology on dreki. I needed one ancient myth to base their origin upon that was not as specific to region. As Mesopotamia predates a lot of other cultures, this fit the bill. The myth of the North Wind scattering parts of Tiamat's body to the four corners of the world, was something that inspired me to work out where the dreki came from, precisely. In my world, the winds scattered her soul, instead, which is why dreki have some Sumerian words within their dialect.

Why Iceland? I could probably admit that I needed volcanoes to play a part in the mythology, but if I'm being honest, this whole world came from an afternoon where I was sitting down with a travel brochure. I don't know if there was a tour called 'Ring of Fire', or just those words mentioned within, but the second I read them the world dumped itself inside my head. I had the dreki. I needed a hero, and a heroine, and some way to pit them against each other. Considering my background as a farmer's daughter, sheep began to intrude in my conscience. Hence Freyja spun herself to life in my mind.

I hope you enjoyed this little detour into a strange world. As you can probably tell, there is more to the story. I have plans for Freyja and Rurik (after all, what exactly is Freyja?), and Haakon and his wife need a confrontation. Plus there is that missing dreki prince, Marduk, and who knows what he is up to?

I enjoyed every second of writing this book, but as with every project I take on, I couldn't have done it without a lot of help from these amazing people:

I owe huge thanks to my editor Olivia from Hot Tree Editing for her work in spit-and-polishing this manuscript until it gleamed; my wonderful cover artists from Damonza.com for taking everything I described and giving me the cover of my dreams; and Marisa Shor and Allyson Gottlieb from Cover Me Darling for the print formatting. To Kylie Griffin and Jennie Kew, the best support team any writer could dream of, and the Central Victorian Writers group for keeping me sane and pointing out the 'fire crotch' on the cover draft! Special thanks to my family, and to my other half–my very own beta hero, Byron–who has always been unabashedly proud of this dream of mine, even when I didn't know if I could do it.

Last, not least, to all of my readers who support me on this journey, and have been crazy vocal about their love for the London Steampunk series, and anything else I write! I hope you enjoy this crazy little detour into a fantasy world!

Cheers,
Bec McMaster

ABOUT THE AUTHOR

BEC MCMASTER is a writer, a dreamer, and a travel addict. If she's not sitting in front of the computer, she's probably plotting her next world trip, and plans to see the whole world, whether it's by paper, plane, or imagination. She grew up on a steady diet of '80s fantasy movies like *Ladyhawke*, *Labyrinth*, and *The Princess Bride*, and loves creating epic, fantasy-based romances with heroes and heroines who must defeat all the odds to have their HEA. She lives in Australia with her very own hero, where she can be found creating the dark and dangerous worlds of the London Steampunk, Dark Arts, Legends of The Storm, or Burned Lands series, where even the darkest hero can find love.

For news on new releases, cover reveals, contests, and special promotions, join her mailing list at www.becmcmaster.com

Made in the USA
Columbia, SC
20 September 2017